BOOK TWO OF THE CHANTERS OF TREMARIS TRILOGY

the Waterless Sea

Kate Constable

PO/NT

SCHOLASTIC INC.

New York Toronto London Auckland Sydney
Mexico City New Delhi Hong Kong Buenos Aires

for Hilary

*I would like to thank Rosalind Price, Eva Mills, and Jodie Webster from Allen & Unwin for all
their help; Lyn Tranter; Jan, Bill, and Hilary Constable, Joy Taylor, Richard Evans, and Elizabeth Reid
for allowing me extra time to work; and Michael Taylor, for everything.*

ISBN 0-439-55481-0

Text copyright © 2003 by Kate Constable
Map illustration © 2005 by Matt Manley

Arthur A. Levine Books hardcover edition designed by Elizabeth B. Parisi, published
by Arthur A. Levine Books, an imprint of Scholastic Inc., March 2005.

12 11 10 9 8 7 6 5 4 3 2 1   6 7 8 9 10 11/0

Printed in the U.S.A.   01

First American paperback printing, February 2006

Contents

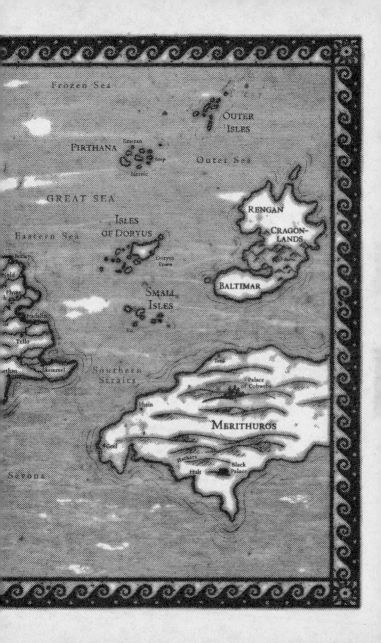

Frozen Sea

OUTER
ISLES

Outer Sea

PIRTHANA

Emeran
Ship
Merric

GREAT SEA

RENGAN

ISLES
OF DORYUS

CRAGON-
LANDS

Eastern Sea

Doryn
Town

BALTIMAR

Birley
Gold
Flyme
h

SMALL
ISLES

dalin
of
Tello

Ela

kemmel

Southern
Straits

rthan

Teni

Palace
of Cobwebs

Ihain

MERITHUROS

Geef

Sevona

Hathea
Hult

Black
Palace

The Serpent-Headed Ship

Dawn had not yet broken over the Straits of Firthana. The sky was a pearly gray, and the three moons gleamed faint and silvery above the western horizon. The sea lapped on all sides, and the fading moonlight picked out tiny silver flecks at the peak of every wave. The boat *Fledgewing* rocked on the water; the dark bulk of the island of Istia lolled beside it, silent as a sleeping cat.

Already it seemed to Calwyn that they'd been waiting half the night. Her fingers twitched, for the hundredth time, toward the thick dark plait that hung over her shoulder. She forced herself not to fidget. Though it was the beginning of summer, there was a chill over the sea that wouldn't disappear until the sun had risen. The air was so crisp, it seemed it might shatter. Calwyn shivered and drew her cloak around her shoulders.

The wheel creaked behind her as Tonno and Mica brought up the nets, heavy and slithering with fish.

"No point sitting about, wasting time, when we can set the nets," Tonno had said in his practical way. "Dawn's the best time for silver-finned jacks." If their adventure this morning came to nothing, they would at least have a hold filled with fish to take home to Ravamey.

"Steady, steady," growled Tonno. "Don't spill 'em all over the side, lass."

Mica snorted and tossed her wild mop of tawny hair as she hauled at the nets. The two of them worked skillfully together: the burly fisherman and the young windworker, both born to the sea and at home on the water.

Not like Trout, Calwyn thought with a smile. The boy sat hunched uncomfortably in the bow, squinting out across the water, though it was still too dark to see much. And besides, he'd taken off the lenses he wore on his nose and was polishing them on the tail of his grubby shirt. Without the lenses, Trout could barely see an arm's length in front of him.

Calwyn started as Halasaa's warm hand fell on her shoulder and his voice sounded in her mind. *Not long now.*

Calwyn nodded to the east, where a line of light glowed at the horizon. "The sun is rising," she said in a low voice. "We should lower the dinghies."

Halasaa smiled, and she could see the gleam of his teeth in his dark face. *The ship is coming.*

Calwyn raised her head, all her senses alert. Yes, she could feel it now, the mixed flicker of lives, jumbled up together, like a buzzing murmur of indistinguishable voices. The ship was still some distance off, but it drew nearer at every moment. She stood up.

"Tonno!" she called softly. "It's time."

* * *

Heben knew that he was dreaming. He curled himself deeper into sleep, to make the dream last.

He was at home, on the lands of the Cledsec in the north of Merithuros. The glorious curve of the sands swept out before him, sculpted by the wind, the same wind that whipped across his face as he spurred the *hegesu* into a gallop. The twins whooped with glee, crouched on their own beast: Gada in front, with Shada clinging on behind, her eyes shining.

They were racing to the top of the dune. Heben heard the soft *splat, splat* as the *hegesu's* feet thudded into the sand and the huffing protest of its breath as he urged it on, and he felt the matted woolly coat under his hands.

At the crest of the dune, Heben saw the whole of his father's lands spread out below: the swell of bronze and golden sands and the silver flashes of the water pools. Far off, a low cluster of tents and flags marked his family's homestead, where they lived in the old way, under canvas. Flocks of *hegesi*, brown and milky dots, shifted slowly across the sands, and above it all spread the taut canopy of the silken blue sky.

The twins were just behind him. Gada stumbled up the dune, dragging the reluctant *hegesu* on its tether, and Shada ran up to tease him —

"Out of the way, you stinking desert dog!"

A sharp kick in the ribs woke Heben. He cried out and tried to roll over, hunched against the pain. Except that he couldn't roll over. He was roped to the prisoners on each side, and none of them could move. His neighbor, a heavy Gellanese whose red face dripped sweat, eyed Heben with displeasure.

"Keep still, can't you," he growled between clenched teeth. "You'll have us all thrown overboard!"

Heben blinked and struggled to sit up.

"I beg your pardon," he said, from force of habit, but good manners were equally unwelcome. The Gellanese curled his lip contemptuously and turned his head away. Heben tried not to grimace at the stench of his companion. After five days without washing, he probably didn't smell very sweet himself.

The pirates' ship was a long galley with a snake's head for a prow, like all Gellanese vessels. But the pirates, rather than feed the hundred slaves they'd need to haul at the oars, preferred to move under sail, and the benches below the deck were packed with treasure and prisoners, not slaves. About a dozen captives were tied with Heben up on deck, roped at the ankles and wrists and crammed into a space barely large enough to hold four men.

It was five days since the ship on which Heben had been a passenger was captured and sunk, and he had almost given up wondering what would happen to him. At first he'd thought he might be held hostage for a ransom from his rich father, the head of the Clan. The pirates weren't to know that his father had disowned him and forbidden him ever to return to the lands of the Cledsec. But the pirates had shown no interest in his parentage. Nor did they ever ask why a wealthy young Merithuran lordling might have gone to sea when it was well known that highly born Merithurans loathed everything to do with the ocean and never went near it except from dire necessity.

The pirates had taken Heben's pouch of gold coins and stripped him of his fine clothes, his curved sword with the gilded handle and leather scabbard, and his golden earrings. The small medallion, the size of his thumbnail, that identified him as a member of the Clan of the Cledsec had disappeared with the coins. Then the pirates had bundled him into a corner with the rest of the captives on deck and paid him no more attention.

"They'll sell us for slaves in Doryus Town," muttered one of the prisoners, but instead of turning to sail south toward Doryus, the stronghold of all piracy in the Great Sea, the serpent-headed ship kept its course to the north. The mutterings grew darker. "Taking us to the tallow pits of Firthana . . . no doubt about it. . . ."

"What are the tallow pits?" Heben asked.

The prisoner on his other side, a bald and bony sailor who had been the cook aboard Heben's ship before it was scuttled, gave an ominous cackle.

"Don't they talk of the tallow pits in them deserts of yours? The tallow pits is where the pirates take them they don't need and them they wants to be rid of." He drew his finger across his throat. "Spit 'em, blood 'em, skin 'em, melt the fat down for candles. You never heard of a dead man's candle? They can burn for a whole turn of the moons without losing the flame."

"They won't get much fat off *you*," sneered the fleshy Gellanese.

The cook leaned over, dragging Heben's arm across his chest as he poked his fellow prisoner in the ribs.

"They'll be getting plenty off you though, won't they! And plenty of hide too, what's more!"

"Hide?" Heben's stomach turned.

"They'll tan your skin and make it into boots," growled the Gellanese. "Pirates all wear man-skin boots."

"They'll make enough boots out of you to shoe the whole ship!" cackled the cook. But the rest of the prisoners sank into despondency, and Heben too was sick at heart to think that his quest might end in such a horrible way.

The cook gave Heben a nudge and nodded over the side of the boat. "Looks like we might be nearly there."

Heben strained to see. Sure enough, the ship was drawing close to one of the little islands that dotted the straits. It was a strangely beautiful sight to someone who'd never known anything but the desert. The sheer rock of the cliffs reared out of the sea, and the deep green of trees fringed the shore. A gull soared overhead, a white flash against the blue. It had rained in the night, and the morning was washed fresh, with a tang of salt that could be tasted on the tongue. The sky shone blue and unblemished, like a glazed bowl filled with clear light.

If this was truly to be the last day of his life, thought Heben, at least he would die in a place of beauty. He hoped he could face death as a Merithuran warrior should: unblinking, straight-backed, so that the ancestors who waited on the other side of the curtain to greet him need not be ashamed.

The other prisoners had fallen silent, their incessant grumbles and curses hushed at last. The brash voices of the Doryan pirates rang out through the clean morning air.

"Boat ho!"

Heben saw a little dinghy bobbing on the water. A scruffy-looking boy was at the oars, and sunlight flashed on the two round glass lenses that he wore perched on his nose. A strange device, thought Heben.

There were two others in the little boat. One was a tall, thin young man who looked about seventeen, Heben's age. He had dark burnished skin, and tattoos spiraled across his face and chest. And there was a young woman about the same age, with a long dark plait over one shoulder. The man with the tattoos was half-naked, but the boy and the woman wore sturdy, plain-colored shirts and trousers, the clothes of people who worked hard with their hands.

Fisher-folk, thought Heben. This must not be the place after all; death would be postponed. He gulped in the cold air with relief. His ancestors would have to wait for him a little longer. To be honest, he was not looking forward to meeting them. They would probably disapprove of him, just as his father did, and the thought of an eternity spent with ancestors pursing their lips and shaking their heads was not a prospect he relished.

"Hello!" muttered the Gellanese, yanking Heben sideways as

he craned to see what was happening in front of the ship. "Pirates won't like this! Can't they see where they're goin'?"

The boy with the strange lenses was rowing directly into the path of the much larger pirate ship. Sailors leaned over the rail, and shouted through cupped hands, "Out of the way! Hey, boy! *Out of the way!*"

"That boy'd better look to his oars," observed the Gellanese. "This ship won't turn aside for *him.*"

"We'll smash 'em like a twig!" The cook rubbed his hands together in glee.

Heben stared. What were the three in the little boat thinking? Still the boy pulled steadily at his oars, without ever looking over his shoulder. He might have been alone on the whole wide ocean, from here to the coast of Gellan. The other two seemed equally oblivious.

The tattooed man sat quietly in the prow and gazed off toward the horizon. Suddenly he lifted his head and stared up at the serpent-headed ship, up at the row of curious faces that peered over the edge, straight into the eyes of Heben. Startled, Heben stared back. For as long as three breaths, their gazes locked. The stranger's eyes were dark and serious, and he stared intently, as if he were trying to find something he had lost.

Then, just as suddenly, he smiled. He tossed back his long dark hair and looked over his shoulder at the young woman who sat behind him in the dinghy.

The dinghy was right under the serpent's head now, in the ship's black shadow. Heben braced for the collision. The pirates raced up and down, waving and cursing, for even though their vessel was so much larger, the little rowing boat might still damage it.

Then the woman with the dark plait did something that made Heben sit up with a jolt and draw in a breath so sharp he almost choked. Slowly she stood up in the center of the little boat, balanced despite the dip and sway of the dinghy. She raised her hands and opened her mouth. And she sang.

Heben felt her song before he heard it. A blast of icy wind hit the galley, so fierce and unexpected that the whole row of roped prisoners was thrown back sprawling. The ship lurched and tilted, and prisoners and pirates alike slid helplessly across the deck. Then another blast of wind roared from the opposite side of the ship and tilted it back the other way. From where he was caught in a tangle of ropes and flailing feet, Heben saw two of the pirates topple overboard and splash into the sea.

The huge vessel plunged back and forth like a toy in a bathtub, gripped by a childish hand. The sky was still a cloudless blue, the sea unruffled by any hint of storm. The gulls still shrieked and swooped, riding the currents of the air on their own errands, untouched by the mayhem below.

The serpent-headed ship was in chaos. Some of the pirates struggled to furl the sails, to reduce the amount of canvas the winds could catch, but the rigging swung about so violently that the task was impossible. The string of prisoners came to rest in a corner beside the wheelhouse. Heben was stuck fast in a pile of heavy bodies, but his head was free so he could see what was going on.

The boy at the top of the rigging, who'd managed to cling on until now, lost his toehold. A blast of wind was directed straight at him. It caught him in the midriff; for a heartbeat, he managed to clutch the ropes while the wind blew him out like a flag. And then he lost his grip. Heben was pleased to hear the painful *crack* as he hit the water far below. Of all the nasty crew on this brutal ship, he especially disliked that boy. He'd seen him set fire to the tails of the ducks that the pirates kept in a coop on the deck; above all else, Heben hated to see anything defenseless suffer.

"Sorcery!" shouted one of the other prisoners, too close to Heben's ear. "This is bleeding sorcery, that's what this is!"

The ship gave another mighty lurch, and Heben could see that there were two little boats besieging the galley, one on each side. He caught a glimpse of a burly dark-haired man at the oars of the second dinghy and another girl, golden-eyed, a year or two younger than the first, with a wild mop of sun-bleached hair. Like the other girl, she was standing, with her mouth open and her hands raised. Then the ship rolled back, and Heben lost sight of them.

"Windwitches!" howled the prisoner who had cried, "Sorcery!" But the rolling was less violent now, the pitching of the ship less extreme. Individual pirates were being picked off, and the whole crew was in a state of utter, gibbering panic, running this way and that in a vain effort to escape the ruthless winds.

The pirate captain had enough presence of mind to lash himself to the foremast with a length of halyard. Now, over the terrified shouts of the crew and the clatter of rolling water barrels, above the whip and crack of ropes and canvas, he shouted, "Stop! A parley, a parley! Witches, hold your song!"

Then Heben heard it clearly: a high, melodious song that threaded back and forth across the ship, carried by the voices of the two girls. It was an unearthly sound, like the faint moan of the wind as it thrummed in the rigging. Or, he thought, like the eerie call of a far-off desert storm as it whipped across the sands. The hairs on the back of his neck stood up, and his fingers twitched in a gesture to ward off evil. Then the song died away, and there was quiet.

The serpent-headed ship rocked slowly into balance on the waves. The few remaining crew, frightened almost out of their wits, clung to the railing. Heben saw a hard-bitten, much-scarred man weeping with terror, and desperate cries and gurgles echoed up from those in the water.

Heben had learned when he first began his voyage from Merithuros that few sailors knew how to swim. He could not swim himself, but he'd expected those who lived on the sea to be better able to survive if they happened to find themselves in it. But an old sailor who'd befriended him had shaken his head.

"If you be washed overboard in a storm or suchlike, better to go quick than be splashin' about." He'd shuddered. "Don't fancy goin' round and round in circles, waitin' till you get so tired you can't lift up your arms no more. Or waitin' for a sea serpent to nibble you up. Hundred rows of teeth, some of them serpents. No, better drown quick and have it over."

The old man had had his quick death in the end. The pirates

had struck him one hard blow on the skull when they first captured the ship, and that was the last thing he knew. Remembering, Heben struggled to free himself from the heap of his fellow captives. He wanted to see what would become of the pirates now.

The disheveled captain yanked at the ropes that entangled him. The dark-haired young woman stood quietly in her little boat and waited, one hand shading her eyes against the sun.

"Come aboard," demanded the captain as he flung aside the last loop of rope. "Come aboard, and we'll parley."

"There's nothing to parley about," said the young woman. "Do you surrender, or must we throw you overboard as well?"

"No! No!" The captain rubbed his hands up and down on his stolen embroidered coat. "Wait on. Let's discuss this sensibly. No need to act like barbarians, is there?" He gave them a nervous grimace that was intended as a mollifying smile.

"Surrender!" a girl's voice rang out from the other boat. "Surrender, you murderin', thievin' son of a dog, or you'll find yourself flyin' over the Sea of Sevona afore you can draw another breath!"

The cook let out a long cackle from under the pile of prisoners. "You let 'im have it, witch-girl!"

"The witches of the Isles," said the prisoner who believed in sorcery. "It's them, by all the gods. I heard tales, but I never thought to see 'em — no, nor hear 'em, neither!"

Heben swallowed. He felt the same way; he could scarcely believe what he'd witnessed. Perhaps *this* was the dream and what he'd taken for a dream was reality. But then someone kicked out a foot and caught him under his rib, and he gasped in pain. This was no dream.

The older girl with the dark plait raised her hands again and sang one clear note. The captain's hands were suddenly manacled, encased in a lump of some stuff that glittered like diamonds in the sunshine. Heben had never seen ice before. The captain gave a yelp of fright and leaped backward.

"It's *cold!*" he spluttered.

"Do you surrender?" asked the girl patiently. "Or shall I imprison your whole body in ice?"

The captain staggered for a few steps, regarding his trapped hands with horror. "I surrender; I surrender!" He sank to his knees and began to thump the block of ice against the deck. But it was impervious and wouldn't even crack.

"Very good," growled the burly rower. "We'll come aboard. You — you with the beard — let down a ladder. And don't think about any tricks."

But the whole crew were so cowed by what they'd seen that they were incapable of thinking up any tricks of their own.

The pirate ship was soon transformed. The pirates were disarmed, trussed up, and herded to the stern of the ship, where the burly man stood guard, his thick eyebrows drawn into a fierce scowl. Those who had been blown over the side were hauled aboard to join their fellows, shivering and chastened. The prisoners were freed. Heben and the others were untied, and those who had been locked up below were released, blinking, into the sunlight.

Briskly, as if she'd done this a dozen times before, the tall young woman took charge. "Where is your windworker?"

The captain shook his head. "Don't have one."

The other girl snorted. "Pirates, with no windworker? S'pose you ain't got no sails to your masts, neither!"

The captain turned pleadingly to the tall girl. "She ran off. With my second mate, half a turn of the moons ago. We haven't found a new one. There aren't as many windworkers for sale as there used to be."

The younger girl laughed. "'Cause we got 'em all on our island!" she crowed.

"Never mind," said the dark-haired girl. "We did come to free your windworker, but there are plenty of other things to do."

The pirates were set adrift in rowing boats, with sufficient provisions to take them back to port, but no more. The serpent-headed ship was handed into the control of the sailors whose own ships had been sunk by the pirates and the stolen goods returned to their proper owners. Heben claimed his sword and his earrings. The little leather pouch hadn't even been emptied; with relief, Heben found his Clan medallion and all his coins still safe inside.

"But you ain't just lettin' 'em go?" objected the Gellanese who had been roped to Heben. "What about cuttin' their heads off? Or even their hands?"

"Take 'em to the tallow pits!" shrilled the cook. "Like they would've done with us!"

Their five rescuers exchanged rueful looks. The younger girl laughed.

"There are no tallow pits," said the boy with the lenses. "They were coming to the Isles for fresh water. The tallow pits are just a story the pirates spread to scare people."

The Gellanese sniffed skeptically. "Well, even supposin' that's true, which I doubt, you should do somethin' more to punish 'em. You can't just let 'em go free!"

"I used to think that," said the younger girl. "But if we cut their hands off, or their heads, then we ain't no better'n pirates ourselves."

"It's not our task to punish," growled the burly man, arms folded. "Only to set things right."

Surprising himself, Heben spoke up. "It's punishment enough to let them brave the Great Sea in rowing boats. They'll be lucky to get back to Doryus without tearing each other to pieces, if they don't drown, or starve, or get eaten by a sea serpent."

The tall girl turned to him. "Yes. At least we give them a chance," she said. "Which is more than they were willing to give to you."

"Will you take somethin' for your trouble?" said the Gellanese. He waved a hand vaguely over the ship. "I'll bet there's enough loot to see us all rich twenty times over. Aye, we'll share it with you, won't we, lads?"

The tall girl smiled, and her serious face lit up. "Thank you for your kindness. We'll take some of the unclaimed goods, if there are any, some food perhaps, and cloth. But you can divide the jewels and the gold coins between you. We don't need them." She tossed her long plait back over her shoulder. "Now, as for your passengers —"

"If you please, my lady . . ." Heben stepped forward, his heart thumping. "I was a passenger, before the pirates attacked, but I — I wish to end my voyage here."

"Here?" The burly man frowned. "There's nothing here but an empty island, lad."

"That's not what I meant," said Heben awkwardly. The five looked at him with varying degrees of interest, amusement, and sympathy. They saw a thin-faced young man, tanned by a harsher sun than shone here in the northern seas. He was dressed in the same filthy rags as the other prisoners, but there was something dignified and self-contained in his bearing, and a courteous tone in his voice that marked him out from the rest.

Heben tried again. What if, after all, they refused him? "I wish to — to come with you. My voyage, my quest — I came seeking you — the sorcerers of Firthana. That is who you are, isn't it? The chanters of the Isles?"

The young girl with the golden eyes grinned. "Some calls us that. But we got names of our own. I'm Mica. She's Calwyn." The girl with the dark plait inclined her head. "That's Tonno." She indicated the burly man with the dark curling hair. "This one's called Trout." The scruffy boy with the strange lenses waved a shy hand. Mica turned to the man with the spiraling tattoos. "And this is Halasaa." Halasaa nodded but didn't speak.

"My name is Heben." He wanted to bow to each of them, as he would have done to visitors at his father's estate, but here on the ship's deck it seemed an absurd formality. "I am —" He stopped. He had been about to say, "I am of the Cledsec, third son of Rethsec," the customary introduction. But since his father had cast him off, he was no one's son, he belonged to no Clan. "I am from Merithuros," he said feebly.

Though he was so young, his troubled dark blue eyes stared out from a fine web of wrinkles, as if he was used to squinting into the sun. Like Darrow's eyes, thought Calwyn with a stab of pain.

"And what is your business with us?" she asked, more abruptly than she'd intended.

Heben held out his hands in the traditional Merithuran gesture of supplication. "You have saved my life. Among my people, that lays a responsibility on you. I need your help."

The five looked at one another but said nothing. Then the tattooed man, Halasaa, who had not uttered a word since they'd come onto the ship, stepped forward and clasped Heben's hands. *Then you had better come with us, my brother, and tell us your story, if there is a story to be told.* Halasaa didn't open his mouth, but Heben heard the voiceless words sound in his mind.

Startled but grateful, Heben smiled. For once, relief knocked the manners out of him. "Oh, yes," he said simply. "There is a story to be told."

* * *

Before noon, they were aboard the chanters' boat, *Fledgewing*, which had been concealed in one of the deep inlets of Istia. They watched as the serpent-headed ship, under the command of its new crew, slid away toward the horizon. Heben overheard Calwyn murmur to Halasaa, "I can never see a Gellanese galley without thinking of Samis and that empty ship of his."

Halasaa must have given a silent reply, because Calwyn grimaced and answered, "Yes. And I suppose it's at Spareth still."

As Heben stood there puzzled, a heavy hand fell on his shoulder. "Know anything about sailing a boat, lad?" barked Tonno. "No? Then you'd best keep out of the way."

Soon they were sailing swiftly toward the chanters' home. The tiny island of Ravamey, one of the hundred islands of Firthana, was half a day's journey from where they'd encountered the pirate ship. Mica proudly pointed it out to Heben when it was barely visible on the horizon, a green mound rising from the dazzling sea. As they sailed nearer, other green shadows loomed into view behind it. It was said that no island of Firthana was farther than a stone's throw from another, and there seemed to be three or four other islands almost as close as that to Ravamey.

"Fisher-folk lived here, years ago, but after the slavers come . . ." Mica's voice trailed away.

"The slavers burned what they didn't steal," said Tonno. "Killed some, kidnapped some. The rest fled."

"But the fisher-folk are beginning to come back," said Calwyn.

She gestured toward a cluster of whitewashed cottages, bright in the afternoon sun, and lines of tall sheltering trees that rose up the slope behind them. "We're not alone here anymore."

They were close enough now to hear the crash of waves against the base of the cliff. Tonno swung the tiller so that *Fledgewing* shot past the rocks into the calm water beyond.

Mica began to sing a chantment, and the sail filled with a spell-wind that carried them easily through the narrow heads and into the bay.

"It's a tricky harbor to get into without just the right wind," said Trout.

"We're spoiled, I reckon," grunted Tonno. "We've rescued half a dozen windworkers from pirates in these straits. And we have Mica and Calwyn too."

"And we'll have another soon," said Calwyn. "That little girl of Fresca's has the gift, I think."

"Calwyn has a dream to set up a college here, like the colleges in Mithates, but for chantment." Trout solemnly pushed his lenses up his nose as he shared this secret.

Calwyn frowned. "Not like Mithates at all. Don't say that, Trout. The colleges of Mithates make weapons and sell them to whomever bids the highest. They do everything for money. Chantment shouldn't be used like that."

Chantment is given to few, but for the use of all. Heben jumped as Halasaa's words sounded in his mind.

Calwyn said, "We must show you Halasaa's garden. You can't

see it from here; it's behind the hill, where it catches the sun. We grow enough vegetables to feed the whole village — and we fish, of course, and keep ducks. And yet half a year ago there was nothing here but derelict cottages and wild berry bushes."

Mica broke off her song. "Mind you, half a year ago we had more help than we got now," she said sharply.

"Mica!" warned Tonno. A look of pain crossed Calwyn's face, and her gaze flickered to a single whitewashed hut perched at the very top of the cliffs, far from the rest of the village. But then she turned away.

They drew close to the jetty, and a little crowd of children came running to greet them. Two women looked up from their baskets of freshly gutted fish and wiped their hands on their aprons, and a man mending the hull of an upturned boat reached to catch the rope that Tonno flung out.

"Welcome, *Fledgewing!*" he called. "Did all go well?"

"Did you catch the pirates?"

"Did you throw 'em all overboard? Did they drown?"

"Did you bring back any treasure?"

"Who's he? Is he a windworker?"

"Boys ain't windworkers, you potato head!"

The children tumbled over one another with eager questions, and the bolder ones caught hold of the side of the boat and clung there, drumming their bare feet on the planks.

"Off the boat!" roared Tonno. The children shrieked with mock fright, leaped back onto the jetty, and ran off laughing.

"He pretends to be a grumpy ogre," said Trout to Heben. "But he's soft as butter underneath."

Heben nodded politely, but the sight of the children had reminded him of the twins, and his heart was heavy.

"All went well," called Calwyn to the waiting villagers. "Linnet, we've brought some sacks of grain, and a bale of fine goats' wool ready to be spun, and a barrel of best wine from the north of Kalysons. And a guest too," she added, smiling at Heben. "Trout, will you take Heben to your cottage and look after him? We'll meet you there at sunset, and then we'll hear his story."

Later, after Heben had washed with water warmed over the fire and changed his clothes, he sat at the long table in the cottage that Trout and Tonno shared, a mug of sweet steaming potion before him.

"Honey brew." Tonno ladled it out. "My own recipe. Not much that this can't cure."

"Now then," said Mica, settling herself. "Give us your tale."

Heben looked around at the five curious faces. At the Imperial Court, and even on his father's estate, storytelling was a far more formal process. He would be standing in the center of the double ring, an inner circle of men and the women seated three paces back. He would strike the drum of stretched *hegesu* hide to mark the most dramatic moments. His listeners would judge him on the flourishes of his rhetoric, the cunning impersonations of well-known people, and the twists of poetry that he could inject into the ancient framework of the tale he had chosen to repeat. But this was not one of the ancient stories. This was his own tale, and he was far from home.

"My name is Heben, of the Clan of the Cledsec," he began. "I was born the third son of Rethsec, son of Cheben, called the Quick —"

"You can leave out the family tree," growled Tonno.

Please go on. That was Halasaa, his face encouraging.

Unsettled by the interruption, Heben faltered. "I — my father — my family is one of the Seven."

"The seven what?" said Trout.

"The Seven. The First Clans."

Still they all looked blank.

"Forgive us," said Calwyn. "None of us has ever been to Merithuros. These First Clans — do they rule the Empire?"

This was not the way storytelling was supposed to proceed. "No, no. The emperor rules the Empire. But the Seven Provinces of the Empire each belong to one of the Clans. My father owes allegiance to the emperor, but he is Lord of the lands of the Cledsec. Nomis is Lord of the Trentioch. Yben is Lord of the Darru —"

"All right, all right," said Trout hastily. "We understand."

"Only members of the Seven Clans are allowed at the Imperial Court. The provincial officials and the ministers of state are always chosen from the Seven. And the generals of the Army, of course. I'm going into the Army —" He stopped. "At least, I was."

Trout said, "Merithuros is one of the chief customers of the weapon makers of Mithates. Their army must be the best-equipped in all Tremaris."

Calwyn frowned. "The Empire is not at war, is it?"

"It's important to maintain a strong army, my lady," said Heben.

"But why?" persisted Calwyn.

"There is much unrest among the outcasts in the coastal towns and the workers in the mines. Bands of rebels stir up trouble. Without the Army, there would be no way to control the uprisings and revolts. The Army is the thread which stitches the Empire together." Heben shifted uncomfortably in his seat. In Merithuros, women did not discuss political matters. In the company of men, women rarely spoke at all. But Calwyn was still curious.

"*Why* is there unrest? Are the miners unhappy? What do the rebels want?"

Heben was lost for words. He'd never wondered if the coast dwellers had reasons to be discontented: It was simply their nature. He admitted, "I don't know, exactly. The work in the mines is — is not pleasant, I suppose. But if the miners didn't work there, they would starve, so they ought to be grateful. . . . And the rebels say they want to overthrow the emperor. But who would rule the Empire, if not the emperor?"

"None of the other lands in Tremaris has an emperor," Trout pointed out. "And they seem to manage all right."

"P'raps they want a different emperor," suggested Mica.

"Now see here," said Tonno severely. "We won't get mixed up in any of these plots and schemes. It's nothing to do with us. If you've come here to ask us to help you overthrow the emperor and put yourself on the throne instead, you've come to the wrong place, my lad."

Heben was angry. He was too well trained to let it show in his face, but his voice shook with suppressed passion. "I'm not interested in the rebels and their plots! And I certainly don't want to be emperor. That's not why I came here. I came to ask you to help your own kind, to help . . . to help chanters!"

At last he had their full attention; they were all silent, waiting for him to go on. He drew a deep breath, but somehow he couldn't speak.

Halasaa's unvoiced words sounded, gentle as a rain of falling dust. *Something has befallen one close to you.*

"Two," said Heben shakily. "Twins. Gada and Shada. It was my fault." He blinked away tears. "I took them with me to Teril. I thought the journey would be a treat for them. But if I'd known that they'd meet that *chanter* —" He was unable to suppress the venom in his voice. He took his hands from the table to hide their trembling and breathed deeply. He didn't see the five around the table exchange glances.

When Heben had composed himself, he went on. "I let them explore the market by themselves while I was on my father's business. That's where they met him. He showed them — taught them tricks, songs. *Why* did he have to choose them?" he burst out. "Why couldn't he have left them alone?"

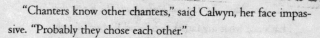

"Chanters know other chanters," said Calwyn, her face impassive. "Probably they chose each other."

Heben was struggling between politeness and his revulsion for all things magical. "I'm sorry, my lady," he said at last. "I had forgotten that you are chanters too."

"Not all of us," said Trout.

Tell us what happened. Again it was Halasaa who urged him on.

"When we came home from Teril, they practiced the — the songs. Secretly. They had enough sense for that. But one day they showed me." He closed his eyes briefly with the pain of the memory. "Of course I told them not to show anyone else, never to tell anyone! I warned them, I tried, I tried to protect them — But someone must have seen them, heard them. Someone told my father."

"What happened to them?" asked Calwyn.

Heben stared at her. "The soldiers took them. By order of the emperor, every child that shows the curse of chantment is handed over to the sorcerers."

They are your brother and sister.

"Yes. Not by blood. I am a third son — not very important, even in the Clans. I spent my days roaming my father's estate, and I found my family where I could. The twins were born on my father's lands, so I am their brother-in-land. Since they were orphaned, I have obligations to care for them, just as if we were related by blood. The land makes a bond between us."

Halasaa nodded. *Yes. The land binds us all. This is as it should be.*

"That's not what my father says," said Heben bitterly.

Heben did not storm and rage; that was not his way. After the twins were taken, he would not rest until he'd seen his father. At last Rethsec consented to receive him, in the lord's tent, seated in the high-backed chair of his lordship, and with all the men of the Clan around him: Heben's brothers, his uncles and cousins. The message was plain: Rethsec spoke as Lord of the Clan, not simply as his father. This was business of the Clan, not merely the family.

"We must ride after them. There's still time to take them back before they're given into the hands of the sorcerers!" Heben cried.

"Those children are dead to us now," said Rethsec coldly. "Tonight we will hold the ceremony of mourning. Their names may not be spoken until the moons go into darkness."

"Gada and Shada belong to us," said Heben, deliberately speaking their names, saying, *They are not dead.* "We cannot give them up; we must not!" A murmur ran around the tent, like the grumble of distant thunder.

His father's anger was swift and terrible. "You do not say *must* and *must not* to your Lord, Heben. The bonds of family, of home and Clan and land, are severed for those children. Beware, my son, lest they be severed for you too."

"Sever them!" Heben threw back his head. He didn't believe his father would act on his threat. "Gada and Shada are my brother and sister. I won't abandon them!"

His father rose and tore Heben's Clan medallion from his brow; it dangled from his hand as he pointed to the door of the tent. "Get you gone! If you care so much for a pair of unwashed chanter brats, then share their fate. Take yourself into the desert; begone from my lands. While I have breath in my body, you shall not return."

In a flash, Heben saw his mistake: to challenge his father in front of all the Clan, all the brothers and uncles and cousins. The Lord of the Clan must assert his authority, even at the cost of losing his own son. Rethsec had no choice. Heben should have dropped his eyes and fallen to his knees to show his humble submission to his Lord. For a long moment he stared at his father.

Then he turned on his heel and left the tent. There was nothing else he could do. Before the sun had inched a handspan closer to the horizon, he had packed his few possessions, buckled on his sword, and ridden away.

He was not far from the homestead when he heard a shout behind him. He thought, *He calls me back, he forgives me!* He turned in the saddle of the *begesu*. It was his younger brother Shabsec who followed him.

"Heben!" he called. "Mother sends you this."

Something sailed through the air; Heben caught it. It was a small leather pouch, oddly heavy in his hand. He undid the thong that bound it; it was filled with gold coins, all the wealth his mother possessed. If his father ever cast her off, she would have nothing. Her own Clan would never take back an abandoned wife. She would be forced to live as a beggar on the streets of Teril or one of the other mining towns of the coast, where all outcasts drifted. There was something else among the coins: Somehow his mother had rescued his Clan medallion.

Heben swallowed hard and looked up to call a message to her. But his brother was already riding away, not the fourth son any longer. Shabsec was the third son now.

"A hard man, your father," said Tonno grimly. "To cast out his own son."

"The twins were just as much his children, under the old laws," said Heben. "If they could not expect protection from him, then why should I?" He swiped at his eyes with his sleeve, ashamed of the tears he could not control. "I did try. I rode after them. But —" He dropped his head. "By the time I caught up to the soldiers, it was too late. The twins had already been delivered to the sorcerers. One of the soldiers took pity on me; he was from my Clan. He told me that he'd seen the sorcerer before, at the Palace of Cobwebs. That must be where they keep all the stolen children."

"The Palace of Cobwebs. That's what they call the Imperial Court, isn't it?" said Calwyn.

Heben nodded. "It's a vast place, and well protected. I have visited it once. I could never hope to rescue the twins from there alone."

"So you came searching for us," said Calwyn. "For other chanters."

"Do they talk about us?" demanded Mica eagerly. "In the middle of the desert?"

"Not there," Heben admitted. "At first I thought of going to foreign lands and seeking out those who could do magic — somewhere, anywhere, Gellan perhaps. They say that tricksters and magicians are as thick in Gellan as flies on meat. But when I came to Teril, I heard the talk of the sailors there. They spoke of a band of chanters in the Isles of Firthana who were preying on the pirates of the Great Sea, and making the waters safe at last for honest traders and fisher-folk. And I thought, *They're the ones I need.* I didn't think then that my own ship would be captured by pirates —"

"And here you are," said Trout.

Heben looked around the table. "I thought you would all be Firthana-born. But you're not, are you?"

Mica laughed. "Only me! I lived in the Isles all my life, till the pirates took me for a windworker. Tonno's a fisherman, from Kalysons. Trout were a student in Mithates, makin' weapons and carts and all sorts of stuff, like them lenses of his. Calwyn's from Antaris, far away in the mountains, and she were a chanter of ice afore she learned any other magic. And Halasaa is one of the Tree People, from the Wildlands."

Heben couldn't help staring at tall, copper-skinned Halasaa, who spoke without a voice. But Halasaa smiled at him serenely. How strange, thought Heben, that all these people, from every corner of Tremaris, from places he had never even heard of, could live together just as if they were a Clan, tied with bonds of blood and land. Indeed, more peacefully than most Clans, he reflected, thinking of the feuds and squabbles in every one of the Seven, which sometimes ended in open warfare.

Tonno thumped his fist on the tabletop. "Who'd have thought it? Did you hear him, Mica? We're the talk of the taverns of Teril and the smokehouses of Har, and every port in between!"

Calwyn frowned and gave the end of her plait a tug. "We didn't begin this just to be the subject of tavern talk."

"Wait till we rescue them children!" cried Mica. "Then we'll be the talk of the deserts as well as the seas!"

"It doesn't sound as though anyone in Merithuros will hail us as heroes for saving chanters," said Calwyn. "And besides, we haven't rescued them yet."

"Yet, she says." Tonno tipped the last spoonful of honey potion into his mug. "You want to go, then?"

"Course we'll go!" Mica's eyes shone. "We ain't cowards!"

These children need our help as much as the windworkers taken by the pirates, came Halasaa's unvoiced words. *Perhaps more. We cannot turn our backs to them.*

"Agreed," said Tonno. "We'll bring back some fine pupils for that college of yours, lass."

A shadow of doubt crossed Trout's face. Calwyn leaned forward. "Trout? Wouldn't you like to see the deserts?"

"Ye-es, but . . ." Trout tilted his cup this way and that. "I'd like to finish that bridge over the stream. And there's my direction-finder —"

Groans and smiles ran around the table. All through winter and spring, Trout had been working on a device to show direction, so they could steer *Fledgewing* without consulting the stars and moons. But he was no closer to perfecting it now than on the day he'd begun.

"Never mind him. The rest of us'll come," said Mica decidedly.

"No, please, wait!" said Heben, with some alarm. "I beg your pardon. You are very kind, but you cannot all come to the Palace of Cobwebs. One or two perhaps, but a group so — so large would raise suspicions." *A group so strange-looking,* he had almost said.

There was a short silence. Heben had the feeling that they had understood him perfectly.

"Calwyn has to go," said Mica flatly. "She's the strongest chanter out of all of us."

And I will go with her. Halasaa's words were firm.

"You'll need someone to take you across the sea," said Tonno. "You'll need me on *Fledgewing*."

"You ain't leavin' me behind!" Mica's golden eyes flashed.

Heben said cautiously, "Calwyn *might* pass as a lady of the court. But you —"

"I'll be her servant," said Mica triumphantly. "A lady ought to have one servant *at least*. Even I know that!"

Calwyn said to Heben, "How many children are there?"

Heben was puzzled. "I've told you, my lady. Two. Gada and Shada."

"But there must be others. You said that every child in Merithuros who shows the gift of chantment is stolen away. How many do you think are held in the Palace?"

Heben stared. "Do you mean to rescue them *all*?"

"Of course." Calwyn's voice was sharp. "Did you think we would rescue your twins and leave the others to their fate?"

Heben dropped his eyes. "I — I didn't think." He paused. With an effort, he said, "Being a chanter is a rare thing. In my lifetime, I have never known another born in the lands of the Cledsec. There might be many children kept in the Palace of Cobwebs. But I don't know. Perhaps they don't keep them locked up for long. Perhaps they —" His voice faltered.

Tonno's broad hand clapped his shoulder. "Don't worry, lad," he said. "I know what it is to lose a brother, aye, and a sister too. If there is a way, we'll save them."

"And the others too," Mica chimed in. "Even if there's a hundred of 'em!"

Calwyn said, "I'm sure Darrow has visited the Palace of Cobwebs. He would know where to begin to look for these children."

An awkward silence fell around the table, and no one would meet Calwyn's eyes.

"Who is Darrow?" asked Heben.

"Our friend," said Calwyn at last. "He's from Merithuros, like you, and he is a chanter too, an ironcrafter. I'm sure all the chanter children of your land are ironcrafters — Darrow led us when we defeated the greatest and most dangerous sorcerer who has ever been."

Almost a year before, in the ancient, derelict city of Spareth, they had faced Samis, a prince of Merithuros who had tried to become the Singer of All Songs. If he had succeeded in mastering all the Nine Powers of chantment — the Powers of Tongue, Beasts, Seeming, Winds, and Iron, the Powers of Becoming, Fire, and Ice, and the Great Power, the culmination of them all — he would have made himself more powerful than any god. But Samis had died in the attempt, and they had left his body there in the ruined city, deep in the Wildlands.

"We all had a hand in the battle against Samis," Tonno reminded her. "Or a voice."

Calwyn ignored him. "If we had Darrow's help in this quest, it would be far easier. But he has . . . gone away for a time. To be alone."

"Alone!" snorted Trout. "Even before he left, he wouldn't talk to us. He hadn't even come down from his hut to eat with us since the last time the moons were all splinters."

"He sat up there and sulked all day," said Mica, and the anger in her voice barely masked the pain that lay behind it.

He is ill. Halasaa's words made them all turn to face him.

"You're supposed to be a healer," flashed Mica. "So why couldn't you heal him?"

The sickness is not in his body, nor in his mind. Darrow's sickness lies in his heart, and in his dreams. It is beyond the reach of my gifts of healing.

"He was so deep in sadness that none of us could reach him," said Calwyn. Abruptly she pushed back her chair. "I'm going to ask Fresca to watch the hives for me while we're gone."

She left the cottage, and after a moment Heben saw her in the moonlight, trailing up the hill toward the tall trees at the cliff's edge, a solitary figure with the dark plait down her back.

"That's not the way to Fresca's house," said Trout.

Mica elbowed him in the ribs. "Can't you see she wants to be by herself? She's gettin' as sad as he was."

Come. Halasaa stood behind Heben, as tall and silent as a tree himself. *I will show you a place to sleep.*

Calwyn pulled a rug around her shoulders and sat down on the broad stone windowsill in the main room of the little cottage she and Mica shared. The window looked out across the dark, curved hand of the harbor and the scattering of whitewashed cottages, where a smear of wood smoke hung in the moonlight. Clouds smudged across the stars and the three moons, and a mist was spreading across the water.

Was Darrow somewhere, in his small boat *Heron*, on that dark sea? It was the time that the sisters of Antaris called the Fingernail and the Quartered Apple. Did Darrow stare at the sky too, at these same moons? Or was he in a tavern in Gellan, listening with his quiet smile to the boasting of men? Or was he wrapped in his cloak, making an uncomfortable bed by a hedge, or snug in a hay-filled barn somewhere on the plains of Kalysons?

She remembered how they'd sat side by side on this windowsill in the autumn sunshine, when they were supposed to be making the cottage more habitable.

* * *

"Not like that. Try it again." Laughter twitched at the corners of Darrow's gray-green eyes. He was trying to teach Calwyn ironcraft, but he was a more patient teacher than she was a pupil. "You must sing the two notes together. One in your throat, and one in your mouth. Like this —" He sang, and the broom swept across the floor by itself.

Calwyn tried to copy him, but the notes buzzed and tickled in her nose, and she burst into laughter. "It's no use, I can't do it! And everyone knows that women can't sing the chantments of iron."

"That's not true. I knew female ironcrafters in Merithuros. It's more difficult for women, but not impossible."

"Impossible for me!" She sneezed. "There's too much dust in here."

Darrow tweaked the end of her long plait. "Calwyn," he said, suddenly serious.

She looked up. "Yes?"

He took her hand between his. "Calwyn —"

But then Mica had come bustling in with a bucket and a brush, and Darrow had let Calwyn's hand drop and turned away.

Darrow had hardly spoken to her again before he went away. That winter, he had gradually fallen more silent. He'd withdrawn to his hut on the cliff top, spending less and less time with her and the others. She noticed that when one of them spoke to him, a swift flicker of irritation crossed his face, like the shadow of a sea hawk flickering across water, and his replies were short and impatient, almost angry.

Sometimes, during those long winter nights when they sat around the fire, sharing songs and stories, Darrow would take out the ring, the bloodred ruby ring that had belonged to Samis, and study it as intently as if he could see visions unfurling in its dark depths. Calwyn saw, and it troubled her, but she said nothing. It was as if the ring had cast some kind of spell over him; she wished that they had left it in Spareth.

At last there came a day, at the beginning of spring, when Darrow readied *Heron* and sailed away. He had told Tonno that he needed time to be alone, to think. To Calwyn, he had said nothing, not even good-bye.

Just once in all the time since Darrow had sailed away, three full turns of the moons, she had asked Halasaa, "Does he still live?"

He hadn't needed to ask of whom she spoke. He had answered her gravely, *Do you think so, my sister?*

"Yes," she'd said. "I think so."

Your bond with him is stronger than mine. If you believe he lives, then he lives.

But she was not as reassured as she had hoped.

With a sigh, she turned from the window. Tomorrow they would begin the long voyage to Merithuros, and it would be wise to get whatever sleep she could while she still had the enjoyment of a soft bed. Yet she lay awake for a long time that night.

DARROW 1

Far away, on a nameless sea, a boat rocked at anchor in the moon-light. It held one lonely, sleepless figure, a slightly built man a few years from thirty, with fair hair and a silvery scar above his gray-green eyes. He stared at the slow-wheeling stars. A dark light glistened from the great square ruby ring he held, so it seemed that a dark ember, the heart of fire, shone on the palm of his hand. He had not yet slipped the ring onto his finger. It weighed in his hand, as heavy as trouble, as heavy as choice. Then he thrust it deep into his pocket, next to his heart, turned his cheek to the hard boards of the little boat, and tried to sleep.

Heron was a light, quick craft and easy to manage when the wind was in her sails, and as Darrow sat in the stern, one hand on the tiller and an eye to the rigging, he was able to let his mind roam. He was speeding back to Ravamey at last, back to Calwyn. But his thoughts returned insistently to Merithuros and to Samis. He remembered the beginning of their last voyage together and how they'd stared across the rail of the big Gellanese galleon, watching as the golden dunes receded into haze. He hadn't been sorry to leave the Empire behind; he was eager to reach the Westlands, the home of chantment, eager to begin their adventures. And Samis — Samis must have been planning even then. As he stared over the rail, did he vow never to return until he was the Singer of All Songs and emperor of all Tremaris?

Darrow shivered. Would he ever stop thinking about Samis? The man haunted him. Since Darrow was a child of twelve, Samis had dominated his life. "Let me be!" he muttered, and hauled the tiller across, so that the wind bellied the canvas of his sail. He'd hoped that when he left Samis behind in Spareth, dead, their bond would be severed.

Impatiently he turned his mind to the time in his life before he knew Samis existed. He remembered another ship, another voyage, and a small boy, hardly big enough to peep over the side —

The boy was born on the ship *Gold Arrow.* The captain is his father, and the captain's wife his mother, but the whole crew is his family. He runs up and down the rigging with ease, so the sailors call him Mouse. They carve toy mice for him out of whalebone and teach him how to play dice and knucklebones. He sleeps in a hammock in his parents' cabin, and he rocks with the rhythm of the ship and watches the shadows swing as the lantern swings. His mother sits nearby with a brush in her hand, and the lamplight glints on the pale shimmering silk of her hair.

The whole ship is his home; he knows no other. He knows that the ship and all the sailors, his mother and father, are from Penlewin, and they teach him to be proud that he is a son of the marshlands. But he has never seen the marshes and has only the vaguest notion of what they are. *A wet land,* they tell him, and he imagines an endless sea like the one they sail, but crowded with other boats, a community of ships and sailors.

Yet when they come to port, the noise and the crowds frighten him. He clings to his mother's side. His father calls him a milksop and sends him back to the ship. "He's only a baby, Jollan," his mother protests, but the little boy is glad to return to the safety of the ship and his own familiar hiding places.

Arram is a wizened old dark-skinned sailor. The other crew treat Arram with a strange mixture of fear and respect and scorn, but Mouse is fascinated by him and his mysterious eye patch and wonders what lies beneath it.

One day Arram sits by himself on the deck, mending a sail. Mouse creeps closer, watching as the old sailor forces the needle in and out of the canvas, pushing it through with a leather pad in the palm of his hand. Then he sees Arram glance about. Mouse shrinks into his hiding place between a barrel and the duck coop. Arram holds the sail out straight and begins to sing, a kind of song that Mouse has never heard before. The little boy sees the needle fly along the seam, darting in and out, but Arram is not touching it at all.

Suddenly Arram looks up and sees Mouse watching. He stops singing, and the needle drops, lifeless, into his lap. For a moment, the two stare at each other, the old sailor and the little boy. Then Arram smiles his toothless smile and beckons Mouse closer. "You never heard a song like that before, eh, boy?"

Mouse shakes his head.

"I'll sing you another, if you like."

Mouse nods. The old man starts a low growling with words that Mouse can't understand, and the carved mouse in the little boy's pocket stirs as if it were alive. He pulls it out, and it sits up on his hand and cocks its head at him.

Arram laughs. "You'll trap a fly in there, boy, if you don't watch out."

With a snap, Mouse shuts his mouth.

Arram winks at him with his one eye. "Our secret, eh?"

Mouse nods his head. Then his mother calls him to a meal, and he scampers away.

Once or twice after that the little boy takes out his toy mouse and stares at it, but it doesn't move. He waits until he sees Arram sitting alone again, and he creeps up with his hands behind his back. "What is it, boy?"

He holds out the mouse on his hand. Arram laughs his silent laugh and sings softly. The mouse's tail flicks; its nose twitches. The little boy laughs too, and he listens to Arram's song and watches the shape of his mouth as he sings.

Night after night in his hammock, swaying with the ship, he practices the song. It's very difficult, but the little boy is clever and patient, and at last he makes the mouse's nose twitch. He does it again and again, laughing with delight, until his mother comes in to see why he isn't asleep. He curls up obediently, clutching the mouse tightly in his hand, but he's too excited to sleep.

The next day he shows Arram what he can do. The old man's face goes pale under its deep leathery tan, and he looks around fearfully. He seizes Mouse's arm and shakes him. "Never let anyone see that you can do that! Understand me, boy?"

Mouse stares at the old sailor in mute rebellion. He wants to learn more. But Arram is afraid. "'Tis a fearful thing to be a chanter, boy. I lost my home, my family, everything I ever loved, for the sake of this magic, and I were lucky not to lose my life." They strike a bargain: The old man will teach Mouse all he knows in return for Mouse's silence. He doesn't have to tell him again to keep their songs secret; Mouse knows. The secret songs are called chantments. The magical tricks are called ironcraft.

Before long the little boy can toss knucklebones without picking them up and lace his shirt without touching the ribbons, and at night he makes the little mouse run up and down his arm.

Night had fallen. Darrow trimmed the sail and let *Heron* rest on the waves, rocking gently just as his hammock had done in those far-off days. He curled himself in the bottom of the boat, wrapped in a blanket, and stared up at the canopy of stars and the three moons. He had made good progress; the northern stars, the tip of the Spear, showed above the horizon.

He had not dragged out these old memories for many years. It was surprising to find them fresh as ever, as if he'd opened an old forgotten trunk, shaken out some ancient garments, and found them scented like wildflowers. But there was an unhappy smell in the old trunk too, a dusty, suffocating smell. And it was that smell that pursued him into his dreams.

The ship comes to a port they've never visited. It's a hot place, with a smell of spices, and Mouse sees people dressed in long robes. He sees strange woolly beasts, and tall thin towers, and golden sand.

Arram does not go ashore with the other sailors. He says he is sick with jawache and stays in his hammock with a cloth wrapped around his head. Mouse goes to visit him. Arram's skinny hand shoots out to grab his arm, and the old man hisses at him, "Be careful, boy! This is Geel. In Geel, when they find little boys who are chanters, they steal them away to the middle of the desert and eat them up! Our secret, boy. Remember!"

Mouse shakes off his grip and goes away. On the ship, the sailors are always warning him not to do this or that, or they'll tan his hide, or throw him to the fishes, or chop him up for stew.

Mouse runs up the rigging to watch the cargo being unloaded. They have big cranes and pulleys here, the biggest he's ever seen. The crew of Mouse's ship hooks ropes around a heavy bale. But the man who operates the crane begins to lift the bale before the ropes are secure. The captain, Mouse's father, is underneath, bellowing orders; he doesn't notice as the bale begins to slip. The sailors shout and wave their arms, but the captain doesn't hear.

Before Mouse has time to think, he is singing a chantment. He leans from the rigging and sings out as loud as he can. The bale hangs in midair; it dangles from one rope, impossibly suspended. The sailors and the men on the dock stare openmouthed, faces turned upward. Mouse sings. The bale floats. The captain steps back, one step, then another, his face ashen. Mouse stops singing. The bale crashes to the deck, on the very spot where the captain had been standing.

The sailors cheer; they don't understand what has happened, but they are happy their captain is safe. The men on the dock seem frightened. They look up at Mouse, who clings to the mast, and they make a sign with their hands to banish evil. And Mouse sees them steal glances at a man in black robes who stands in the shadows, watching the scene, watching the little boy.

Suddenly Mouse is afraid. He scuttles down the rigging and darts across the deck toward his favorite hiding place. He scrambles out onto the bowsprit and perches there. The man in black robes steps onto the ship. The captain strides forward, frowning, his arm raised. No one comes onto the ship without the captain's permission. But the man in black robes sweeps the captain aside with a wave of his hand, like a fly. His eyes are fixed on Mouse.

The little boy inches his way to the very end of the bowsprit. He is more frightened than he has ever been. Arram's warning comes back to him with terrible force. The man in the black robes stands in the bow. He stretches out his hand, and Mouse feels a rush of relief. The man cannot touch him; he's safe.

Then the man begins to sing. Mouse is lifted by the loop of

his belt. The bowsprit snaps off beneath him and falls with a splash into the water. An invisible hand tosses Mouse roughly onto the deck, and the man in the black robes sweeps him up under one arm. The captain runs toward them, shouting. The captain's wife throws herself at the feet of the man in the black robes and tears at him with her fingernails, screaming. Mouse wriggles and bites and kicks. But the man in the black robes strides swiftly on, with Mouse under his arm, off the ship and away.

Mouse is smothered in the black robes. He will never forget their choking, dusty smell. He can't see where they're going; all he sees is the man's calloused, sandaled feet. The feet move rapidly, down steps, through doorways, along streets, and into buildings. He can hear his mother's voice as she pursues them through the winding streets. Mouse wriggles and twists more than ever. The man raises his hand and clouts Mouse hard around the head. Mouse gives one little gasping sob.

"You'll thank me for this one day, boy," hisses the man. Then he hits Mouse again, and he knows no more.

The Deadly Sands

Mica leaned over the side of *Fledgewing*, staring through a narrow tube. Heben came up behind her. "What is that?"

"Trout made it. You can see far-off things like they was at the end of your hand. Here, look."

She passed him the tube and he stared through it. At once the faint line on the horizon, the shore of Merithuros, sprang into sharp focus. Heben could see the dunes, like frozen waves whose shape echoed the waves that curled onto the beach. He swung the tube back and forth. For as far as he could see, the desert stretched away, fold after fold.

"I thought Doryus were a bleak place," said Mica. "All rocks and little stunted slava bushes. But this —" She shivered. "It's so dead. Don't nothin' live there?"

Heben stared at her in amazement. "The desert is filled with life. There are all manner of creatures: flocks of *hegesi*, and *wasunti*, the wild dogs. Snakes and lizards, and birds and little *nadi* —" Seeing her blank look, he held his hands about one span apart.

"Little burrowing creatures, about so big, with long snuffling noses. Every child in Merithuros, I think, has a *nadu* for a pet."

Halasaa stared toward the shore, his tattooed face difficult to read. *So many creatures in such emptiness?*

Heben laughed. Their voyage had lasted a half turn of the moons, and he was becoming accustomed to Halasaa's silent speech, though it still startled him to hear that quiet voice inside his head.

"Wait, and I'll show you! The desert is far from empty. Not like this —" He gestured with a grimace at the sea that lapped all around them.

"By the gods, you must be joking." Tonno, at the tiller, had been listening to their exchange. "Why, you can't put a bucket into the ocean without drawing out a dozen different kinds of fish and weed."

Mica said, "There's islands near Doryus where you can dive for shellfish, and there's gardens all across the bottom of the sea. There's beautiful corals taller'n a man, and flowers bigger'n your head."

"You dive — into that?"

Calwyn smiled. "You and I have something in common, Heben. We who were not raised by the shore have to learn not to fear the sea."

"My people do not trust the ocean," he admitted.

"But Merithuros has ports, and traders, and fisher-folk, same as every other land. Except Antaris," Mica said.

"Yes. But the coast dwellers are not true Merithurans. Once they leave the desert life, once they leave the sands, they turn their backs on their true heritage. Criminals and outcasts work in the mines on the coast, and only misfits and orphans, people without family, live by the sea."

Calwyn shook her head. "Don't forget you're one of those orphans now," she reminded him.

Half to herself, Mica sang a scrap of a song from her native island.

> *"From the river, the sea;*
> *From the sea, the rains;*
> *From the rains, the river . . ."*

Calwyn said, "The sea connects us all; it's the lifeblood of Tremaris. You will have to learn, as I did, to embrace the ocean, and not to be afraid of it."

Heben looked away. It was true, he had forgotten that he had no family now; he was no different from those outcasts he had always scorned and pitied.

"Ho, Mica!" called Tonno. "Sing us a breeze, lass. This wind is slackening."

"Are you sure we're far enough from Teril? It would be a pity to be arrested as chanters at the very beginning of our quest!"

Calwyn's tone was light, and Heben said with a slight bow,

"My lady jokes, but I fear it is no joking matter. If anyone were to discover you were chanters, your fate would be no better than the twins'. Perhaps worse."

Calwyn was contrite. "I'm sorry, Heben." She and Mica exchanged a look, and when Mica sang up a wind for the sails, she sang so softly that Heben could barely hear the music weaving through the breeze.

The next day they came to Teril. At Heben's insistence, they entered the port without the aid of Mica's or Calwyn's chantment.

Tonno grumbled, "It's a long time since I had to rely on my skills alone to bring *Fledgewing* into harbor."

"It'll do you good," teased Calwyn. "We don't want our chief sailor's skills to get rusty."

Halasaa moved about the boat in his deft, silent way, hauling in canvas and loosening ropes before Tonno could give the order. Tonno had taught him well, and he was almost as at home on the waves as he had been in the dense forests of the Wildlands. But as soon as they drew near the teeming jetties of the port, Heben asked him to go below. "Once we reach the court, we will dress you as a foreign servant. There are many such there, and no one will look at you twice. But here you will be conspicuous until we find you some proper desert dress."

Halasaa merely bowed his head and disappeared into the cabin.

Once at dock, Heben did not want Calwyn and Mica to go ashore and help purchase the supplies they would need. "The ladies will find it dull and dusty work," he said with a bow. "And the town is too rough a place for women."

Mica's eyes flashed. "You can't stop me comin'; just you try!"

"You expect me to carry all the parcels, do you? Like one of those beasts of yours?" Tonno glowered.

"Surely it wouldn't hurt if Mica and I came along," said Calwyn. "We're not so delicate that we can't deal with a little dust." Heben's gallantry was beginning to grate on her nerves.

Heben pressed his lips together and gave another of his stiff bows. "Very well, my lady," he said, but he was not pleased.

He shepherded his small band of foreigners around the marketplace, relieved that they attracted less attention than he expected. The market was a shabby, depressing place, buzzing with flies and inhabited by skinny dogs who slunk along the streets, tongues lolling. It was very hot. The stallholders were slumped beneath their drab awnings, and their goods were shoddy. There were beggars on every corner; one old man looked up pleadingly at Calwyn and shook the stumps where his hands had been. Calwyn was horrified. "Heben! Look!"

Heben threw the old man a swift glance. "He must have been injured in the mines."

"Can we give him something?"

"You give to one, they'll all be crowding round us for the rest of the day. Leave him. They're all thieves. Some of them cut off their hands on purpose, so they can have a lazy life as beggars." And he hurried on.

Calwyn was sorry she'd asked to come. Even Mica was uncharacteristically subdued, and she trailed behind while Heben doled out coins from his diminishing store to buy food, tents, waterskins and cooking pans, and long dust-colored robes.

"But what are these?" Calwyn said when Heben loaded a new bundle of cloth into her arms. She fingered the bright swaths of embroidered cloth, in every color of the rainbow.

"Court clothes, for you," said Heben.

Calwyn slid the silken lengths between her hands. The cloths were beautiful, without a doubt, but she was not looking forward to wrapping herself in these heavy sheets.

There was one last thing to buy. Heben led them to a silversmith's and had the man make a copy of his Clan medallion.

"When we come to the Palace, you must wear it all the time," he explained to Calwyn. "Otherwise no one will believe that you are one of the Cledsec." They had agreed that Calwyn should pose as an obscure cousin of the Cledsec Clan, come to the Palace to acquire some polish.

Calwyn held the small medallion to her forehead. The cool metal scratched uncomfortably between her brows. She sighed; it was one more thing she would have to get used to.

They were all laden down with packages and ready to return to the boat when Mica's head swiveled around. "What's that? Sounds like a parade!"

There was a commotion in the far corner of the marketplace; they could hear shouts and yells, the beating of a drum, and the blaring of horns, and the noise was drawing nearer. "I can see banners!" cried Calwyn, who had a better view than the others.

Heben looked worried. "Are the banners yellow and red?"

"Yes! Is it a festival?"

"No," said Heben. "Not a festival."

Mica's eyes lit up. Laden as she was, she scrambled up onto the rim of a fountain. "I can hear what they're yellin'! Somethin' 'bout bread . . ."

"It's a protest march, to complain to the governor of the province." Heben frowned. "These sea-towners are always whining about something. The rebels stir them up." Without thinking, he echoed what he'd heard his father say. "What they need is a good stint in the desert. That would toughen them up. All these towners are the same. They're soft. They have no honor."

"They say they have no bread," said Tonno grimly.

"They don't look soft," said Calwyn. "They look hungry."

The marchers were almost upon them now; the crowd that pressed around Calwyn and the others was so dense, they could scarcely breathe in the crush. "We should get back to the boat!" Heben shouted, but any kind of movement was impossible. Calwyn could see the faces of the protesters clearly: men and women, children and old people. The force of their emotion crashed over her like a wave in the surf, even more violent than the crush of their bodies. Hunger, fear, anger, and desperation churned all around her. The tattered banners of red and yellow, the rebel colors, fluttered in the hot, dusty wind. The dull, hopeless chant,

"Bread, bread," swelled out in time with the beating drum, and deep in the middle of the throng, invisible, someone shouted, "Death to the emperor!"

"Ought to be locked up," muttered Heben.

Someone knocked the parcel of embroidered cloths from Calwyn's arms, and as she bent to pick it up, she was shoved sideways, lost her footing, and was swept into the thick of the mob. "Tonno! Mica!" she called in panic, unable to see her companions.

"I've got you, lass," grunted Tonno, gripping her sleeve.

Mica was still perched on the edge of the fountain, scanning the crowd. "Somethin's happenin'!" she yelled. "More marchers comin'!"

Incredulous, Heben hauled himself up beside her. "That's not more marchers," he said, and relief showed on his face. "It's the Army. This will sort them out."

But even he was shocked by what happened next. All at once a mass of soldiers burst into the square in a storm of flashing dagger blades. The well-trained troops thrust at the unarmed protesters with square metal shields. Screams rang out as people were trampled underfoot, slashed by the soldiers' daggers, struck down by the heavy shields. Without a word, Tonno lunged toward Mica, plucked her off the fountain, and swung her to the ground. Snarling ferociously and using the force of his broad shoulders, he burrowed his way out of the crowd, clearing a space for Calwyn and Mica to follow. Somehow Heben managed to keep up with them, and soon they were clear of the marketplace, running down a side street, bruised but safe.

"I dropped that cookin' pan!" wailed Mica, as soon as she had breath to spare.

"Never mind," said Heben shakily. "I'll buy another."

Calwyn halted, staring back toward the square. "We should go back. Perhaps we can help —"

"Keep out of it, lass," said Tonno. "I'm not going to scrape you off the street after those soldiers have cut you down."

Mica said scornfully, "You still plannin' to join the Army, Heben?"

"They wouldn't take me without my father's blessing," replied Heben mechanically, but he seemed hardly to have heard her. He was as shaken as the rest of them by the casual violence of the Army.

"There were children in that crowd," said Calwyn.

"The Army has to keep order." But Heben sounded less certain than before.

"They was only marchin' and chantin', they wasn't doin' no harm!" cried Mica.

"They did look hungry," said Heben, almost to himself. "But it has been a harsh year everywhere. Even my father said grain was more expensive than usual."

"Some of them kids had legs like sticks. Didn't you see 'em?" said Mica.

"Mica, leave it," said Calwyn quietly. "Let's go back to the boat."

Tonno hoisted the sack that contained their brand-new tents onto his shoulder and put his arm around Mica, and in silence they walked after Heben.

Calwyn followed, deep in thought. The words of the evil sorcerer Samis came back to her: *Merithuros trembles on the brink of chaos . . . when the Empire falls, all of Tremaris will shudder . . .* She was beginning to realize how little she knew about this place, how ill-prepared she was for this adventure. If only Darrow —

She made an impatient gesture with her hand, cutting off the thought before she could complete it. Couldn't she take ten breaths without thinking about Darrow? Gathering her parcels, she hurried after the others.

The next morning, Heben set off early for the livestock market and came back with half a dozen sturdy *hegesi*. The backs of the woolly animals stood as high as Calwyn's chest, and their long necks gave them an imperious look.

"By the gods!" exclaimed Tonno when he saw the six expressionless animals lined up on the dock, all staring at him from beneath their long, dark lashes. "What are you going to do with *them*?"

"We'll ride them," said Heben. "And they will carry the packs. We'll milk them. And use their dung for fuel."

"Do they lay eggs too? And pack up the tents when you're done with them?"

"The *hegesi* can travel over sand faster than any man can walk," said Heben, in his polite tone, ignoring Tonno's sarcasm. "We need them."

Mica came out on deck, clad in the garments that would protect her from sun and sandburn, her new turban and the long robes of a desert dweller. She squealed at the sight of the *hegesi*. "Halasaa won't never be able to ride one of them big goats! His feet'll be scrapin' on the ground!"

"He and the beast can take it turn and turn about," said Tonno. "It can carry him awhile, then he can carry it!"

Heben was adjusting a saddle strap, but it was his shoulders that were tight, with disapproval.

They set out at midday; Heben was anxious not to lose any more time. He was taken aback that Tonno was to wait behind with *Fledgewing*.

"But you are the captain!" he said.

"The captain doesn't leave his ship unprotected." Tonno's bushy eyebrows beetled down with a warning look.

"So you would rather abandon your crew?"

Halasaa's dark eyes gleamed with laughter. *On land, Calwyn is our captain.*

Heben made no reply; he was sure that Halasaa was making fun of him. Calwyn did not hear this exchange, and in private, she told Tonno to wait for them until the end of summer, but no longer.

"Don't be daft. I'll be here until you get back," he said gruffly and gave her a rough hug.

"What'll you do without us, Tonno?" asked Mica cheekily.

"What I did before I got mixed up with chanters and magic tricks. I'll be fishing." He tweaked Calwyn's turban. "Take care you don't melt away to nothing, eh?"

Already Calwyn could feel an uncomfortable prickle of sweat on her brow. "Mica and I can sing up a breeze to cool us all," she said with a cheerfulness she didn't feel. "That's the advantage of traveling with chanters."

"Not until we're out of the town, I beg you!" said Heben, in a low, anxious voice.

Mica gave Tonno one final farewell squeeze, and Halasaa gripped his hands, and then it was time to go.

In silence, they trooped through the streets of Teril. The noon-day sun blazed down, white-hot, on the grimy buildings, and the marketplace was deserted. There were one or two dark dried blood-stains on the stones, and a crumpled scrap of red-and-yellow cloth had been trodden into the dust, but otherwise there was no sign of yesterday's troubles. Calwyn thought she saw someone peering out at them through a narrow window, but when she turned to look, the figure vanished.

Heben set such a fast pace that the *hegesi* bleated in protest, and before long they were at the outskirts of the town. A scattering of dilapidated huts petered out beside the dusty track. A landscape of rolling dunes confronted them, unmarked by any sign of human habitation. The waves of sand rose and fell, each one sculpted with small ridges, on and on, as far as the eye could see. It was like a sea, thought Calwyn, a waterless sea.

They stopped, and Heben helped them to clamber onto the *hegesi*. Calwyn said to Mica, "Here's a place where Trout's direction finder would be useful."

"You think he knows where to go?" Mica hissed, nodding to Heben.

"Of course he does," said Calwyn. "This is his country, re- member."

As if he had heard them, Heben said, "There is much traffic between Teril and the Palace, but we don't wish to be seen. I will take us a different way." Urging on his *hegesu* with a dig of his heels, he trotted off over the first rise, leading the pack animal by a strap in one hand. Mica, keen as ever, followed as close behind as she could. Calwyn and Halasaa came after, swaying precariously on the woolly backs of the *hegesi*. Even before Teril had dwindled to a series of black dots behind them, Calwyn's legs ached from the effort of gripping the beast. Halasaa's feet didn't quite scrape the ground, as Mica had predicted, but he was uncomfortable, and his long limbs were hunched and tense.

All too soon, the town behind them had vanished. The shining blue line of the ocean disappeared, and the *hegesi* trudged up and down the baked, shimmering surf of golden-white sand. The sun burned down, a white spot of light high in the sky. Halasaa kept one hand up to shield his eyes from the glare.

At first Calwyn was as good as her word and sang a lilting chantment that blew a soft breeze across their faces. Mica joined in eagerly. But it was difficult, with the jolting of the *hegesi*, to find the breath to sing, and after a time, Mica's chantment faltered. Presently Calwyn too began to pause as she sang, and as the day wore on, the pauses grew longer.

Halasaa didn't remain on his *hegesu* for long. Soon after they lost sight of the town, he slipped out of the saddle and began to walk, lifting his feet laboriously. Calwyn watched as he tugged his head cloth over his lean, bronzed face. It was strange to see him completely swathed in cloth. Like a corpse in its shroud, thought Calwyn, and shivered.

Following Heben, they moved across the dunes. Each fold of the desert was striped with dizzying ripples of shadow. To gaze at the harsh lines of light and dark hurt Calwyn's eyes, but the blue glare of the sky made her head swim too. So she stared down at the hypnotic rise and fall of the muscles on the *hegesu*'s back.

Mica took up her chantment again, and the dry air blew stray tendrils of hair across Calwyn's nose and mouth. Her clumsy head-dress, so different from Heben's neat turban, began to fall down, and impatiently she wound it up. She would have to ask Heben to show her how to hold it in place. The jolting of the *hegesu* made her stomach churn. She slid off its back, like Halasaa, and began to walk. The shifting sand dragged at her feet like glue. Heben was right; the padded feet of the animals were better suited to the terrain. But if she didn't walk, she'd go mad.

She kicked out against the long robe that hung down to her ankles. It was impossible to walk when a curtain of heavy cloth struck against your knees with every step! She struggled on for a time, but at last she could bear it no more and returned to the queasy sway of the *hegesu*.

She looked ahead at the tall silent figure of Heben, upright and easy on his mount as he moved steadily onward, a little way in front. Since they left Teril, he had barely spoken a word. Did he regret bringing them here, to this dry, bright place where they did not belong? Perhaps because she sensed that his gallant manners concealed a lack of respect, she did not feel at ease with Heben. But then, she had never known any young men before, except for Darrow, and that was different. And Halasaa, of course, and that was different again. But if anything happened to Heben, how would they survive? Already they had walked so far that she could no longer tell which direction led back to the sea. This would be an easy place to die, she thought, and despite the heat and the sweat that made her clothes stick to her back, a chill ran through her.

It was late in the afternoon when Heben came to the crest of a dune and stopped. He slid off his *hegesu*, his robes billowing about him, though he stood as still and stern as a pillar of stone. In that moment he reminded Calwyn of Darrow, and she felt the familiar pain that stabbed her every time she thought of him.

"Heben's sorry he brought us here," Calwyn murmured to Halasaa.

He sees how helpless we are here. Halasaa's face was grim. *He knows that our lives rest in his hands.*

"Then we must show him that we're not helpless after all!" said Calwyn.

Behind them, Mica shouted, "Cal! Cal! Race you to the bottom!" The younger girl hurtled by with a gleeful shriek, running full tilt and dragging her reluctant *hegesu*, which let out a high-pitched squeal of disapproval. She flew past Heben, tripped over her cumbersome robes, and rolled to the foot of the dune in a laughing, breathless heap.

Heben followed more sedately, a frown creasing his face. "If you please, it isn't wise to run. You will make yourself too thirsty."

Calwyn trotted down the slope and helped Mica to her feet. "He's right, Mica. We must be careful."

But Mica let out a furious cry. "Oh no! My waterskin!"

She had worn the bag, fat with fresh water, slung across her back, and she'd landed on it with all her weight. The skin hung limp; the precious water seeped away, a gleaming puddle absorbed by the sand. Then it was gone, and only a patch of damp showed where it had been. Calwyn shot a look at Heben; he had an expression of horror on his face.

"I'll sing up some ice," she said quickly. "Don't worry, Heben, we can replace it with chantment."

His face recomposed itself into its customary polite, distant look. Clearly he didn't believe her.

"If Darrow was here, he could mend it," lamented Mica, turning the empty waterskin over in her hands. "See, it's the seam what's split. The skin ain't torn at all."

Heben examined the bag and tossed it back to Mica. "I can stitch it," he said dismissively, and despite herself, Calwyn had to smile.

"You're right. We chanters are too quick to think we should use magic for every little task. I could sew it up myself, I daresay, though the sisters in Antaris never thought much of my skills with a needle —"

Heben interrupted. "Forgive me, my lady, but there is no time to mend it now. There is a sandstorm ahead. We must go on before it catches us."

The little band set off once more, in grimmer silence than before. Calwyn sensed dismay rising in Heben now, stronger with every step, though he urged on his *hegesu* more and more swiftly, as if he could outpace his own misgivings as well as the sandstorm. The wind had changed; at the crest of each dune, Calwyn could see a smudge on the horizon, a dirty smear that grew larger and larger. She dug her heels into her *hegesu* until she had caught up with Heben. "Should we take shelter?"

Already the wind was whipping at their ankles, stirring up the golden sand around the hems of their robes. Calwyn saw Halasaa, a long way behind, cough noiselessly and pull a fold of cloth across his mouth.

"There's nowhere to take shelter, my lady," said Heben. He looked to the horizon. "I'm afraid we'll have to sit it out as best we can."

Mica ran up to them. "Cal! Why don't you and me sing up a wind to hold it back?"

"We could try, to keep it at arm's length."

Heben hesitated, then gave a brief nod. They all dismounted and drew the *hegesi* into a close huddle at the top of one of the dunes. The animals were distressed, bleating and pressing together for comfort. Heben tried to persuade them to kneel, but they would not. At last Halasaa laid his hand on the head of each beast between its eyes, and, one by one, they knelt in the sand. The travelers piled their packs in the center of the tight circle and sat, knees touching, with their backs to the desert. As the wind howled higher, Heben showed Halasaa how to wrap his head cloth across his face. Calwyn and Mica left their faces uncovered as the sand whirled about them.

Calwyn began a low chantment, a song of the Isles, and Mica joined her. Their two voices rose together, intertwined, sounding frail beside the ever-growing roar of the storm. Calwyn saw doubt in Heben's eyes; he feared that their voices were too flimsy to pit against the might of the approaching storm.

There was a flicker of movement beneath the stirring sand as a small snuffling animal scurried for shelter, its ears as long as a rabbit's: one of the *nadi* Heben had described. Calwyn saw the white flash of its rump as it whisked into a hole. If only they could do the same . . .

The wind was rising, and their song rose with it, steady and lilting, still audible as it threaded through the howl of the storm.

Mica's wide golden eyes were fixed on Calwyn's face as they sang. Together they wove the chantment, the wind that wound about their huddle of bodies like wool about a spindle, shielding them from the whipping sand. The storm looked like a yellow mist, creeping ever closer. But it was a hot, stinging mist, a deathly cloud.

Then it was upon them. Heben's eyes narrowed above the tight wrapping of the cloth over his face, but he did not flinch. Halasaa had curled himself into the shape of a rock, his knees pressed against his eyes. Calwyn held the cloth up close to her face with both hands, afraid the wind would tear it away. Outside their tight circle, the sand rose in a blinding cloud that blotted out the sky, the sun, the harsh light. The scream of the wind rose too, drowning out Calwyn and Mica's song.

Mica was still singing; Calwyn could see her lips moving, and she herself was singing too, though she couldn't hear her own voice. The spell was holding. The space in which they crouched was untouched by the storm, the sand beneath them a smooth circle of calm. But outside that circle, nothing was still. The suffocating sand whirled and stung and moaned. How long would it go on? Did these storms blow through a whole night? Already it seemed that she and Mica had been singing for half a day, and the wind that beat against their magic was as strong as ever.

And then, more suddenly than it had come upon them, the wind passed. The fine grains of sand floated, a choking cloud suspended in the hard light, and then, slowly as drifting snow, the sands settled. The white sun beat down on them again. The blurred haze that was the storm diminished, moving toward the horizon. The inquisitive face of the little *nadu* poked out of its hole. Its nose twitched once, then it bounded away. Calwyn nodded to Mica, and they let their song drop into silence.

Heben unfolded himself and extended his hands to help Calwyn and Mica up. "Let us go on," he said, as if they'd stopped for a meal, and he clucked the *hegesi* to their feet. But Calwyn thought that after the storm, he spoke to her differently: with less courtesy, and more respect.

They stopped just before dusk, while there was still enough light for Heben to mend Mica's waterskin. They had come to the edge of the dunes. A flat, rocky plain stretched before them, pocked with stones and stunted vegetation, gray-green against the burnt hue of the rocks. There were no more rolling waves of golden sand; that was all behind them. Ahead lay just this red flat, stony plain.

"Let me sing up some water for the *hegesi*," said Calwyn, eager to make amends for their carelessness.

Heben looked up from his neat stitching. "Thank you, but they don't need it," he said. "So long as they eat enough *arbec* leaves, they will have all the moisture they need."

The *hegesi* were already tearing at the juicy leaves of the low-growing *arbec*.

Calwyn squatted beside Heben. "So, if we ran out of water, could we chew the *arbec* too?"

"No," said Heben briefly. "It is poison to men."

And women? Calwyn bit her tongue. "All the same, wouldn't the *hegesi* enjoy some cool water?"

"My lady is more than kind, to think of the comfort of the *hegesi* before her own," said Heben, and bit off his thread.

It took her several attempts to get it right. At first she sang up a thin sheet of ice that melted quickly on the warm ground, but it vanished into the dirt before the *hegesi* could come near it. Then she sang a solid block of ice that Heben eyed with astonishment. But the *hegesi* didn't know what it was and wouldn't lick it. At last she found a hollow in the top of a rock and sang up a handful of snow that melted into a little crystal pool that the *hegesi* lapped at eagerly. When Mica's waterskin was mended, she filled it with the same swift-melting snow and filled the waterskins of the others too. "There," she said, proud of her efforts. "You need never go thirsty in the desert with a chanter of ice in your company!"

Torn between admiration and suspicion, Heben dipped his finger in the pool and tasted the water. "How can it be? How can you make water out of nothing?"

"Not from nothing. Out of the air. There's water in the air, even here, all around us, always. All chantment does is wring it out." Calwyn pressed her hands together as if she were squeezing a sponge. "We can't make something out of nothing. Even the illusions of the Power of Seeming only draw out what's already in the mind."

"What is this Power of Seeming?" asked Heben.

"Chanters of seeming create illusions. They can make you believe you see and feel things that aren't real."

"Samis once made himself look like Darrow, and even Cal couldn't tell no difference," put in Mica.

"Only at first!" said Calwyn, slightly stung.

All life, everything that is, is the river. Halasaa's eyes were bright. *Chantment is only an alteration of the river's flow.*

Involuntarily Heben made the gesture to ward off evil, then looked embarrassed. "I know nothing about sorcery. I could never understand how the twins could make solid objects fly through the air or spin about. Or how they could crack open a log of wood for kindling without an ax. It is a fearful thing."

Calwyn said, "One day, no one in Tremaris will think it fearful or strange to see chantment at work, and it will be as commonplace as mending with a thread, or harvesting vegetables from a field, or fishing with a net."

"I am a son of the deserts, and those last two things are strange to me also," said Heben with a small, tight smile. "You should say, as common as milking a *hegesu*, which I must do now."

Darkness was falling fast as Heben squatted beside one of the *hegesi* and squirted yellow milk into a battered tin cup. He held out the cup to Calwyn. The milk tasted almost sour, but it was more refreshing than her own snow-water, and she drank every drop.

As they crossed the stony plain, they spent the nights under the shelter of the tents. As soon as the sun set, the cold came crashing down with the force of a rockfall. They would light a fire and sit shivering around it; apart from *hegesi* dung, there was little to burn. The low *arbec* plants were not good fuel, and the clumps of dry-grass that grew here and there as high as Calwyn's throat had razor-sharp leaves that crackled up in a flash: good for starting fires, but useless for sustaining them.

On the third night of their journey, Heben shyly took out a flute made from the leg bone of a *hegesu*. He played a thin, eerie melody that wound its way into the night; the canopy of stars and moons shone with a brilliance that was almost violent in its intensity. Mica was nodding with sleepiness. Before long she and Halasaa crawled into one of the tents and lay down on the hard sand, with nothing beneath their aching bodies but the folds of their robes, which were so hot and cumbersome by day yet so thin and inadequate by night.

Heben and Calwyn stayed by the glowing pile of coals. Heben put his flute away, and Calwyn began to sing: no chantment, but a melancholy song of her childhood, a song of the Goddess bereaved, a song of cold and loneliness and aching sorrow. When it had finished, Heben bowed his head toward her.

"Is that a song of Antaris?"

"Yes. It's a winter song. It seemed cold enough to sing it here." Calwyn smiled. Her breath made white clouds in the icy desert air.

Hesitantly Heben said, "I have brought you a long way from your home, my lady."

"And you had to travel far from your home to find us. Don't fear, Heben," she said. "We won't let you down."

A distant howling broke through the silence of the night. On and on it echoed, a deep, sinister call, unutterably wild.

"What is it?" asked Calwyn. "Not a *hegesu*?"

Heben laughed grimly. "No. That's a *wasuntu*, a wild hunting dog. The *hegesi* are their prey, and people too, if we don't take care. They hunt in packs, but they won't come near so long as we have a fire. I'll tend it. You go and sleep."

"I'll tend the fire," said Calwyn firmly. "And when I'm tired, I'll wake Halasaa. You don't have to coddle us, Heben. You forget, we're used to sailing through the night, taking turns at the tiller. You can trust us to mind a campfire. Go and sleep. I'd like to sit up for a while."

Heben hesitated, then bowed deeply. "Thank you, my lady."

"Heben!" Softly Calwyn called him back. "Heben, my name is Calwyn. There's no need to call me 'my lady,' as if I were a High Priestess. We must be equals in this quest, or we will fail."

Heben looked startled. Unwillingly he admitted, "I did not expect your sorcery to be so useful. We might have perished in that sandstorm, if not for you. And it is good to have water whenever we wish it."

Calwyn inclined her head. "And without your desert-craft, Heben, we would have perished a dozen times over."

"Thank you — Calwyn." With a bow and a whisk of his robes, Heben disappeared inside the tent.

Calwyn looked up at the sky. How far away Antaris was, and yet the same three moons sailed here, huge and very clear, so that she could see every mark on their silver faces.

As always when she stared at the moons, her thoughts turned

to Darrow. Where was he now, and when would she see him again? Did he ever think of her? Did his heart ache, as hers did? She laid her cheek against her knee and began to sing the sad winter song once more.

The next day Heben did not ride off ahead as usual but waited so that Calwyn could ride beside him. For a time they went on in silence; Calwyn had little energy for talking. Her whole body was sore to the bones, and her eyes ached from squinting into the glare. Yet she had begun to see a harsh beauty in this parched land, with its red sands and blazing sky. Presently she sang up a breeze that cooled her face and Heben's before drifting to Mica and Halasaa behind them. Halasaa was trudging on foot again, his face lowered, and puffs of dust rose where his bare feet shuffled. When he felt Calwyn's breeze, he looked up with a brief smile of gratitude. Calwyn felt a stab of worry for him. This journey seemed to be harder for him than the rest of them.

Heben cleared his throat, looking at her sideways, as if he had something to ask but was too shy to begin.

"What is it, Heben?"

"Can any sorcerer do what you've done, turning the storm aside and making water out of the air? Could the twins learn to do as you did?"

She shook her head. "No. Only a daughter of Antaris can sing the chantments of ice. And the winds can only be controlled by one born to windwork, like Mica, a daughter of the Isles."

"But you sing up the winds just as she does. Weren't you born in the mountains?"

For a moment Calwyn didn't reply. She didn't like to speak of the fact that she, like the dead sorcerer Samis, possessed the rare gift of mastery of more than one kind of chantment. Samis had thought that gift entitled him to rule the whole of Tremaris. Calwyn didn't think that. She didn't want to think about it at all; her mind shied away from the matter like a mackerel from a shark.

"I was raised in Antaris, but not born there," she said at last. "I'm not certain of my fathering. I must have some island blood too."

Shock flashed across Heben's face. "You are not certain? But —"

Calwyn gave a dry, forced laugh. "Fathers are important in Merithuros, I understand that already. But where I come from, it's mothers who matter more. Any child born to a priestess of Antaris after the Festival of Shadows will always be a little uncertain of their fathering, though boy children, and the girls who have no gift of chantment, are often fostered by their fathers. But the girl children who can sing are raised as sisters together, and the High Priestess is mother to us all." She fell silent, remembering Marna's kindly blue eyes and her regal smile. Would she ever see her again? Would she ever return to Antaris? Suddenly the mountains seemed so far away, they might have been on one of the moons. She shook herself. "My mother's name was Calida," she said briskly, to forestall his pity. "She bore me somewhere in the Outlands and took me back to Antaris before she died. I was only a baby then. I don't remember her."

"I'm sorry," stammered Heben. To be a fatherless child in Merithuros was an unthinkable misfortune. Even though his father had cast him out, he knew who he was: Heben, son of Rethsec, son of Cheben, called the Quick, and so it went on, back and back. He said proudly, "I can trace my ancestry back to Cledsec himself, who was one of the Seven, the first warriors of Merithuros."

Calwyn had to smile. "And who was Cledsec's father, Heben? Who was his mother?"

"The legends say that the gods sent the Seven from the sky in a silver ship."

Mica had been listening. "Then you got sailin' in your blood after all, same as me!"

"It's only a legend." Heben frowned. "And after twenty generations in the deserts, I think we can claim to belong to this land."

No! Halasaa's voice was savage inside Calwyn's head. A quick glance at the others confirmed that they had not heard him; Halasaa's words were for her alone. Halasaa was never violent, never anything but gentle and calm. But the words that tumbled from him now were harsh and disturbed. *This land does not welcome his people any more than a corpse sits up and bids welcome to its murderer!*

Calwyn stared at him. "Peace, Halasaa!" she murmured.

His face set, her friend strode ahead, and the subject of ancestry, whether it was Heben's, Calwyn's, or Mica's, was dropped.

But the image of the murdered land stuck in Calwyn's head, and as the day went on, she found herself listening intently to the small sounds of the desert: the shuffling of the *hegesi*, the crunch of Halasaa's footsteps, the scamper of a startled *nadu*. After a time, she fancied she could hear the breath of the land itself, as if the endless plain sighed like the ocean, or the whispering forests of the Wildlands. But this land seemed to murmur of death and decay. The gnarled, stunted shrubs looked like bundles of dead twigs stuck into the dirt. She noticed tiny piles of *nadi* bones heaped up like abandoned birds' nests. The scattered rocks and boulders lay inert and lifeless. The air was so dry in her throat that she couldn't sing. At that, panic gripped her, for without chantment, she was no longer herself, and she stopped and took a gulp from her waterskin.

Despite the protection of the long robes and turban, Calwyn's face was flayed by the sun. When at last night fell, the cold air was as welcome as a cool bath on her burnt skin. The others were all darker-skinned and stood the fierce sun better; certainly she was the only one who glowed red at the end of every day. Halasaa laid his cool hands against her cheeks, and even before he began the subtle movements of healing, she felt better at his touch.

That night Calwyn slept badly, despite her fatigue. Cold and sore, she found no comfort on the hard ground, and every rustle of a night creature or crackle of the fire jerked her awake. When at last she did doze off, she was tormented with nightmares and woke clammy with sweat, heart hammering, unable to remember her dreams.

* * *

On the fifth day they came through the hills and saw it.

The Palace of Cobwebs lay along the top of a ridge. At first, except that the hills were too low, Calwyn might have taken the Palace for a snowcap: it was a glistening of white marble, the froth on a wave of red rock, a layering of light that burned across her eyes. That was all that could be seen at first: light, and whiteness, and a shining like glass.

As they drew nearer, she could see the texture of the whiteness, the shapes of the interlaced buildings with their curved and gleaming roofs, some high, some low. There were domes and slender turrets and towers as fine as needles; there was one tower that seemed to pierce the sky. Calwyn, who had visited the most ancient of all cities of Tremaris, the abandoned city of Spareth, felt her memory catch at those shapes. She wondered at the builders who had copied them, and the stories of their patterning that must have been passed from generation to generation, until they flowered into being here, carved from the white stone.

"We'll make camp here." Heben led them down a narrow path, almost invisible, into a hidden place between two hills, where a small creek ran. There was shelter and shade beneath an overhang of rock, and green plants feathered the banks of the stream. "There is plenty of *arbec* here; the *hegesi* will be happy, and should not wander. And for us, these fruits are sweet; they are in season now."

Halasaa smiled at him serenely. *This is the way all your lands used to be, wild and green. In this place, the memory of the lost land still lives.*

As if to prove his point, he threw back his head and gave a silent call, and after a moment a bird appeared, circling overhead: the blue flash of a kingfisher. It hovered above them for the space of a heartbeat, no more, then darted away upstream. But a few moments later it returned, with a silver fish in its beak, and it dropped the fish at Halasaa's feet and flew away.

Supper for us all. Halasaa looked at Heben's astonished face and smiled his slow, wide smile, but it was Mica who laughed on his behalf.

After they had pitched camp and eaten, Calwyn wrapped herself in her cloak and walked through the dusk back up the path to a place where she could see the Palace of Cobwebs clearly. As near as this, she could make out some of the intricate lacelike patterns carved into the white stone walls. But no, they didn't look carved; it was as though the Palace had somehow grown into being, a tangled mesh of silk and gossamer, light enough to blow away at a puff of wind, so delicate and fine that it seemed to shimmer and billow in the air.

The light of the setting sun stained the white walls in more colors than Calwyn could have imagined: deep and bloody reds, rich mauves and purples, blue and gray, pale as winter clouds, a bright flare of yellow, then rosy pink like the cheek of a sleeping baby. And as the colors of the Palace shifted, one blending into the next, so the sky behind it changed, flaring and fading, blue into purple into deepest indigo, then black. Then the stars and the three moons shone out, and the Palace was cold and sparkling against the black velvet of the night.

"In the morning," said Heben behind her, "you will see it gold and white and blue."

"It's truly a marvel," said Calwyn. "I never thought I'd see such a thing built by human hands. It's a most exquisite sight."

"Wait until you've seen the walls up close. The carvings are so fine, so delicate, they could make you weep."

"And the people who dwell inside the walls?" Suddenly Calwyn felt nervous. It was not fear of the danger that lay ahead, though she felt that too; this was the same shy awkwardness that she'd felt before the village boys of Antaris. Tomorrow she would bind Heben's medallion to her brow and put on the robes they'd bought in Teril, and they would enter the Imperial Court of Merithuros. She would pretend to be an aristocratic lady, even though she did not know how to speak, or how to dress, or how to hold her spoon. She could not dance, nor flirt, nor play at dice.

Heben flashed her a grin, the first unforced, wholehearted smile he'd given since they'd met.

"Oh, have no fear," he assured her. "The courtiers will make you weep more than the carvings."

Calwyn smiled back at him weakly, and then they were both silent, gazing at the silver confection and thinking their own thoughts, until at last they turned and made their way back to the camp.

Darrow 2

Pleased with himself, Trout stood back and wiped his lenses on the tail of his shirt. The bridge was coming along nicely; within the next day or two, the ends of the archway would meet above the stream. This bridge would stand for hundreds of years, he thought with satisfaction. Even after the stream itself had changed course, this bridge would still be here. Trout's Bridge, they'd call it, long after everyone had forgotten who Trout had been —

A shout from below made him jam his lenses back onto his nose. He frowned. Fresca was coming up from the village, waving furiously. Surely it couldn't be time for lunch already? Fresca shouted something. A few steps nearer and he could make out the words.

"Trout! He's back, Darrow's back!"

Trout flung down his trowel and hurried along the muddy path to the harbor, with Fresca at his heels. Even without a looking-tube, he recognized *Heron*'s brown sail as it swayed to and fro across the mouth of the bay.

By the time Darrow's little boat reached the jetty, half the village was there to greet him, and the children jostled to catch the rope that he tossed out.

"He went away to rest," Fresca murmured to Trout. "But he looks more tired than the day he left. Shoo, shoo, children!" She strode forward, clapping her hands to clear a path for Darrow. "Let the poor lad be! Can't he have a breath to himself?"

Darrow gave her a distracted smile, and he nodded to Trout, but his eyes traveled searchingly across the little crowd and swept up the hill. Trout knew who he was looking for, and so did Fresca. She laid a hand on his arm.

"Come to my house," she said. "I'll warm you a cup of broth, and you can wash. Better than going up to that old hut of yours with no fire laid, and no welcome."

Darrow hesitated, and Trout saw him glance swiftly to the cottage that Calwyn and Mica shared. He frowned at the fastened shutters and the closed door, which the girls usually left flung open to weather and visitors alike.

"They aren't there," said Trout. "They've all gone off in *Fledgewing*."

Darrow's face cleared. "Chasing pirates? So they'll be back tonight?"

"No. Not tonight." Fresca hooked her hand beneath his elbow. "Come inside, and we'll tell you."

Darrow kept his hands wrapped tightly around the bowl of soup while Trout told the story. Darrow said not a word to interrupt, and he didn't touch the broth until Trout was finished. His face was set like a mask; he looked more *foreign* than usual, Trout thought, and his gray-green eyes were unreadable.

He swung around and asked Fresca, "This Heben. What is he like?"

"He's just a boy," said Fresca. "Trying to be brave like a man, but he's a little boy underneath it all."

Darrow looked relieved, which puzzled Trout. Wouldn't Calwyn be safer with a man than with a half-grown boy? But Darrow had turned back to him. "And they have gone to the Black Palace? That's what they said?"

Trout frowned. That didn't sound quite right. "It was some Palace or other."

"But they have gone to find the chanter children?"

"Oh, yes. Definitely."

"Then it must be the Black Palace."

Fresca said, "Eat your broth before it's cold."

Darrow put the spoon into the bowl and left it there. Then he pushed back his stool and went to stare out the window.

"If only she had waited," he said under his breath. "She doesn't know what she's facing. The Black Palace, by herself! She thinks she is equal to anything. And Tonno is worse. I told him to take care of her. I told him —" Abruptly he turned, as if he'd suddenly remembered that he wasn't alone. "Forgive me," he said. "I'm used to thinking aloud, day after day on *Heron*, by myself."

Fresca and Trout exchanged glances. "Don't mind me," said Trout uncomfortably.

"I didn't hear a word," said Fresca, unperturbed. "My hearing's not what it was before the slavers came. Come back and eat your soup, Darrow, for the sake of Si'leth! You look as if you need some good food and some comfort."

Darrow's face closed as he returned to the table. It was true, he had come back to Ravamey in search of comfort, but he'd expected to find it in Calwyn's cottage, not here. In Calwyn's bright eyes and the warmth of her smile, he'd thought he might find the answers he sought, answers that months of solitude had failed to show him. He'd pictured their meeting a hundred times as he sailed back to the island. Would she run down to the jetty? Would he surprise her in Halasaa's garden, or by the hives, with that absurd straw hat falling over her eyes? Or would he knock at her door and see the light come shining into her eyes as she leaped up to greet him?

Moodily he spooned up the soup. Then he gave a grim little laugh. It was what he deserved, to come back and find her gone off on an adventure of her own. He had no right to expect that all her thoughts and her actions should revolve around him, that she would sit quietly by her hearth and wait for him to return. But he wished with all his soul that she hadn't chosen this particular quest. To venture into the heart of Merithuros, to the Black Palace, the secret stronghold of the chanters of iron: She had no idea what she would have to face. Even with Halasaa and the others to help her, he feared for her.

With a clatter he pushed away the empty bowl. "When did they leave?"

"Let me think." Fresca leaned against the table. "It was when

Big Fish Swallows Small Fish. The Fingernail and the Quartered Apple, Calwyn calls it."

"Twenty days ago," said Trout.

Darrow groaned. If only they had waited! He could have persuaded her not to go, or if that failed, he could have gone with her. But that chance was lost. There was only one thing to be done now. Perhaps this was his answer, after all. . . .

"I'll go after them," he said. "I have business in Merithuros in any case. *Heron* is not so fast as *Fledgewing*, but I know the deserts, and I can travel swiftly once I arrive. With luck, I might find them before they reach Hathara."

"Tonno told me he'd wait for them in Teril," volunteered Trout.

Darrow nodded. That was good; they could take *Fledgewing* round the coast together. "I'll leave tomorrow at dawn," he said.

Fresca looked at him in horror. "But Darrow, you've only just arrived! You need to rest, you'll have to stock your boat. Wait a day or two at least. What difference can it make?" But she knew as she looked at his face that no amount of argument would dissuade him. With a sigh, she began to bustle around. "Let me wash your clothes at least. Trout, fetch him something clean to wear, go on now. Darrow, you can lie down on that bed and sleep. You'll be no use to anyone without a good night's rest behind you."

"I would rather go up to my own hut."

"Rubbish! That cold, damp shack! No one's aired it out for a turn of the moons. You won't sleep there, you'll catch your death."

"No, he won't." Trout turned back to argue. "It's the middle of summer." Darrow gave the smallest of smiles.

"I don't care. Get along, Trout! Darrow, you go and lie down on that bed. When Trout comes back, we'll see to your boat, we can get your supplies together. Go on now! I've enough to do without chasing around after you." She scolded Darrow out of her kitchen as if he were one of her own children.

He allowed her to shoo him into the other room. After all, it would be pleasant to sleep on a feather bed after so many nights on *Heron*'s hard planks. Fresca's bed was covered in a cheery patchwork quilt. Darrow sat down and tugged his boots off; it would be a shame to dirty that quilt with his muddy feet. . . .

But he got no further before sleep overtook him, and when Fresca came in to fetch his clothes for washing, she found him sprawled across the bed, fully dressed and fast asleep.

Darrow woke in a lather of sweat. The covers were twisted around his neck, choking him, and he fought his way free with his heart hammering. The cool night air dashed against his face, and he gulped it in with relief.

For a moment he didn't know where he was. Moonlight streamed through Fresca's window. He wondered how many other people all over Tremaris lay awake, staring at the moons. Some herders, perhaps; fisher-folk, waiting for the schools to rise. And the astronomers of the Black Palace, who slept by day and made their observations all night long. Was Calwyn awake somewhere in those deserts to the south, watching the moons? He thought of her long hair, the way it fell in a shimmering curtain to her waist, darkly glinting.

Darrow hunched the quilt over his shoulders, turned his face toward Merithuros, and tried to sleep.

Mouse has gone. The boy is older now, and when he is called anything, he is called by the name of the ship he was stolen from: at first Gold Arrow, then Darrow. When he came to this place, he dreamed every night that the captain and his mother and Arram and the other sailors would come storming over the dunes and take him away, back to the ship, back to his home. But that hope has faded slowly, and the boy's memories of his parents and the ship grow dimmer with every turn of the moons.

It's hard to measure the passing of the years, for the days are all alike, and there are no seasons in the Black Palace. The chanter children live day and night, year in and year out, within its dark walls; among themselves, they call it the Black Place. The sorcerers light the rooms with dim lanterns, continually refilled with oil by some complex mechanism that the children are not permitted to understand. Without sunlight, the children are as pale as ghosts, and the sorcerers are pale too, gliding about silently in their long black robes. The boy does not know which of the sorcerers stole him from his parents, so he hates them all with an equal, secretive passion. There are one or two girls among the children, but all the sorcerers are men.

He understands now that Arram, the old sailor, was once one of these children. *They steal them away to the middle of the desert and eat them up!* It's true. He is being eaten up; day by day, a little more of him disappears.

The Black Palace has no visible doors, no gates or windows. When the sorcerers wish to leave or enter, they cut open a doorway in the smooth sheer walls with chantment and seal it behind them. The boy has never forgotten his first sight of the huge black monolith, when he was carried here on the back of a *hegesu* with a band of other abducted children. The Palace rises on a plateau in the center of the vast plain called the Dish of Hathara: a polished black cube, stark against the red dirt.

Inside, the cube is a succession of vast empty rooms, mostly of polished black stone, relieved here and there with geometric patterns of dull red or bone white to mark out a passageway or frame a door. The sorcerers' robes whisper on the smooth floors. It's possible for the boy to tell where he is inside the cube by the temperature of the rooms. Near the surface, it is baking hot; in the depths, chillingly cold.

The sorcerers have their own way of keeping time. There is an enormous sand-clock at the foot of the central staircase, connected to a series of bells and hammers that strike out the quarters of the day. At sunrise, noon, sunset, and midnight, the deep bells ring, up and down the spine of the staircase that links the many floors of the Palace.

The chanter children are told to be grateful. They are told they have been rescued from the dangerous, ignorant world outside. They are told, "There are no Clans here. We are all brothers." The children are forbidden to speak of their homes or their Clans, but stubbornly, children of the same Clan affiliation seek out one another and cluster together. Children from the same province eat at the same table, sleep in the same dormitory, lend washcloths and blankets and hand down clothes to one another. The boy has no Clan. He eats and sleeps alone and rarely speaks. At first he finds it difficult to understand what the sorcerers and the children say. That passes, but when he speaks, he has an accent different from theirs, and they mock him. He finds it simpler to be silent.

He is always hungry. The children and the sorcerers eat the same monotonous diet: tasteless leaves, mushrooms, soft *hegesi* cheese. There are arid gardens on the plateau all around the Palace, and flocks of *hegesi* graze close to the monolith. One turn of the moons he spends outside the walls, helping to watch over the flock, milking and shearing.

One day during that time, he sees something among the *arbec* plants. Curious, he wanders over to investigate. It is a long black-wrapped bundle, stretched on the red dirt. He turns it over with his foot and then jumps back. A mummified skull grins up at him, and a skeletal hand dangles from the folds of a sorcerer's black cloak.

A voice sounds behind him. "We are not prisoners. We may

leave if we wish." It is a young sorcerer, tall and very thin. His name is Amagis. The boy does not like him; he is cruel to the younger children. Amagis lifts the corpse's dry, fleshless hand, shakes it gruesomely at the boy, then lets it fall. He grins at the boy, without warmth. "Do *you* wish to leave?"

The boy shakes his head. He takes a step backward, and Amagis laughs.

The boy does not forget the mummified skull of the runaway, dried by the winds. But he also remembers Arram. Arram must have escaped. Others must have escaped too. But the boy is not a child of the deserts. He knows nothing of how to live in the barren lands. This is not his place. He could never survive.

But he dreams of his time with the *hegesi* for a long while after he is sealed in the Palace again. He dreams of the sun on his skin, the smell of the clean wind, the warm greasy wool under his hands. Another time, he takes his turn singing round the great millstone that grinds flour out of dune-grass seeds for their bread. He hopes that one day he might be sent to gather the dune-grass, and then he might see the ocean. But the sorcerers never assign him to that task.

No one knows when one of the sorcerers might swoop down like a vengeful crow and carry off a child for the Testing. It might be in the middle of a meal or halfway through a lesson. Sometimes a child vanishes from his bed. Those who have passed never speak of it. Nor do those who fail: They disappear. The girls always disappear; they always fail. Like the dead, the ones who disappear are not spoken of. But unlike the dead, the names of the disappeared are never mentioned again, even after the moons emerge from darkness. It is as if the unlucky ones had never existed. The boy works feverishly at his studies. He knows he is in the first rank of the chanter children, but still he lives in terror, as they all do, of failure in the Testing.

The boy still carries the carved mouse in his pocket. Occasionally he takes it out and turns it over in his hands, but he never makes it dance or twitch its nose anymore. In secret, he has made himself a tiny knife, which he also keeps in his pocket, and from time to time he steals a wooden plate from the dining hall. He sits by himself and carves. It is an eccentric habit; if he wished, he could carve without the knife, and a hundred times quicker, but the subtle movements of the knife comfort him, and in the act of carving he keeps alive the memory of the sailors who carved toys for a little boy, long ago. He makes tiny wooden fish and boats and seabirds. When they're finished, he hides them around the Palace. It gives him a sense of power to know that his carvings lurk in unsuspected corners, safe from the sorcerers' eyes, tucked in a nook behind a lantern or pushed into a crack under the stairs.

One day, between the end of lessons and the evening meal, he sits in a cold corner, absorbed with the scratchings and gougings of his little knife. Something makes him shiver, and he looks up to see black robes looming over him. He jumps up, expecting to be punished. But the sorcerer ignores the knife. He is a grim man with darting eyes and very long arms and legs; the children call him the Spider. He gestures to the boy to follow. The boy feels a shiver of fear that runs from the top of his head to the soles of his feet. This is the Testing.

Terrified, he follows the Spider down the shadowy corridors. His feet slip on the polished stone, and the whispers of the other children echo after him. They avert their eyes as he goes by, as if from a corpse. He doesn't blame them. How many times has he done the same? How many times has he given thanks that some other child has been chosen, not him?

He follows the Spider down corridors he has never entered, into a part of the Palace he has never seen. Soon he is shivering with cold as well as terror.

At last the Spider leads him to a room with white walls. The room is empty. The Spider motions him to go inside. Dry-mouthed, the boy asks what he must do.

The sorcerer smiles a mirthless smile. "Nothing," he replies. He stands outside the room and sings a droning chantment, and the wall seals itself.

The boy cries out. He is in pitch-darkness. And once again he is a small boy, suffocated by musty black robes, borne away from his mother and father and everything he knows. He opens his mouth and gasps for air; his throat is dry with fear.

Blindly he walks forward, hands outstretched, until he bruises his hands on the cold stone. He feels his way around the entire room; it is small and polished and featureless. Blood beats in his ears. He feels the walls again. The room is smaller than before; it is shrinking around him, the walls are pressing in. He cannot sing, he cannot breathe, he cannot stand. Now he is on the floor. His mind is blank with fear. The room tips and spins around him. It makes no difference if his eyes are closed or open. He gasps like a fish out of water. He is dying; that is all he knows, and that knowing swallows him like the dark.

When he wakes, he is in a red-walled room. He sits bolt upright, gasping again for breath, his heart clutched by remembered fear. But it is not dark now. He can see, he can breathe, he is alive. Trembling, he rests against pillows. All around the walls are ranged black-robed sorcerers. The Spider stands beside the bed, next to a very old man the boy has not seen before. The old man's hands are clasped on top of an ebony staff. When the boy sees those hands, wrinkled and blotched like old leather, he knows who this is. The old man wears the Ring of Hathara, Lyonssar's Ring, with its great square red stone. This is the Lord of the Black Palace, the unseen ruler of the sorcerers. He bares his toothless gums in an imitation of a smile.

"Well done, boy," he quavers. "You are one of us now. You will join our brotherhood and become a guardian of the secrets of chantment. For this you were rescued. For this you were brought to us. For this you were Tested."

The boy gapes in confusion. He looks around; each of the sorcerers wears a look of grim pleasure. Uncertainly he says, "I have passed the Testing?"

"Yes."

"But —" He is too afraid to tell them that he sang no chantment, in case somehow they do not know.

The Spider says, "You did what was asked of you: nothing. Even as the room grew small, and smaller still, you did nothing. The Testing is not a test of your skills in chantment. We know your skills. We watch you every day. It is a test of your obedience. You were obedient. Get up, boy. You may go. Or rather —" The Spider gives his leering grin. "You may stay."

The Palace of Cobwebs

"But when will you begin searching?" asked Heben, his courtesy barely restraining his impatience. It was the third day after their arrival at the Palace. He and Calwyn were walking, slowly, because of Calwyn's robes, around the walled courtyard attached to their apartments. Far above their heads a pocket handkerchief of blue sky was visible, but the garden below was all moist greenery and perfumed flowers. Not one direct ray of sunlight penetrated the lush patch of green.

"We've begun already," said Calwyn.

Heben frowned. "Forgive me, but all you've done is walk the public galleries and the halls and gardens. The twins will be hidden somewhere, in a dark corner, in a dungeon —"

Have patience. Halasaa walked behind them, silent and soft-footed as a manservant should be. *We have been listening.*

"Listening for chantment," said Calwyn.

Not here. Halasaa touched his ear, then his forehead, between his eyes. *Here.*

"And have you heard anything?"

"Not yet." Calwyn reached out a fingertip to the ivory-colored wall. The walls of the courtyard were so delicate that they were almost translucent. Shadows could be seen moving within. As they approached one particularly transparent section, a skull-shape suddenly jumped at them: eyes, nose, an open mouth, dark hollows pressed against the other side of the wall.

This was a favorite game of the courtly gentlemen, to startle the ladies through the delicate screens or to loom up behind the curtains that fluttered in every doorway. Their aim was to force an unseemly shriek, but Calwyn was hardier than the courtly ladies, and she had never yet uttered even a squeak, disappointing the pranksters. Now she merely passed a hand over the dark shape and walked on.

The surface was rough to her fingertips. When she looked closely, she saw that it was carved with intricate figures, no bigger than her thumb, who danced in stately procession, their tiny hands interlinked, their skirts swirling. Each one had a different expression: this one proud, this one laughing. But most of them, thought Calwyn, looked rather sad.

There might have been a hundred little figures on this panel. Anywhere else in Tremaris, such a fine piece of work would be a treasure beyond price. Yet here it was just another panel on a nondescript wall in an ordinary garden, half-hidden with leaves; possibly she was the only person who had ever noticed it. In this courtyard alone there were dozens of panels just as intricate, and everywhere throughout this vast Palace it was the same. Every curving wall, right up to the arched ceilings, was covered in carvings, a miniature reflection of courtly life: tiny people hunting, dancing, feasting, stealing kisses, arranging their hair . . .

There was not a single plain surface anywhere in the Palace, nor any straight lines. Everywhere there were curves and arches and bends and twists, as if the Palace were a vast organism that had sprouted up out of the desert, rather than something constructed by builders and masons.

Heben had winced when the face appeared. When they'd entered the Palace, he'd posed as one of Calwyn's servants, his head cloth obscuring his face, and now he was confined to their apartments and the adjoining courtyard, lest any of his relatives see him and send word to Rethsec that his disowned son was flaunting himself at court. But even if he had been free to wander, he would have been as uncomfortable here as Calwyn. It was no wonder he had sought help. He was a fish out of water in this place — or a *wasuntu* caged, Calwyn thought wryly. All the confidence he'd shown out in the desert had melted away.

Calwyn too found the Palace of Cobwebs unnerving. She had been raised in the simple dwellings of Antaris, and on Ravamey she shared a two-roomed cottage. The endless rooms of the Palace and its corridors, its galleries, its unfolding courtyards, its slyly curved walls, its niches and alcoves and unexpected doorways, its screens and curtains bewildered her. The passageways echoed with secretive whispers and rustlings as the courtiers and their servants tiptoed in their dainty slippers from room to room, passing snippets of gossip behind their hands, scrutinizing the robes of other courtiers, sneering, smirking, scheming, snubbing one another.

This behavior was not entirely strange to Calwyn. The closed community of Antaris had its share of gossip and intrigues, and there were those who sought favor with the High Priestess and those who sniped sarcastically at other women. Even so, this was beyond anything she had known in Antaris. There, at least everyone had useful work to do; here, idleness and inventing insults had been elevated to a way of life. Somewhere, she supposed, the real work of governing Merithuros must go on, though she had yet to see any evidence of it. It seemed that the rebels might indeed have cause to complain that the Empire was poorly ruled.

She sighed and touched Heben's arm. "Don't worry. If the twins are here, we will find them."

But privately she was not so certain. At first, they had had some idea of conducting a systematic search of the Palace. Now she knew how immense and how convoluted the Palace was, she suspected that such a search would be impossible.

That afternoon, Calwyn planned to walk with Halasaa around the area that the courtiers called the Garden of Pomegranates: a long colonnaded terrace with secluded nooks and alcoves leading from its shaded walkway. It was a favorite haunt of the minor members of the royal family, and Heben was nervous about their exploring it alone, though he agreed that it was an ideal place for concealment.

"I pray you, don't speak to anyone if you can avoid it," he begged Calwyn. "Even as a country cousin, you're not yet ready for a conversation with one of the Imperial Family. And please, please, don't take Mica with you!"

"Mica's searching the laundries today," said Calwyn. Posing as a maidservant, Mica had worked tirelessly since their arrival, scouring the immense labyrinth of servants' quarters, kitchens and store-rooms, cellars and sculleries that teemed beneath the fine rooms of the Palace.

"I reckon there's more below than there is above!" she'd declared. "You got the easy job, you two!"

Heben looked relieved. Then his forehead creased with worry again, and he cleared his throat. "There is one more thing, Calwyn. Your hair."

Calwyn raised her hands to her head in a fleeting defensive gesture. She was proud of the effort she'd made in transforming her thick plait into a twisted rope, fastened precariously in a knot on top of her head. "What about my hair?"

"Your hair is beautiful," said Heben diplomatically. "But —"

"But?"

"If it were arranged ... differently ... perhaps more people would appreciate its beauty."

I will help you. Unexpectedly Halasaa's words sounded in her head.

Calwyn stared at her friend skeptically, but he smiled with gentle confidence. *In Spiridrell too we arrange our hair. Let me try.*

"Well, if you like," said Calwyn doubtfully, and she pulled out the pins that held the shaky bun in place and let her thick mass of hair tumble down.

Halasaa's hands were deft and skillful. With the aid of pins and combs, he built a swift, complicated edifice of hair that towered high above Calwyn's forehead. Staring into the mirror, she had to admit that now she could pass for a lady of the court, though she felt wary of turning her head too quickly, lest it all come cascading down.

"I still can't drape these robes properly," she complained, turning this way and that before the long mirror of polished silver.

But they all confessed defeat on that score. It was clear from the moment they arrived that the robes Heben had bought in Teril were not *quite* the right ones, and Calwyn didn't wear them in *quite* the right way. To a casual observer, she would pass as a noble lady. Unfortunately, there were no casual observers in the Palace of Cobwebs.

Halasaa picked up the folding stool of ivory that every servant carried for his master or mistress, for there was no permanent furniture anywhere in the Palace, and held back the door curtain for Calwyn to pass. Calwyn sighed, gathered her heavy skirts, and went through.

Many of the courtiers chose to nap in the afternoons, saving their energy for the evening revels that could last all night, and Calwyn and Halasaa found the Garden of Pomegranates almost deserted.

They had already realized that this and early morning were the best times for searching, and they moved as rapidly as Calwyn was able along the sleepy shaded terrace, alert for chantment.

Calwyn said in a low voice, "Sometimes I wonder if this quest is hopeless. We could wander this Palace for a lifetime and never find them. We don't even know for certain that they're here!"

There are chanters here, Calwyn. I sense them.

"Are you sure that's not Mica and me you can sense?" she asked tartly, but Halasaa only smiled.

The garden's alcoves were perfect for secret assignations. Several times that afternoon, Calwyn and Halasaa stumbled upon a guilty-looking or languid pair of entwined lovers and had to turn hastily away.

"Don't they have their own rooms?" muttered Calwyn in embarrassment, letting a curtain of ivy fall back into place.

Look. Halasaa dropped the word into her mind as quietly as a pebble slipping into a pond.

Calwyn looked.

A man stood in a patch of sunlight between the graceful pillars of the colonnade. He was tall, and his long face was as pale and waxy as a corpse's, but his eyes burned like coals. His hair was slicked back, reaching almost to his shoulders. He was austerely clad in black, with a collar of gold and silver lace. He was staring directly at them.

Calwyn held her breath. For a long moment there was no sound in the garden but the faint tinkling of an unseen fountain.

The gentleman in the black robes held her gaze; there was infinite menace in that stare. Calwyn felt herself revealed and utterly vulnerable, as though his stare were a knife that gutted her like a fish. He looked at her, and through her, and beyond her. Only the presence of Halasaa at her side prevented her from falling to her knees, weak as a rag doll.

At last he curled his bloodless lip in a suggestion of a sneer and turned away. In a heartbeat he had vanished behind the elegant rows of the pomegranate trees.

Calwyn let out her breath and clutched at Halasaa's arm. "He — he —"

Come away. Halasaa propelled her to a shady nook; deftly, he unfolded the ivory stool and pushed her into it.

"That man — he's a chanter, Halasaa!"

Yes. Halasaa's face was troubled. *And he knows that we are chanters.*

"What will we do? He'll have us thrown out of the Palace!"

We should wait. Perhaps he too is here in secret. He cannot reveal us without revealing himself.

"Yes. Yes, you're right." Decisively Calwyn stood up. "Let's finish searching. Perhaps Heben knows something about him. Or we'll see what Mica can discover."

Heben did not recognize their description of the gentleman in black. Mica went away and talked to her new friends among the kitchen staff. Despite her complaints, Mica was enjoying herself. While Halasaa followed Calwyn about, carrying her stool, Mica was free to roam as she pleased. No matter where she was, she could pretend to be on some errand for her mistress. The court teemed with intrigue, and the passages crawled with servants scurrying to and fro with private messages for this lady or that gentleman. No one ever questioned her.

She returned that evening with some information. "His name's Amagis. He's the ambassador from Hathara, wherever that might be."

"Hathara is in the south, the harshest part of Merithuros," said Heben. "Hatharan ambassador! That must be someone's idea of a joke. No one lives in Hathara. No one even goes there. There is nothing in Hathara but a dead, dry plain."

Calwyn frowned. "Darrow's ring, the one he took from Samis, is called the Ring of Hathara."

"Perhaps the gem was mined there, long ago," suggested Heben.

I have heard Darrow call that ring by another name.

"Oh?" Calwyn looked up quickly at Halasaa.

"We talkin' about Darrow or Amagis?" demanded Mica. "Thought we was here to find them chanter kids, not moon about Darrow all the time."

Calwyn flushed.

Mica helped herself to the platter of food she'd brought back from the kitchens. "These pastries ain't bad. Shame they're cold by the time I get back here."

"Did you find out anything else?" asked Calwyn.

Mica shrugged. "He come back from Gellan not long ago.

That's all. Keeps himself to himself. He comes and goes. No one likes him. And he ain't got no servants."

"That is strange." Heben frowned as he paced up and down the room. "But if he had reported you to the Imperial Guard, we would all have been arrested already. I think we're safe for now."

"All the same, I think we should avoid him if we can." Calwyn plucked at the stiff embroidery of her skirt. "No more questions about him, Mica."

"All right," agreed Mica cheerfully. "I s'pose if he is an iron-crafter, he don't need a servant, even with his gloves on. If he wants to pick up anythin', he can just *sing* it."

One thing they hadn't managed to buy in Teril was a pair of the long embroidered gloves that the courtiers wore, ladies and gentlemen alike. The gloves were made of supple leather, richly decorated with gold thread and jewels and festooned with silk ribbons. Holding one's hands elegantly to show off one's gloves was an important art of the court, and the gloves could only be obtained from the master glove-makers of the Palace. Calwyn had come to court without them. Every day she endured the titters of ladies who passed her in the corridors; she had learned to thrust her bare hands into the folds of her robes whenever a stranger approached.

"It's so strange," she complained to Mica. "I've never worn gloves in my life, except rabbit-skin mittens in the snow, and now I feel naked without them. I feel ashamed to walk around with bare hands."

"That's how they want you to feel. Like you don't belong here."

Mica sniffed. "Stupid gloves. Do you think, if these fine sirs and madams get an itch, they ask their servants to scratch it for 'em?"

Calwyn laughed. "I haven't seen anyone do that yet. But perhaps they do." She lowered her voice and cast an anxious glance at Heben. "I must have gloves. Even now my hair looks right, I'll never be allowed into the courtly gatherings until I have a proper pair of gloves."

"Can't Heben get you some?"

"Heben has spent everything he had." She sighed. "Never mind. I'll manage without them. I'll just have to lurk around outside their storytellings and their banquets." She shuddered. "I don't want to go to the banquets anyway. Did you know, Mica, because there aren't any tables and chairs, they sit on those wretched stools, and their servants fetch them food on a tray? Then the servants kneel down and feed them with golden forks so they don't soil their precious gloves! I'd rather stay and eat here in our rooms where we can all be together, and sit on the floor, and eat with our hands if we want to."

"Much better," said Mica stoutly. But she knew that it was a blow to Calwyn, and especially to Heben, to have come so far and still be unable to penetrate the inner salons of the court. The poetry tournaments and banquets and smoke-parties were held in closed galleries; they would never be able to examine the rooms unless Calwyn was invited inside.

*   *   *

The next day Mica went to the bazaar. Every day a hundred craftsmen and merchants set up their stalls inside the covered market. There were aisles of goldsmiths and fan-makers, shoe-stitchers and sweetmeat cooks hunched under striped awnings with their wares heaped before them, while a crowd of courtiers and their attendants buzzed all around.

Mica made her way slowly down the aisles, pausing to inspect the fine necklets and shiny buckles spread on the counters. She looked up at the delicate gossamer lattice that held out the sun's glare. The bazaar was cool and shaded; it was easy to forget that they were in the center of the desert. She leaned forward to admire some silver bangles. They were very large, too large for a human wrist, and Mica puzzled over them for a moment before she realized that they were meant to be worn over the embroidered gloves.

Next to Mica, a lady with towering hair pointed to a tray of extravagant hair ornaments. Seeing Mica's brown skin and cropped hair, she drew herself away with a little shudder of distaste. Mica had come to expect that, though she didn't like it. What made her angry was that the lady's manservant, himself burnt bronze by the sun and wind, gave her a snooty look down his nose as well. "Puffed-up swanker!" muttered Mica as she moved on.

At last she found the aisle of the glove-makers, stall after stall fanned with the enormous glittering gloves. Eagerly she scanned the array of goods. There was a pair that would do for Calwyn: not too flamboyant but very beautiful, made of soft blue-dyed leather and stitched with golden birds and moons. The crowd pressed against Mica's back as she bent forward, careful not to stare at the pair she really wanted but at some gaudy ruby-studded gloves nearby. Swiftly, casually, she glanced about. The vendor was attending to a lady in pink and white, who was examining a pair of green gloves with silver lacework and lilac ribbons. Behind her, the crowd rippled and parted, and she saw, not far away, a sinister dark-clad figure. That must be Amagis! He was the only one at court who dressed so severely. Her heart quickened. It would be a double challenge to get away with it under the nose of the Hatharan ambassador.

Without hesitation, she reached for the blue gloves and tucked them quickly into her robes. Then with a nonchalant toss of her head — not too fast; be casual about it — she turned away.

"Hey!" The heavy hand of the vendor clamped her arm. "What do you think you're doing?"

"I dunno what you're talkin' about!" Mica struggled to shake herself free, but he gripped her too tightly.

"Hark at her! You know exactly what I'm talking about, girl! Maybe you don't pay for your purchases in Phain or Geel or whatever sea-town you come from, but here in the Palace we do!" His contempt as he spat out the word *sea-town* was palpable. The murmuring crowd gathered around the stall. Lords and ladies shook their elaborately coiffed heads, carefully, so as not to disarrange their hair.

"Sea-town savages . . . Riffraff . . . Shouldn't be allowed!"

"Let me go! I ain't done nothin'!" Mica was truly desperate now. If she were caught stealing, it would mean all kinds of trouble. Perhaps they would all be interrogated — tortured — expelled from the Palace. . . . She tossed back her head and tried to glare down the stallholder with all the venom she could muster, but he was grim and self-righteous.

"Undo your robe. Go on! Or I'll send for the guards to do it for you!"

She could see that he meant it. She couldn't hope to get away; the crowd was too thick. She would just have to find a way to keep the others out of it. Slowly Mica reached into her robe and drew out the blue gloves. The crowd gave a moan of disapproval.

"It's quite all right. Those gloves belong to me."

Mica turned in surprise and saw the young lady in pink gesturing to her manservant to open the purse he carried. "I can pay with silver or gold, whichever you prefer," she said to the glove-maker.

"You're too kind, my lady. This young — person — were stealing. That's the point of it."

"Not at all," said the pink lady calmly. "I asked my maid here to hold these gloves for me while I looked at the others, these green ones here which you *kindly* showed to me. I hadn't quite made up my mind which I liked best. But now I *have* decided. I'll take both pairs."

"Now, my lady, you know that's not what happened."

"Are you calling me a liar? *Me?*" The lady's ice-blue eyes flashed dangerously. Her blond hair was arranged in an elegant fan shape, and even Mica could see that her pink and white robes were as stylish as could be.

The vendor swallowed uncomfortably. "Well, now, my lady, I wouldn't say that."

"Then I'll thank you to unhand my servant, and to cease making such a fuss about my property." Silently the pink lady's manservant laid some gold coins on the counter. The vendor, abashed, removed his hand from Mica's arm. Furiously she began to rub the place where he'd clutched her.

"Thank you." The pink lady turned to Mica. "Come," she said imperiously. "I must attend the emperor at noon."

A shiver of delight ran through the onlookers, and the lords and ladies cleared a respectful space for the pink lady and her servants to pass. In a few moments Mica found herself swept away from the bustle of the bazaar. The milling crowd closed up behind them and they stood in a quiet inner corridor.

"You may thank me now," announced the lady in pink. She gestured to her manservant, and he thrust the blue gloves at Mica. "But do, please, tell me *why*. Surely you don't intend to wear them yourself?"

"They're for a friend," said Mica in some confusion. "I mean, for my — for my lady —"

"Commendable loyalty! *Most* amusing. I only hope that Immel would do the same for me!" The pink lady nodded toward her impassive manservant and gave a trilling laugh. "Well, my dear, I give you the gloves, but on one condition. Your lady must attend my poetry tournament tomorrow. I simply *must* meet the person who can command such touching devotion that her maidservant would risk the dungeons to steal her a pair of gloves. If she doesn't come, I'm afraid I might have to make some teensy trouble for you both. Do you understand?"

"Yes. But —"

The lady narrowed her ice-blue eyes. "You don't know who I am, do you?"

"No," said Mica bluntly.

The lady gave another of her trilling laughs and tipped back her head so that her hair ornaments tinkled together. "You must be the only person in the Palace who doesn't know me! *How* delicious! In fact, I've made up my mind not to tell you, so I can enjoy the sensation a while longer. You must find out for yourself. But by tomorrow! I do insist on your lady's attendance at my little tournament. I do believe we'll be friends! How *delicious!*"

With a charming smile and a flurry of blown kisses, the lady disappeared up a private staircase, her pink and white skirts rustling.

Her manservant lingered for a moment. "Her name is Keela," he hissed. "The tournament is tomorrow evening in the Gallery of Birds. Tell your mistress not to be late." And with that, he vanished after the pink lady, leaving Mica to stare openmouthed after him.

When Mica returned to their apartments, she pulled out the gloves and tossed them to Calwyn. "I got you these, Cal."

Calwyn gazed at the gloves in dismay. "Oh, Mica! They're beautiful, but — these must have cost three gold pieces, at least."

Mica shrugged. "No need to worry 'bout that. Some lady took a fancy to me. She bought 'em for me." She reached out for a slice of spiced cake. "Mm, I'm starved, I could eat a whale!"

"What lady?" asked Heben in alarm, looking up from his cushion on the floor.

Mica swallowed. "Keela," she said indistinctly, through a mouthful of crumbs.

Heben sank back with a groan. "Keela! She is the Third Princess, the chief gossip of the court, a notorious intriguer. My sisters schemed for a whole year for an invitation to one of her famous poetry tournaments, but they never managed it."

"That's right." Mica wiped her mouth. "She said she wants you to go to her poetry whatsit tomorrow night, Cal, in the Gallery of Birds. Wants to see what you're like."

Calwyn turned to Heben. "What is a poetry tournament, exactly?"

"All the most fashionable courtiers gather and try to best each other in poetry. Someone starts — the princess decides the order — they invent a verse, and then the next person has to use the last words of that poem to begin their own. And you must insult the person who went before, as wittily as you can. And you must try not to give the person who follows you any ammunition to insult you. And you must be original."

"You mean they make up the poems on the spot?" cried Calwyn. "And speak them, in front of everyone? How many people attend these tournaments?"

"Oh, only thirty or forty," said Heben reassuringly. "It takes too long otherwise." Reserved as he was, Heben had been brought up with public storytelling and versifying and it held no terrors for him. But Calwyn had never done such a thing. In Antaris, the rituals of the priestesses were shared, many voices together, not one lonely individual standing up in front of a crowd. Calwyn had never liked crowds.

"I suppose I'll have to go," she said dismally. "It's the chance we've waited for, to get into one of those galleries. But —"

Do not fear. I will be with you.

Across the room, Halasaa's dark eyes smiled at her. Calwyn smiled back, but she was not entirely comforted. She would rather have gone to sea in a hurricane than stand before a group of powdered Merithuran courtiers and make up poetry. At least she had the right gloves now, she consoled herself, pulling the soft blue leather over her hands. The embroidered moons winked at her. "The Goddess will help me," she said, more cheerfully than she felt. She was beginning to wonder if the Goddess's gaze could penetrate these ivory walls that shut out the sun.

*   *   *

> *"The sword's edge of the shadow*
> *On the red sand*
> *Sharp as your sleeve when you turn from me."*

A ripple of applause greeted the poet as he bowed modestly, then resumed his seat. The next contender rose to his feet. Heart sinking, Calwyn saw that it was none other than Amagis, forbidding in his stark black clothes. She shrank in her seat, trying not to catch his eye.

> *"As sharp as your sleeve*
> *Is the raven's beak*
> *Descending on the nadu from the fierce wind."*

Amagis's voice was low but commanding, and the poem was met with an appreciative rustle of laughter and much more enthusiastic applause. The Third Princess, who had seated Calwyn beside her, leaned across and whispered, "Amagis is very clever at this. That's the only reason I invited him. *Nadu* is Jamin's nickname, he's such a timid little thing. And Amagis is known as the Raven. That's why everyone laughed."

"I see, thank you," Calwyn whispered back. Amagis stared coldly around the assembly as though daring anyone to better him. Calwyn was almost sure he hadn't seen her.

Keela nudged her elbow. "Come on, my dear. Your turn. It's not polite for newcomers to wait too long."

Calwyn stared at her in horror. "I — I can't —"

The princess's blue eyes crinkled with amusement. She laid a slim green-gloved hand on Calwyn's glove: a gesture of great intimacy. "I'll help you. Stand up!"

Reluctantly Calwyn rose from her stool. She felt the piercing gaze of forty pairs of eyes as everyone in the crowd turned to face her. There was Amagis, his black eyes burning in his deathly pale face. Calwyn swallowed and stared over the array of complicated hairdos to the back of the gallery. All around the walls, with their frieze of swooping birds, were the servants who had carried the stools. They stood silent and immobile, hands folded, as if they too were merely furniture. Halasaa stood among them; his face leaped out at her, and his bright eyes smiled.

Courage, sister!

He was joking, but in truth, Calwyn's heart beat as fast as it had ever done when she was faced with true danger. Keela smiled up at her. "*From the fierce wind falls the raven*," she whispered.

"*From the fierce wind falls the raven*," repeated Calwyn. Her voice was steady and clear; years of practicing chantment had given her that at least.

> "*Bitten by the slithering serpent*
> *Beneath the flame of the sun.*"

Calwyn repeated the whispered words. There was an immediate gasp of horrified laughter, and a few cheers among the applause. It seemed that Calwyn had said something very daring or very rude. She shot a quick glance at Amagis. His face was livid with anger. Calwyn sat down, too furious to bow. The Third Princess touched her hand; she was laughing.

"'Bitten by the serpent,' means he's been disappointed in love. And 'the flame of the sun' means he's been burned by trying too hard at a sport he's not fit for. Very good, my dear! You've managed two wonderful insults in the space of one poem!"

"I would rather not have offended him," whispered Calwyn fiercely.

Keela bit her lip in mock contrition. "Forgive me! But everyone will know it was my fault. No one will think that — pardon me for speaking frankly — a girl so new to the court, fresh from the wilderness, would be capable of two superb insults, and in such an elegant verse, too! Amagis won't blame you."

Calwyn was too agitated to pay attention to the next poem, which, naturally, contrived to insult her. But she did catch something about "*a disheveled tent, blown in the sandstorm.*"

After the poems were over, the servants fetched delicate glasses filled with cool, frothing drinks, and the courtiers mingled, strolling about the gallery, arm in arm. This intimacy, "touching gloves," was the highest mark of friendship at the court. At the first opportunity, the Third Princess drew Calwyn's arm through hers. Calwyn was still upset and would rather have been left alone to explore the immense gallery, but Keela was insistent.

"Come, my dear, don't be cross! This is what life at court is all about! The cut and thrust of wit and so on. You're lucky I've taken such a liking to you. There are ladies in this room — and gentlemen! — who would willingly scratch out your eyes from sheer jealousy! And you'll find me a very valuable friend. We *will* be friends, Calwyn, you know, even though you do dress so badly." She plucked at Calwyn's sleeve. "Did those Cledsec girls help you pick out your clothes? Now, let me see, what *are* their names?"

The ice-blue gaze was uncomfortably piercing. Calwyn stammered, trying to remember the names of Heben's sisters. Luckily for her, the princess was soon whisked away by some other ladies, who cast derisive glances at Calwyn, evidently sharing Keela's judgment of her dress sense, and Calwyn was left alone to wander the perimeter of the gallery. It took her a long time to walk all the way around it, with Halasaa at her heels, and when they were done, the gathering had almost dispersed, and a stony-faced servant was waiting to usher them out. Neither Calwyn nor Halasaa had sensed any hint of chantment.

As they departed, Keela blew Calwyn a kiss and tweaked at her robes. "I'll teach you to drape them properly," she whispered. "Come to my reception rooms tomorrow."

"Well, really!" said Calwyn crossly, watching her sweep away around a bend in the corridor, trailed by a little group of her admirers and their servants.

You dislike her. Halasaa was at her elbow.

"Yes, I do. Tricking me into insulting Amagis! How can someone be so polite and so rude at the same time? But I suppose she'll be useful."

She is no more rude than others in this place.

"That's no compliment," said Calwyn ruefully. "For all their fine manners, I don't think I've met a more unpleasant collection of people in my life."

Halasaa smiled peacefully, and his words were typically diplomatic. *They are unlike any people I have known.*

"A pampered, perfumed pack of idlers!" After her uncomfortable experience at the tournament, Calwyn felt the need to vent her feelings. "Did you hear them, taking images from the desert for their poems? I'm sure none of them has ever set foot in the desert!"

It would be possible to live in this Palace for a lifetime and never see the sands outside. A shadow crossed Halasaa's face. *This place is more dead than the desert itself. It is like the coral gardens Mica spoke of, built from the bodies of dead creatures.* Coming from the thick forests of the Wildlands, teeming with life, he could not have said anything more damning.

It was long after midnight when Keela heard the discreet tap at her doorway. She frowned at her reflection in the polished silver mirror, slowly removed her earrings, and handed them to her maid. "Leave me, Riss," she said. "I'll manage the rest myself." The maid bowed and silently withdrew. The Third Princess, like most of the ladies of the court, often received visitors in the middle of the night.

Keela called, "You may enter."

The heavy curtain at her doorway lifted, and a dark, shadowy shape appeared in the mirror. Keela did not turn around. Languidly she reached up and extracted a long tortoiseshell pin from the elaborate arrangement of her hair. "Really, my dear, must you skulk about like that? Can't you whistle, or sing? Oh! How foolish of me!" She lifted her naked fingertips to her lips and looked coyly over her shoulder. "Of *course* you can sing!"

Amagis stood at her shoulder, his pale face impassive. "You will have your jokes, my lady."

"Oh, yes . . . I am sorry about tonight — I couldn't help myself. You forgive me, don't you?"

"I would forgive you anything, my lady." Amagis's voice was taut with suppressed emotion.

"I know you would." Keela blew his reflection a kiss. "And I did well, did I not, pretending friendship with that *unwashed child*? But must I go on pretending, my dear? She is so tiresome."

"Yes. I must find out why they are here."

"Oh, very well. If you insist." Keela withdrew another pin. A flaxen lock of hair, smooth as silk, fell to her waist. "But who is she, Amagis? Why must I be charming to a little *nadu* from the wilderness?"

"A little *nadu* she is not. Watch her carefully, my lady. She is a chanter, and her servants are both chanters too, of some sort."

"She is a chanter? Really? How extraordinary. Well, I knew *at once* she was not one of the Cledsec, in spite of the medallion she wears." Keela touched a fingertip to the golden pendant on her own brow. "I could see *that* from one glance at her face. Would you like me to speak to the emperor? We could have them thrown out like *that*." Keela snapped her fingers.

"No. Not yet. I would like to find out why she is here. It's possible she is in the pay of the rebels. There has been violence in Teril. The rebel leaders may be plotting some action against the Palace, using foreign sorcery. Or even against the emperor himself. It would be a perfect way for an assassin to infiltrate the court; no one but another sorcerer would ever suspect her of being dangerous."

"My dear, you're not serious! That little *nadu*, dangerous?"

"Even a little *nadu* may give a sharp bite to the emperor. Or even," added Amagis slowly, as if he formed the thought as he spoke it, "to one greater than the emperor."

"You think she plans to harm *me*?" Keela swung around on her stool.

"You, or — I was thinking of our master," Amagis admitted.

"Oh. Him." Keela turned back to the mirror. "*He* is far away. Surely you ought to be more concerned about *me*?"

"Of course, of course." Boldly Amagis picked up the lock of blond hair in his gloved hand and caressed it. "Never fear, my lady. No one would dare to harm you. Nothing will disrupt our master's plans."

"Our plans," drawled Keela. For a heartbeat, her cold blue eyes met his dark gaze in the mirror. Then suddenly she was the charming, flirtatious princess once again. "Amagis! You're frowning. You know perfectly well that you're forbidden to frown in my presence."

"Forgive me, my lady. The arrival of these chanters has disturbed me."

Keela said shrewdly, "You don't like having other sorcerers

about, do you? You'd rather it was just *you*. And those children, of course. . . ."

"My lady, I beg you, do not speak of *them!*" Amagis glanced swiftly at the curtained doorway. "I have told you many times, *they* are a sacred secret! If anyone, my brother sorcerers, or the emperor, were to discover that I have shared that knowledge — particularly with a woman, even one as — as extraordinary as yourself, the consequences would be unspeakable!"

"If that's the way you feel, you shouldn't have told me about them in the first place," said Keela petulantly, plucking out more pins. "Anyway, what does it matter? Our master will be here soon enough, and then he'll be the emperor and Lord of the Sorcerers too, and I'll be empress, and there'll be no one to care what I know or don't know!"

Amagis's long, cadaverous face looked even more somber than usual. "So long as our master arrives to carry out his revolution before the rebel leaders can carry out theirs," he said. "These are uncomfortable times, my lady. Discontent ripples all through the Empire; I have seen it on my travels. Strange things are written in the stars. If the rebels succeed, then our world will be turned inside out. I say again, my lady: Watch the girl."

"Yes, yes. Why don't you watch her yourself?"

"Ah, my lady," murmured Amagis, raising the smooth lock of hair to his lips. "I would rather spend my time watching you."

Keela smiled, and another hairpin fell to the floor.

* * *

The Imperial Court had been settled in the Palace of Cobwebs for so many generations that everyone had lost count of how long it had been. Yet in some ways the courtiers lived as their desert-dwelling ancestors had done long ago, when they roamed with flocks of *hegesi* and camped under woven tents, with no possession too heavy to be loaded onto a *hegesu's* back.

The seasonal shifting of the entire court from one part of the Palace to another marked a memory of those days, and each piece of furniture was light enough to be transported from place to place by a single person. There were screens carved from ivory, so thin that the light shone through them, and feather-light woven mats and curtains and cushions. Even the most elaborate painted cabinets that housed the ceremonial robes of the courtiers were built from the lightest, most precious wood, and rested on casters so they could be rolled along the twisting corridors with ease.

On this day, Calwyn had been invited to watch the Midsummer Procession from outside the rooms that Keela would be vacating. The Third Princess was famously in the thick of everything, even in her choice of apartments, and from the gallery outside they would have an unparalleled view of the whole Imperial parade.

"I'm sorry I can't be with you myself, darling," said Keela regretfully. "But I have a role to play, you know. How delicious it would be to watch everyone go by! But then, of course, I wouldn't be able to see the most gorgeous creature of all — *me!* Now, sweetest, this diamond necklace, do you think? Or the sapphires?"

Now Calwyn and Halasaa and Mica were crowded along the edge of the gallery with the other eager observers. Mica leaned so far over the delicate railing that Calwyn feared she might topple down onto the Fifth Prince's head.

"Look, look! He's got *gold* in his hair! What a goose! Do you think Heben's wishin' he could see all this? Look at that one! Her gloves go right up to the top of her *head!*" With an excited squeal, she turned to tug at Calwyn's arm, but in the crush, she found herself clutching at the sleeve of a stranger.

The elderly gentleman in scarlet and gold drew himself back as far as the press of the crowd would allow and looked down his nose, not at Mica, but at Calwyn. Mica was so far beneath his notice that she didn't even exist.

"I beg your pardon, sir," said Calwyn hastily.

"Ladies who cannot keep their attendants under control should not be permitted to spoil the parade for the rest of us," pronounced the scarlet gentleman haughtily.

"It won't happen again," said Calwyn, thrusting Mica firmly behind her.

"They say those who dwell in the desert never wash themselves." The scarlet gentleman wrinkled his nose fastidiously. "They don't have water to spare."

"We're clean as you," retorted Mica. "Cleaner, I reckon, 'cause we ain't hidin' behind the stink of no perfume." She glared at the elderly gentleman, who did smell very strongly of artificial scent.

"Mica!" hissed Calwyn, but luckily the gentleman in scarlet had moved away and seemed not to have heard her. "Mica, you'll have to go back to our rooms if you can't keep quiet."

"Ever since we come here you been orderin' me around," grumbled Mica. "You're so scared of this lot of painted-up puffer fish, you think I should be too. Anyway, it's all right for you," she added crossly. "You're tall, you can see. I can't see nothin'!"

It was true. Halasaa and Calwyn had a fine view of the courtiers assembling in the Long Gallery. There were the ladies in elaborate costumes, hair pinned up so high that they had to carry their heads with stilted care. There were the lords and princes dressed up in warrior gear that hadn't seen the heat of battle for centuries: unnaturally bright, polished breastplates, curved swords, engraved arm guards, and their own intricate hair arrangements incongruously floating above. Musicians had gathered in the court-yard, quietly tuning their flutes, and now began to beat softly on their drums.

Amagis, somber and sinister in his customary black, stood not far from the Third Princess, resplendent in silver and golden robes. Calwyn shot a glance at Mica, then she began to sing, very, very low. Even Halasaa could barely hear her through the excited buzz and clamor of the crowd. Down below in the Long Gallery, the ornament at the top of Keela's headdress gave a sudden tug. Startled, her hands flew to her head, then, satisfied that all was well, fluttered down. Calwyn saw her turn and stare sharply at the Seventh Princess, who stood behind her.

Halasaa looked at Calwyn, his eyes dancing.

"Do you dare me?" whispered Calwyn. She felt like the naughty little girl she had been in Antaris. And perhaps she wanted to show Mica that she wasn't so scared after all. She sang again, just two quick notes, a high, clear chantment of the winds.

The comb snagged, twisted, and leaped free, clattering to the ground, and Keela's hair tumbled down around her face. Desperately she clutched at her hair, as if she could hold its intricate loops and swirls in place with her gloved fingers, but it was hopeless. Her hair was in utter disarray, a bird's nest of tangles. Flushed with anger, the princess fled the gallery, leaving a ripple of titters and even outright laughter in her wake. There were many in the Palace who had little love for Keela.

Mica stifled her laughter behind her hands.

Halasaa shook his head gently. *She will not forgive such humiliation.*

"Then it's lucky she doesn't know who caused it," said Calwyn, a little shamefaced but unable to restrain a giggle. She hadn't seen Amagis, sensing chantment, raise his head sharply like a raven with a sight of prey.

The musicians, thrown off guard by the brief commotion, settled down and began their music in earnest. The murmuring crowd fell quiet, and the watchers on the balcony could see that the Imperial Family had arrived.

First came the empresses; there were seven of them. The most senior wife, draped in unbecoming mustard yellow and violet, was ancient and wrinkled. She leaned wearily against the arms of her carved chair, which was carried by two burly manservants. Her hair, dyed harsh black, made her wrinkled face look even older, and her eyes and lips were painted so thickly that Calwyn could see the brushstrokes even from this distance. The First Empress must be the same age as Marna, she thought, yet how much more dignified was the High Priestess of Antaris, with her kindly seamed face that wore every year of experience and wisdom with pride.

One by one the junior empresses paraded by, each carried in her carved chair. Some were more popular than others, and they each belonged to a different Clan. Different sections of the crowd cheered as each went by. The youngest wife, the Seventh, was pregnant. Her enormous belly jutted out, dwarfing her, and her face was swollen and miserable. She looked as if she would rather be lying on cushions in her rooms than taking part in a procession and a feast. Calwyn felt a pang of sympathy; she looked scarcely older than Mica.

Next came the princesses. Keela had scrambled her hair back into a semblance of order and rushed to rejoin the parade. Even with her hair slightly tousled, she was easily the most beautiful and the most spectacularly dressed of the ten princesses. Beside her, the others were pallid, mousy little things. The crowd cheered loudly when she went past. Mica gave Calwyn a nudge. "Them other princesses're lookin' sour, ain't they?" she whispered.

Then came the princes, a veritable horde of them. Samis had been part of this preening company once, Calwyn reminded herself. It was hard to imagine him, so arrogant and so imperious, being one of this anonymous crowd. He always wanted to be first, to stand out among others. Seeing the fifty princes milling about in their polished armor, indistinguishable, she could almost feel his frustration. The First Prince, with a golden circlet on his head, strutted in front of the others; he was not the oldest, nor the strongest, nor even the most handsome, but somehow he had won the emperor's favor and been appointed his father's heir. He was plump and spoiled, with a self-satisfied smile.

Mica whispered, "How come there's so many princes and only ten princesses?"

"Heben told me," Calwyn kept her voice low, "they make certain that there aren't too many princesses."

Mica's eyes widened. "You mean they *kill* 'em?"

"Ssh! They call it an offering to the desert. . . ."

"That's horrible!" said Mica loudly, and glared around at the crowd. "Murderers!" she muttered fiercely.

Finally came the emperor himself. The crowd fell silent as His Imperial Majesty passed by. There were none of the shouts and cheers that had accompanied the parade of the Imperial wives and offspring; rather, a hush swept over the crowd of onlookers. Reverently people pulled off their gloves and held them above their bowed heads like banners, as a mark of respect; hastily Calwyn stripped off her gloves and did the same. No one dared to look at the face of the emperor. But Calwyn was so curious about this powerful man that she couldn't resist peeping down at the figure in the huge carved chair that swayed slowly past.

She had heard much about the emperor's great age and his feebleness, but it was still a shock to see the wizened figure, with a face like yellow paper, in the chair that towered above him. He seemed no bigger than a child, shrunken into his embroidered robes and elaborate gloves, peering out without interest at the silent crowd that thronged the winding corridors. As he passed beneath where Calwyn and the others stood, he glanced up. His eyes met Calwyn's and locked there, and she gave an involuntary shudder, for his eyes were the same as Samis's eyes: dark and cruel and ruthless, piercingly intelligent, utterly arrogant. His cold stare seemed to say, "Who are you, to gaze at me?"

She forced herself to stare back without flinching. *I am a daughter of Taris, a chanter. I am no one's servant but the Goddess's. I will not bow down to you.* She thought of the hungry, miserable people of Teril and felt a pang of anger. But then she remembered: *We killed this man's son.* And her eyes dropped.

The crowd remained silent, heads lowered, while the shuffling feet of the emperor's many attendants went by. Then people began to cough and chatter and pull on their gloves and move away. Now would follow the great feast in the Midsummer Banqueting Hall.

Mica stretched her arms above her head. "You'd best get on, Cal, if you want to see that hall. Today's the only time it's ever open."

Calwyn pressed her lips together; she loathed crowds, and today's procession had been trying enough already. The prospect of another half day's noise and jostling was almost unbearable. But it must be done.

She was pulling on her gloves when she felt it.

At first she thought she'd imagined it. She stopped still and closed her eyes. Someone pushed her from behind.

Mica snapped, "Watch where you're goin'!" She tugged Calwyn back against the curved wall as the crowd surged past. "What's wrong? You feelin' all right? You ain't goin' to faint?"

Halasaa was at her side. Calwyn knew at a glance that he had felt it too. *Here. Close by.*

"Yes." The three of them stood in a tight knot, an obstacle to the ceaseless forward surge of the crowd, which parted around them. Calwyn's and Halasaa's dark bright eyes, so alike, met and held. There was chantment nearby, very near.

Not yet.

Calwyn nodded. "There are too many people around. We'll come back when the corridors are clear, during the feast." She turned to Mica and said in a low voice, "Go to Heben. Tell him we've found what we came for."

The food was laid out at one end of the banqueting hall; servants swarmed around the long tables like ants to a lump of honeycomb. Halasaa made a brief foray to the tables so that Calwyn should have something in front of her, and returned with some slivers of marinated *hegesu* meat and a chunk of marzipan from a model of the Palace that took pride of place high on the central table.

It looked to Calwyn very much like her first glimpse of the real Palace, shining white against a red cloth. It seemed a long time ago. With a sudden pang, she thought of Tonno, waiting with *Fledgewing*, and Trout, busy on the island. And, fleetingly, she thought of Darrow in his little boat, wherever he might be. What would he say if he knew they were here now?

The model Palace was already partly demolished. The servants competed fiercely to grab the choicest tidbits for their masters and ladies, and greedy hands had clawed away all the eastern half and left nothing but a heap of crumbs and marzipan rubble. Someone grasped a handful of the remaining walls and tore it away. A turret collapsed, lopsided, into a pool of custard.

Presently a murmuring hush fell over the hall as the courtiers settled down to eat. Lords and ladies sat in clusters, their servants kneeling to one side with their trays. At the far end of the hall, on a raised platform, sat the Imperial Family and their intimates; Calwyn was relieved that today she didn't seem to be considered Keela's best friend. She could see the Third Princess, looking bored, opening her rosebud mouth to receive the sweetmeats that her servant delicately laid on her tongue. The First Prince sat beside her, trying to engage her attention, but Keela ignored him. The emperor's heir looked annoyed.

Calwyn glanced about for Amagis; she was particularly anxious that he shouldn't notice their departure. She spotted him near the edge of the platform. His back was to the hall, and he was staring at the Imperial Family, perhaps at Keela herself.

Calwyn could do no more than pretend to pick at the tray that Halasaa held up to her. Anxiously she scanned the hall, alert for the best moment to sneak out unnoticed. She could see musicians and dancers and jugglers waiting near the doors for a signal that the entertainments should begin. That would be the best time to go.

But before the musicians could file into the central space, there was a disturbance up on the Imperial platform. One of the empresses let out a piercing scream; most of the royal family leaped to their feet. Calwyn jumped up from her stool, but she couldn't see what had happened, and neither could Halasaa.

At the next moment they heard the whispers flying through the hall. "The emperor — The emperor's collapsed — The emperor is ill!"

Courtiers bounded to their feet, the banquet abandoned, trays overturned on the floor. Lords and ladies and servants eagerly pushed toward the platform, ghoulishly craning to see, forgetting that the emperor was not to be gazed upon.

"Where are the healers? Clear a space, get back! Move away! Take off his collar, take off his gloves! How dare you lay hands on his person! I have as much rank as you —" The princes were all shouting orders at once, but no one seemed to be doing anything to help the emperor.

Halasaa touched Calwyn's sleeve. Quickly they turned and slipped through the chattering, excited crowd toward the wall of the great hall. Unnoticed in the commotion, Halasaa clambered nimbly up the carved wall, inserting his toes into the crannies and ledges of the stone. Encumbered by her gloves and heavy robes, Calwyn could only watch. "What can you see?" she called.

Halasaa's face was as still as one of the carvings he clung to. *The man is dead.*

A gap had formed in the center of the crush. The princes and empresses and their attendants had fallen back, leaving a space around the shrunken, tiny body of the emperor. Halasaa caught one brief glimpse before the gap closed again: the yellow face, already waxy with death; the limp hands, shockingly naked and gloveless, curled on the embroidered robes. And the whisper traveled through the hall, shivering through the courtiers like a breeze rippling across the sands: "He is dead. . . . The emperor is dead. . . . The emperor is dead at last!"

Halasaa leaped lightly from his perch, and he and Calwyn slipped from the hall. No one paid them any attention. Everyone was caught up in the horror and excitement of the moment: After so many years, the unthinkable had happened, and happened in the presence of all the court. The emperor was dead. Most of the courtiers had known no other ruler. The Imperial Court, where every moment of every day was governed by ceremony and strict rules of etiquette, was thrown into chaos. No one knew what would happen now. The emperor was the center, the focus of every activity of the court. Without the emperor, the entire fabric of the Empire might begin to unravel.

As she and Halasaa set off down the wide, twisting corridor that led from the Midsummer Hall, Calwyn pulled off her gloves and thrust them safely in her belt, then she ran, holding her stiff skirts aside. The corridors were almost empty. A middle-aged official, clumsily pulling on his gloves as he ran, shouted to Calwyn, "Have you heard? He's dead, the emperor's dead!" The official halted, puffing for breath, in the middle of the corridor. "The First Prince has been plotting this for years! He pushed him off the platform!"

"That's not true!" cried Calwyn. "I was there, I saw — the prince was nowhere near him!"

"Poison then," said the official, half to himself. All the normal rules of behavior were suspended. He was a stout, self-important man who, on an ordinary day, would never have dreamed of speaking to an ungloved woman in a public corridor. But today was not an ordinary day.

Come. We should hurry. Halasaa was ahead of her, poised to fly around the next corner. Suddenly Calwyn was confused. Was it this passage or the next that led to Keela's rooms? The foamy white tunnels all looked the same. But Halasaa's sense of direction was as unerring as a bird's, and without faltering he darted around the next bend and the next, and then they were in the gallery where they had watched the procession.

Here, Halasaa's quiet speech sounded in her mind.

"Yes," breathed Calwyn.

The chantment was still there. It shimmered in the air; though she couldn't hear it, she sensed it all around. Only the press and confusion of the crowd could have prevented her from noticing it earlier. It was as clear as the echo of a bell, as plain as a breath against her skin. Without hesitation, she and Halasaa followed the silent call, until they reached the doorway of Keela's private quarters.

They halted. Calwyn had never been inside Keela's apartments; she had only visited the princess in her official reception rooms. A heavy silken curtain hung in the archway. She glanced at Halasaa.

His eyes were steady. *We must go in.*

There might be servants still inside, packing the princess's possessions, but they had to risk it. The chantment came from somewhere within. Calwyn pushed aside the curtain.

The room was empty. No screens or cabinets or hangings or cushions or mirrors remained; everything had been removed, by servants as busy as ants, to Keela's rooms in the Summer Quarters of the Palace. Before the day was out, the apartments where Calwyn and Heben and the others were staying would be emptied too. The gentle curves of the walls and ceiling glowed bare and ivory-colored, the intricate carvings outlined sharply, black and cream and gray-shadowed, without the distraction of colored tapestries. A long window sent a shaft of dazzling light slicing across the room; with no veil to soften it, the light was as harsh as a knife blade.

Calwyn moved toward one of the walls. She and Halasaa had no need to speak. They both knew they were drawing closer with every step.

Suddenly a brisk voice rang out from deeper within the apartment. "You take those stools, Riss, and I'll fold these. That'll be the last of it —"

Halasaa touched Calwyn's sleeve and nodded to a little doorway. Unusually for the Palace, rather than a draped curtain or a sliding screen, it contained a door. It fell open at Calwyn's touch. In an instant they'd ducked through the archway; both of them had to bend their heads. Calwyn closed the little door behind them.

They found themselves in a dark place; the only light seeped from under the tiny door. As her eyes adjusted, Calwyn saw that they stood at the foot of a steep flight of stairs. The ceiling was very low; neither of them could stand upright, and the walls curved around them, enclosing them like a clutching hand.

Up and up, Calwyn and Halasaa climbed in the dark, while the stairway twisted and turned. The steps were irregular, and it was hard work to stumble upward, barking their shins on the edges of the steps.

After a time, a faint light shone through the walls, as if the stone were a closed eyelid, and they found they could see their way at last. In the gray light, exhausted, they climbed on, heads bent beneath the stone roof. In silence Calwyn briefly reached out a hand behind her, and in silence Halasaa grasped it, then let it go. Still the chantment vibrated all around them, stronger all the time.

Presently the stairs narrowed; Calwyn was crouched almost double. Halasaa spoke into her mind. *I can go no farther.*

"Wait for me here," whispered Calwyn. Though she spoke

softly, her voice seemed loud after the long silence in which they'd climbed, with no sound but their stumbling feet and the quiet panting of their breath. Calwyn went on alone.

At the very top of the gray-lit stairs stood another tiny door, twin to the one below but even smaller. It reached only as high as Calwyn's waist; Halasaa could never have fitted through it. Calwyn was a tall woman, but she was slender. She would just be able to squeeze through.

She thought that the door might be locked, but as she reached out her hand, it swung open. She bent down and crawled through the doorway.

The sun's glare hit her like a hammer. She was on the roof of the topmost tower of the Palace of Cobwebs, the high, thin spire she'd seen on the first day, the spire that had seemed to pierce the sky like a needle. Beyond the frothing white and cream of the Palace, the vast red desert spread on every side; the blank blue sky stretched from one horizon to the other.

The space of the roof was barely three paces square. A shallow wall ran around the edge, as low as Calwyn's knee. The sun burned on the patch of roof, bright white; there was a thin line of shadow along one of the ramparts. And in that shadow lay a child.

Heron sped on, skimming over the waves of the Outer Sea. The night before, Darrow had passed the western coast of Baltimar and seen the shore fires burning. Now only open ocean stood between him and the Empire of Merithuros. Once he had sworn never to return there. But now two things drew him back, as the moons drew the tides. One of them was a tall girl with a dark plait down her back. The other was in his pocket. He sat with one hand on the tiller while the other fingered the ruby ring, turning it and turning it until his fingertips were raw. And even then, he couldn't let it go.

Passing the Testing has changed something of the pattern of the boy's daily life. He no longer eats and sleeps with the younger children but lives in a different part of the Palace, on the western side, which is hotter during the afternoons. He is aware, even now, three years later, that his reprieve was a mistake, that his safety was purchased with false coin. He expects at every moment to be found out for a coward and a cheat. He has learned what happens to the children who fail the Testing: Sufficient in skill but deficient in obedience, they are sent away, to the north, to the Palace of Cobwebs, to be sacrificed. The handful of girls who arrive at the Black Palace are always deemed to be too willful; they are, without exception, sent away. The children are the price the sorcerers pay for their solitude. A bargain has been struck; in return for the children, the sorcerers may remain in the safety of Hathara, to pursue their magic and guard their secret craft.

The boy has begun to comprehend the brotherhood of the sorcerers and what binds them. He sees their fear of the world outside, their absorption in their traditions, their reverence for the ancient scholarship they guard. And he too derives a fierce delight from the exercise of his gift. One of the oldest of the sorcerers tells him, "Out there — that is not freedom. Freedom is here, within these walls. Eh? Do you understand me, boy?" And he does understand.

The boy does not know exactly what happens after the failed children reach the Palace of Cobwebs or the manner of their sacrifice. He prays that he will never find out, for it is not unknown for a rebellious adolescent to be banished long after he might have thought that the Testing had bought him safety forever. But a limit is observed. After the boys' voices drop and they are considered men, they are no longer sent to the Palace of Cobwebs.

The boy longs for the sorcerers to assign him a room of his own and a set of black robes, for that is the mark of manhood, the guarantee of safety. The black robes mark his entry into the covenant of the sorcerers. After that, he can bully the children himself, preside over their lessons, and learn the most secret lore of the adult chanters. The boy loathes the sorcerers as much as ever, yet he longs to be of their company, and these conflicting emotions tear at him daily as he walks the dim corridors.

In the boy's twelfth year, he is told he will learn the movements of the stars and moons and their meanings. For a year he will join the astronomers on the rooftop every night and sleep during the day.

To his surprise, he enjoys the lessons in astronomy. The star-seers are scholarly men, sunk in the deep mysteries and speculations of their study, detached from the petty intrigues that flow through the rest of the Black Palace. They rarely practice chantment, regarding themselves as astronomers first and ironcrafters second. The boy even finds himself liking several of them, who speak to him kindly and draw him into their work. And it is a great joy to see the stars again, and the moons, and to feel the breath of the night air on his face. For the first time since he's come to the Palace, he feels some measure of contentment.

It is because he is with the star-seers on the rooftop that he sees Samis arrive. The roof of the Palace is more complex than he had ever imagined, crowded and muddled in a way that would never be tolerated below. It is crammed with ramshackle structures, boxes of equipment, and odd protruding lengths of pipe and chimney, necessary for the provision of air and heat within the Palace. There is one particular long, thin pipe, played by the desert winds, that whistles with an eerie high-pitched wail, night and day. There are wild eagle nests up there too, and the birds gaze balefully at the sorcerers, believing that the roof belongs to them.

Every night he and the star-seers — they are seventeen in number, always with one or two pupils among them — pick their way across to the bare patch of roof in the southwestern corner where they make their observations. The wall that runs around the edge of the roof is low here, barely waist-high, and when he is not required by the star-seers, the boy leans his elbows on the wall and stares across the sands and up at the sky. Silently then he repeats the names that the sailors of *Gold Arrow* gave the constellations, imposing them over the names the Merithurans teach him, keeping alive something of the little boy called Mouse.

He is leaning on the wall one night when he catches sight of a moving dot, far off on the flat plain. He watches it with curiosity, because it seems to advance deliberately toward the Palace, which a *hegesu* would not do. Then he sees with a shock that it is a man, traveling on foot and walking with great purpose directly to the plateau where the Palace stands.

The boy lets out an exclamation, and soon the wall is crowded with the star-seers, leaning over the edge and remarking on the marvel in their gentle voices. There are no visitors to the Palace. No one knows where it is except the sorcerers themselves, and it lies so deep in the wilderness of Hathara that it could never be discovered by chance. They are too high up to see the traveler's face. But they watch him come to the foot of the doorless, windowless monolith and stand staring up at it. Then he moves around to the other side, out of sight.

"Come, my brothers," chides the most senior of the star-seers. "There is no profit in this idle talk. Let us work. It will be dawn soon."

And so they return to their observations, but they are alight with curiosity.

The next night, one of their number has news of the strange visitor. He is no ordinary traveler but a Prince of the Imperial Court. And he has come to the Black Palace of his own volition, to learn chantment.

The astronomers buzz with wonderment. Not one of them has come here of his own will; every one of them was stolen or thrown out from his Clan; every one of them knows himself to be an outcast and a pariah. Yet this man — this prince! — has chosen to exile himself here, he has chosen this life. It is an astonishing event.

Living his back-to-front life, the boy has no opportunity to see the stranger. Occasionally one of the star-seers picks up a piece of gossip and relays it to his fellows. The visitor is imperious, demanding particular foods and comforts in his lodging room. The visitor is gifted: He sang his own way into the Palace without help or guidance from anyone. Without being taught, he knows many of the tricks of ironcraft, and some that the masters did not know. The visitor is dangerous; he discovered the location of the Palace from the sorcerers' representative at court, the so-called Hatharan ambassador. There are whispers that the Hatharan ambassador is dead. A hasty embassy is dispatched. The whole of the Black Palace has been turned upside down by the presence of this stranger.

Despite the threat he poses, the visitor remains. Is it possible that the sorcerers are afraid of him? The embassy to the Imperial Court returns. The ambassador was not dead, after all. The visitor has been seen laughing. Who is this man, that the sorcerers are so cowed by him? He goes everywhere, he pokes his nose into everything.

One night, the visitor decides to poke his nose into the business of the astronomers. He ascends the ladder and steps onto the roof. It is the first time the boy has set eyes on him since the night of his arrival, when he was a tiny figure swathed in dusty robes. The star-seers fall back in a dismayed flutter of black crows round a bird of paradise.

The prince dresses as though he were still at court, in embroidered gloves, bejeweled shoes, a short brocade cloak that stands out stiffly from his shoulders like the ruff of a lizard. Yet the boy's eye is drawn at once to the stranger's large head, to his face. The prince's face, in contrast to his foppish attire, is strong-featured and contemptuous. His lips curl, his eyes are hooded, as he stares about disdainfully at the star-seers' shabby equipment, the tarnished astrolabes, the chipped stone wheels that serve as starmaps. He is a young man, strong and proud and fearless. This is a man, thinks the boy, who should be emperor.

The prince makes his way to the edge of the roof, where the boy stands. The boy has never seen a prince before. The prince's gaze is cool and haughty. The boy thinks, You may be a prince, but you are not my prince. I am a man of the marshes, not a Merithuran. I will not be cowed by you, no matter what the rest may do.

The prince halts before him. One of the star-seers pulls timidly at the boy's sleeve, but the boy stands his ground. The prince is not a tall man, but his massive, imposing head makes him seem bigger than he is. The boy and the prince stare at each other. The prince's eyes are as dark as the spaces between the stars, but they flash with glittering light and power. The boy trembles. Suddenly he knows that this man is stronger and more dangerous than all the sorcerers of the Black Palace combined. Yet he cannot look away, he cannot move. It is the same paralysis that gripped him during the Testing. And like that paralysis, this inability to act will purchase him a reward he does not deserve.

The prince speaks. His voice is deep and powerful. "What is your name, boy?"

The boy feels a jolt of surprise. It's so long since anyone asked that question, he has to think for a moment before replying. Perhaps his hesitation looks like arrogance. "They call me Darrow."

The prince nods. "My name is Samis." He puts his hand to his lips, then holds out his palm in greeting. Mechanically, as if in a dream, Darrow returns the gesture. His heart beats hard. He knows, dimly, that something important has happened, though he doesn't know what it is.

As if he is no longer interested in the star-seers and their complicated work, Samis turns away and goes down from the roof.

The next day, just as he has ordered cushions for his chair and plums for his dinner, Samis demands that Darrow be sent to him, to be a companion in his work. "That boy is the only one of you sniveling wretches who is not afraid of me," he says.

And so for a second time Darrow finds himself unjustly saved.

The Captive Children

Calwyn dropped to her knees on the glaring white roof of the tower. The child stared at her with wide, terrified eyes but did not move. A low, continuous growl issued from it, like the warning growl of a frightened animal. But Calwyn knew that this was no animal's sound: It was chantment, the throat-song of ironcraft. The child was singing. This was the song that had drawn Calwyn and Halasaa here.

The child was so filthy, so thin and ragged, that Calwyn couldn't tell if it was a boy or a girl who peered at her through a tangle of matted, dirty hair. In one corner of the roof was a pot, and the stench that rose from it was indescribable. Beside the child was an earthenware water jug, the plainest, shabbiest object Calwyn had seen in the Palace.

Calwyn held out her hand. "I've come to help you."

The child shook its head, still growling out that low, almost inaudible chantment.

"What's your name? Can you understand me?"

This time the child nodded. But the big eyes were still wary, and the ceaseless chantment droned on.

"I know you can speak," said Calwyn. "I can hear you singing."

The child reached up a skinny paw and pushed back the tangle of hair. "Can't stop." The words were whispered so low that Calwyn had to lean forward to hear them, and the chantment began again at once.

"You can't stop singing? Why not?"

"Palace will fall."

"But you must sleep, you must stop to eat and drink."

The child shook her head — Calwyn was almost sure it was a girl — and a look of panic came into her eyes.

Gently Calwyn asked, "Are you Shada?"

At this, the girl gave a moan. Her hands crept to her mouth, muffling the chantment, and she began to rock back and forth. Her eyes were fixed on Calwyn's face with a new expression, part greedy hope, part terror. A single tear trickled down her face, leaving a trail in the mask of dirt, and dripped onto the roof.

Calwyn moved nearer, trying not to alarm the child. "Heben sent me to find you. He's here, in the Palace. We've been searching for you and your brother. You're safe now, we'll take care of you." She held out her hand, but the child batted it away and shook her head more vehemently than ever.

"We'll take you, we'll hide you. You're safe now!"

The girl, Shada, broke off her drone of chantment just long

enough to mutter in a fierce whisper, "No! Can't! *He* knows. If I stop, *he* —"

"He? You mean Amagis? Is he the one who keeps you here?" Calwyn's mind was busy. Did Keela know what was hidden behind the little doorway in her rooms? Calwyn dismissed the thought; the Third Princess was too shallow and too frivolous to be involved in anything like this. "Come with me," she urged.

Shada shook her head again, singing softly, her eyes filled with tears, and she gestured to her grubby feet.

Calwyn stifled a cry. The child's feet had been broken. Calwyn knew something about injuries and healing. Skillfully and deliberately, someone had snapped the bones. Shada could not run, nor walk; she could not even stand.

Calwyn touched the child's thin arm. "The emperor is dead. The court is in chaos. This is our best chance to save you."

Shada's dry lips never ceased moving, the soft growling never paused, but slowly she nodded her head.

"My friend can heal you. Don't be afraid. He's waiting for us, just down the stairs. Be brave. I'll carry you down to him."

Calwyn put her arms under the child's frail body and lifted. Shada gave a cry of pain and bit her lip. At last the chantment fell silent. The child was small, and Calwyn was strong, but she staggered under the sudden weight.

Shada whispered, hot and urgent, into her ear, "The others? He'll kill them! He'll know I've stopped; he'll come!"

"You mean the other children?"

"There are five of us, five came from — from the Black Place."
She shuddered and hid her face in Calwyn's shoulder.

Calwyn stood in the harsh sunlight, thinking hard. "Five
chanters, like you? Only five? What about all the other chanter
children?"

"They're in the Black Place. There are only five of us here, all
over the Palace."

"With their feet broken, like you?"

A grimace, something like a smile, flitted across Shada's face.
"Locks and chains can't hold ironcrafters."

"But why — why keep you here, like *this*? Who could be so
cruel?"

Shada peered into Calwyn's face. "We sing, night and day, all
the time. We keep the Palace whole. We take turns to sleep." Her
eyes were huge, staring urgently into Calwyn's. "If we don't sing,
the Palace of Cobwebs will crumble into dust."

Calwyn took a breath, but there was no time to wonder at it
now. "We'll find the others, we'll take you all away. The Palace will
have to fend for itself. But we must hurry."

Staggering, she stooped before the dark doorway. Shada cried
out. The stairway was so narrow that they couldn't fit inside it together. Calwyn thought rapidly. She set the child down and tore off
her stiff outer skirt. "We'll make a sled. In Antaris, where I come
from, we slide down the snowy hills on sleds — of course, I'm
forgetting, do you know what snow is? Here, sit on the skirt, and
I'll pull you down the steps. It will hurt, Shada, I'm sorry —"

But the child understood. "Like a sandskin, for sliding down the dunes," she said. Her dark eyes were large with pain as she shifted herself onto the folded square of fabric. Calwyn was careful, but it was a rough, bumping journey down the winding stairs. And slow — so slow. One step at a time, they descended, down through the thickening darkness.

"Halasaa, oh, Halasaa —" Calwyn wasn't sure if she said the words aloud or only called them with her mind, but at last an answering call sounded inside her head.

I am here.

"I have the child. I have Shada." He was just ahead of her, waiting at the place where the stairs widened. His hands reached out and held her firm. Calwyn let go her grip on the folded skirt and steadied herself against the cool stone walls. "She's hurt, Halasaa. Her feet . . ."

Calwyn could just see him in the dim light, kneeling before the frightened child. Gently he picked up one of the small feet and held it between his thin brown hands. Shada gasped and flinched. "No — no!"

"Halasaa won't hurt you, Shada; I promise."

Be still, little one. Halasaa's calm, reassuring voice sounded in both their minds, and then Calwyn heard, for herself alone, *Who would hurt a child like this?*

"I don't know," she said helplessly. "It must have been Amagis. They are Keela's rooms, but I'm sure she knows nothing."

He has broken more than her bones. Her heart and her mind are damaged also.

"Can you heal her?"

Halasaa nodded. *The injuries to the spirit are more serious than the broken bones. But I can help her.* Already his quick caressing hands were moving over Shada's foot in the silent magic of healing, the Power of Becoming that belonged to the Tree People. Calwyn sat back against the cold stone and allowed herself to rest. Her hands tingled, and her head buzzed with the pleasant, familiar sensation of chantment. As she watched Halasaa's deft movements, she felt herself fall into a kind of dreaming trance, and unconsciously she began to move her own hands in an echo of his. Such a precious gift he had, this dance of healing, and he was the last to know its secrets. . . .

She became aware of a noise in the rooms below. Instantly alert, she shot a look at Halasaa, but his face was severe with concentration. There it was again: a faint rustle of robes on the stone floor. Perhaps the servants had come back to fetch one last bundle of mats.

Quickly, without disturbing Halasaa, Calwyn crept downstairs to the little doorway. Rods of light pierced the shadows of the staircase; like everything else in the Palace, the door was made of carved stone, and there were tiny chinks in the carving. Calwyn put her eye to one of the gaps.

For a moment she saw nothing but the empty room. Then a swish of black crossed her vision, and she fell back, heart thudding. It was Amagis, his gaunt face hard with anger, and he was striding purposefully toward her.

She took one step back and began to sing, a swift quiet chantment of ice. Praying that he couldn't hear her, she sang up ice all
around the door, to hold it fast in its frame. Even before the song
was complete, the sorcerer reached for the handle. Calwyn sang
on, to reinforce the spell, her mind working frantically. She knew
she had trapped them, but somehow she had to hold off the sorcerer until Shada was able to run.

Amagis rattled the door, expecting it to swing open. Then he
swore and pounded on the door with his fists. Tiny splinters of
ice flew from the door frame. Calwyn took a step back, then another, singing under her breath.

Calwyn.

Halasaa and the child were behind her. Shada was on her feet,
eyes wide with terror.

"It's *him*," she whispered. "He brought us from the Black Place."

Amagis's fists pounded on the door, a regular double thumping. Then Calwyn heard the sound she'd been dreading: a low
throat-song, the gurgled notes of a chantment of iron. Amagis
was tearing down the wall around the doorway; bit by bit, it crumbled away. Calwyn sang on, blocking the gaps with ice. More and
more light flooded into the narrow stairwell. She could see
Amagis's grim face clearly now, and his hands raised for the chantment.

Suddenly Calwyn flung her arms up and sang out strongly, a
different chantment, a song of the winds. She blew the door away.
The force of the wind caught the sorcerer utterly by surprise;

Calwyn glimpsed the shock on his pale face as the door hit him with full force. Its top edge clipped him beneath the chin and knocked him flat.

"Run, run!" Calwyn sprinted across the empty room and out into the maze of corridors. Halasaa hared after her, pulling Shada by the hand. The little girl stumbled, her legs weak from long imprisonment. Halasaa scooped her up onto his back and ran on, fleet-footed, barely breaking his stride.

Calwyn ran blindly. On an ordinary day, the Palace hummed with activity: There were concerts and parties and assignations; couples met and sighed in the courtyards; music wafted through the winding corridors; there was the sound of laughter and the swish of robes. But now Calwyn and Halasaa ran through deserted corridors and galleries. Calwyn dropped her gloves and kicked off her dainty sandals so she could run barefoot.

Mica spun around as they burst into Heben's rooms. "Where *were* you? We been worried sick!"

"*Shada!*" Heben gave a choked cry and gathered the little girl just as Halasaa set her down. Shada flung her thin arms around his neck and clung to him.

"What's goin' on? I been out, but no one knows what's happenin', not even in the kitchens, and they know *everythin'*. They said the emperor's dead, and no one wants the First Prince to be emperor, and the Army wants the Fifth Prince instead, and the rebels are comin' to kill everybody. . . ." Mica paused for breath at last.

Calwyn ducked behind a screen and stripped off what remained of her heavy court garments, the stiff bodice and rustling petticoats. No more posing as a courtly lady now. She pulled on her own loose shirt and trousers. It felt so good to stretch her legs and arms, to know that she could run and climb and leap!

"I don't know what's happening, but we can't wait," she said as she laced her boots. "We have to find the other children." She put her hands to her head. Half the pins and combs had tumbled out, all the careful coiffure ruined. She shook her hair free, then with fingers as quick and deft as Halasaa's she braided it into her customary heavy plait and threw it over her shoulder.

"I know where they are!" Shada dropped from Heben's embrace, though she kept her hand wound firmly in his tunic and his arm was tight around her thin shoulders. "But how long before *he* wakes up? Or . . ." Her voice lowered, heavy with the weight of hope. "Did you kill him?"

"Amagis," Calwyn explained to Heben and Mica. She pictured the black-clad body, spread-eagled on the floor. "He cracked his head, but I don't think he's dead." Her eyes sought confirmation from Halasaa's.

He shook his head. *No. Not dead.*

"Then we have to hurry!" There was panic in Shada's voice. "He'll hurt the others! He says, if one of us stops singing, the others —" She began to sob, terrible dry-throated sobs that racked her frail body. "We came here together, and we'll die together, he says. He says, if one of us tries to kill ourselves, or get away, the others will all die! That's what happened to the five who were here before us. . . ."

Heben knelt and tried to soothe her.

"We'll find 'em!" cried Mica, eyes flashing. "We'll get to 'em afore he can, won't we, Cal?"

"Four more," said Calwyn. "Hidden all over the Palace. All hurt, with their feet broken, and worse. . . ."

Heben said nothing, but his arms tightened around Shada.

"Heal them, hide them, take them out of the Palace, all without being discovered." Calwyn passed a hand over her eyes.

If they can be found, they can be healed. If they can be healed, they can be taken away. Halasaa's warm hand gripped her shoulder. *Have courage. We have come so far. We cannot abandon them now.*

"No. No, of course not." Calwyn shook herself.

"I know where they are," said Shada again, staring fiercely from one to another, as if daring them to change their minds. "Ched is in a tower above the Autumn Quarters, not as high as mine. Haid and Vin are together, down in the dungeons. And Oron's in the heart of the Palace, the very center."

"And Gada?" asked Heben eagerly. "Is he here?"

"No." Shada dropped her head. "Gada is in the other place, the Black Place. He must have passed the Testing. I didn't. Girls never pass; that's what *he* said, Amagis. They don't want girls there. They took me away. There's so many, from all over the Empire, all the stolen children." She peered up through her tangled fringe of hair. "Can you help them too?"

"Don't you fear," said Mica confidently. "When we've got these kids out, we'll go and help the others."

Shada did not smile, but a light came into her huge eyes. "The Black Place is in Hathara," she said.

Heben's face went still. "Hathara is the harshest part of the desert. Those who venture there seldom come out."

"That Amagis come out of there, and these kids come out," cried Mica. "We'll come out too!"

Calwyn swallowed and wished that for once Mica could be a little less enthusiastic, a little more pessimistic, like Trout. The task ahead was daunting enough without piling another on top of it. What was this Black Place? What would they do when, *if*, they reached it? A memory flickered, just out of reach: something Darrow had once told her — She felt a stab of longing for Darrow, for his experience, his guidance. She would have given her right hand at that moment just to see his gray eyes meet hers across the room, to feel the warmth of his hand on her own. But they had come here to find the chanter children, and they could not turn back now.

As if he read her thoughts, Halasaa unfolded his long legs and stood. *Come. The four children first. Then the rest.*

"Will you heal them, like you healed me?" Shada gazed solemnly at Halasaa. "How did you do that?"

It is a gift of healing, a gift of my people. You can sing. I can dance.

"We should split up," said Calwyn. "Shada, which way do we go?"

Shada said, "I know every corner of this Palace, every room and every passage, every stair and every balcony. I've sung them up, day and night."

Calwyn nodded. "I have an idea." Inspired by the sled she'd made for Shada, she ripped down one of the large wall hangings and spread it on the floor. "Halasaa, come and hold up one end. No, stand on it, in the center — yes, like a mast on a boat." She sang a quiet chantment of the winds and the mat bellied out in front of Halasaa. "You see? It's a sail! We can slide down the corridors much quicker than if we went on foot. Mica, you and Halasaa take one and I'll take another. And once we've found the children, they can hold the mat up with chantment."

Mica grinned at her in admiration. "You been spendin' too long with Trout! That's good as any idea he ever had!"

Calwyn flushed. "Shada, you wait here for us with Heben. Save your strength; we may have a long journey ahead."

But Shada shook her head. "No. The room in the center of the Palace has no windows and no doors. You're not an ironcrafter. You'll need me."

"I will come with you," said Heben firmly, his hand on Shada's shoulder. His steady dark blue eyes met Calwyn's for a moment, and suddenly she was very glad that she wouldn't be alone.

They agreed that Mica and Halasaa should go in search of the two children in the dungeons beneath the Palace, territory that Mica knew well. Calwyn, Heben, and Shada would rescue the others.

Each group would find a way out of the Palace and return to the camp where they'd left the *hegesi*.

If not for the chaos in the public rooms and corridors and the general upset of the court, they never could have done it. Mica and Halasaa sped off down the passageway, Mica whooping with excitement, while Halasaa held up the mat, his long hair streaming behind him. Shada growled out a chantment to hold up the second mat, and Calwyn sang a blast of wind to propel them forward, leaning precariously to the side to steer. Relieved to be out of their confined rooms at last, Heben gave a broad grin as they rushed down the smooth tunnel of the first corridor, swooping and gliding around the bends and turns.

The sailing sleds were no use on the stairs. But Shada directed them to the passages the servants took when they shifted furniture, where they could wheel the cabinets on their castors along ramps rather than haul them up and down steps.

They shot along the smooth slopes faster than Calwyn had ever slid down any snow-covered hill in Antaris. It was an exhilarating way to travel, from one side of the Palace to the other, up and down between the levels, for Calwyn could propel them up the ramps with chantment just as quickly as they slid down. Room after empty room flew by in a blur of creamy stone.

When Shada tugged at Calwyn's sleeve and pointed to a wide archway on the right, Calwyn turned the mat and they shot out onto a promenade that twisted along the length of the Palace. The floor was made of thousands of small tiles, each grained differently, so that the surface caught the light of the setting sun and glimmered like mother-of-pearl.

Now Calwyn could truly use the power of her chantment. "Hold on!" she cried, and she sang up a wind into their makeshift sail that was as strong as she dared. The mat swelled out before them, and Heben gasped as they zoomed onward. The promenade ran along the side of the Palace, but it didn't overlook the desert. A high wall enclosed it, covered in flowering vines that flashed by in a blur of green. But the walkway was open to the sky, and Calwyn could see the light fading fast, bleaching the sky to the color of bone. Soon it would be night. Had Amagis recovered consciousness? Would he find them? Were there other sorcerers hidden somewhere in the Palace who would help him, or was he alone?

"Please, be careful!" cried Heben. They were veering close to the wall, and Calwyn hastily corrected her course. Torn and scraped by the Palace floors, the wall hanging was beginning to wear thin, and a rip had appeared at one edge.

They were near the Summer Quarters now, and for the first time, there were people about. In the dimming light Calwyn saw astounded faces in the archways of the promenade. A knot of startled courtiers had to leap out of their way. The sailing sled moved too fast for anyone to catch them on foot, but they had been noticed. Even on a day of bizarre events, the sight of a wall hanging laden with people, flying along the promenade like a boat under sail, was a spectacle to set tongues busy.

They swerved off the walkway and back inside. Deeper and deeper toward the center of the Palace they sailed on their ragged raft. Even with the help of chantment, it would not serve them for much longer. The threads were fraying and falling apart, and no amount of magic would hold them together.

Presently Shada whispered, "This is the way to the room where Oron is."

Calwyn halted the raft. The passage before them twisted abruptly. Shada leaped up. "It's a maze. I'll show you the way."

While Heben kept guard outside, Shada led Calwyn through the twists and turns of the maze, confidently doubling back and darting forward; the path was so narrow that the two girls couldn't walk abreast. At last they reached the center. The wall that confronted them was blank and featureless, about four paces wide, its surface bulged and pitted.

Shada took a deep breath and began to sing, unsteadily at first. Gradually her voice grew stronger, and the wall quivered and trembled.

"Keep singing, Shada!" cried Calwyn. "I'll help you."

The top corner of the wall started to crumble like a piece of cheese. Calwyn summoned up a breeze to blow the crumbs of stone away. Soon dust blew all around them; they kept their eyes screwed shut against the storm of white grit.

Now Calwyn could hear a third voice: another child, adding his chantment to the struggle, punching out from the inside with all his force. When the wall was breached, Calwyn opened her eyes and saw a small form crouched inside the whirl of white dust and chips of stone. The wall was collapsing fast, the room dissolving before their eyes. Calwyn stepped inside and snatched up the boy. Oron clutched at her neck, just as Shada had done, shielding his eyes from the sudden burst of light after being sealed in the dark for so long.

Calwyn, Heben, Shada, and Oron sailed on, deep into the deserted rooms and cold corridors of the Autumn Quarters, moving more and more slowly. Calwyn urged the frayed raft onward with her spellwind, fearing that every corner they turned might be their last. She nudged Oron and gestured to the biggest tear in the wall hanging, but he stared back at her blankly. Calwyn looked to Heben for help.

"Please, can you mend it?" he asked the boy. Oron shrugged and reluctantly began to sing, binding the threads tightly together. Calwyn felt his hostility, and she remembered what Halasaa had said, that Shada's spirit had been more badly hurt than her feet. It must be the same for Oron.

At last they reached a small door at the base of the second tower. Calwyn and Heben left the children huddled on the mat while they climbed the dark stairs. These were wider than those inside Shada's tower, and Heben was able to climb to the top.

When they came out at the roof of the tower, the sky was ablaze with stars, thicker than Calwyn had ever seen. This was the first time since they'd come to the Palace that she had seen the night sky.

It was only at Heben's sharp intake of breath that she noticed the dark figure outlined against the shimmering backdrop of the stars. Marked with a vicious gash across the chin, Amagis's ghastly white face loomed out of the dark. Calwyn heard a muffled cry of pain and saw that the sorcerer held a boy, smaller than the others. He had one hand clamped hard over the child's mouth to stop him from crying out or singing. Ched struggled fiercely in the sorcerer's grip, though every movement must have caused him agony.

Amagis's lips were moving. Calwyn was jerked violently to one side; the sorcerer's chantment had seized her shirt and dragged her toward the low railing, to hurl her over the edge.

Calwyn had no time to think. Already she teetered at the edge of the tower. Heben flung himself forward without hesitation and grappled her to the ground. Calwyn couldn't sing; she screamed in pain as the twisted cloth of her shirt bit into her flesh.

The next thing she heard was a small angry voice from the doorway. Shada had followed them. She faced Amagis, hands clenched, head lowered, growling defiance like a *wasuntu* pup. She was singing; she sang a spell that grasped the sorcerer's fine embroidered collar and pulled it tight around his narrow throat, choking him, choking his chantment, and Calwyn's head banged against the roof as the grip on her shirt was suddenly released.

Even before she could sit up, she was singing. Amagis's hands flew to his throat, tearing uselessly at his collar, and he released the boy. Without the use of his feet, Ched dropped as if he'd been poleaxed. Calwyn sang out a spellwind to throw Amagis off balance, a wind that caught his black cloak and billowed it out behind him, like a bat against the night sky.

But the wind she sang was stronger than she knew, and Amagis was already off balance, struggling against the stranglehold at his throat. The wind lifted in the folds of his black cloak. Calwyn saw the gaunt white mask of his face split in a grin of horror, like a skull's. He flung his arms wide, suspended against the diamond glitter of stars. Calwyn cried out, her song abruptly cut off. But it was too late. She rushed forward as Amagis toppled back over the railing.

With his black cloak spread in the air like wings, outlined against the white froth of the Palace, he hung for a long moment like a hovering bird. "He'll sing!" gasped Calwyn. "He'll save himself —"

But the sorcerer had no time to gather the breath that might have saved him. The dark figure plummeted down, down into the jumble of small domes and turrets and palisades that sprouted from the Palace roof. The final impact made no sound. But they all saw the crumpled body, far below, a small black shape on the white stone.

Calwyn turned away in horror. "I didn't mean it!" she cried. "I didn't mean to kill him!"

"He would have killed you," said Heben. "The fight was fair." Matter-of-factly he turned to the boy. "Put your arms around my neck." Shada gave Ched's shoulder a warm squeeze as he pulled himself painfully onto Heben's back.

"The Palace is crumbling," Ched whispered as Heben carried him down the stairs. "I can feel it; it's beginning. I'm the last. The song, the song was too hard —"

"I'll help you, Ched!" cried Shada. "Oron's here, too. We'll all sing! We won't let the Palace fall down, not yet."

They settled Ched in the center of the raft. He was trembling all over, his eyes bright and feverish. Was he weaker than the others because he had borne the whole burden of holding the fabric of the Palace together as Calwyn and Mica and Halasaa plucked away his helpers, one by one? Oron and Shada bent their heads in concentration, and a low growl of ironcraft droned from their lips. Ched joined in, but feebly.

"The mat is falling apart," Calwyn said. "It won't carry us any farther. We need to find another tapestry, something . . ." Her voice trailed away. This part of the Palace was unfurnished and bare. The nearest hangings were in the Summer Quarters, too far away and too dangerous.

The image of Amagis, crumpled on the white stone, rose unbidden before her eyes. She shook her head fiercely to banish it, then suddenly she buried her face in her hands, overwhelmed. Ched and Oron, helpless with their broken feet, depending on her; Shada and Heben, waiting for her decision; the Palace, crumbling around them. How could she get them all out safely?

In despair, she called out with her mind, *Halasaa! Where are you?*

Sister, I am here.

She hadn't expected a response; when his voice sounded in her mind, she leaped up.

"Halasaa!" *Our sailing sled is worn out. I don't know what to do.*

Wait. We are near. We have been in the dungeons. We will come.

Wild-eyed, almost weeping with relief, she turned to Heben and the children. "The others are coming! Halasaa will heal your feet! You'll be able to *run* out of the Palace!"

Shada stopped her chantment to hug Heben, and Ched smiled weakly, uncomprehending. Oron stared skeptically at Calwyn, his lips barely moving as his song of ironcraft droned on.

Calwyn looked away, to the curving wall they crouched beside. The elaborate carvings had begun to blur slightly, like a melting candle. The delicate edges of the stone were losing their sharpness, as if wind and rain were wearing them into softness. She touched the floor; it was dusty beneath her hand. Even if she had set off for the Summer Quarters, by the time she returned with a new mat, the floors might have been impassable. . . .

Calwyn.

She looked up. A little band hurried toward them on foot, their sailing sled abandoned: Halasaa, Mica, and two children, moving tentatively on their newly healed feet.

Mica broke into a run when she saw them. "Our sailin' sled fell to bits!" she shouted. "And somethin's happenin' to the Palace!"

The voices of all the children broke out in a frightened, jostling babble. " 'Course it is!"

"Nothing to hold it together now!"

"It's going to come crashing down!"

"Got to keep singing, till we can get out!"

"Got to go now!"

"Halasaa?" Calwyn turned to her friend, and he gave her a weary smile.

I will begin.

He knelt beside Ched, the youngest of the children, and took his foot between his hands, his fingers moving in the swift, deft dance of healing. Calwyn pressed his shoulder. *I'm sorry to ask so much of you, my brother.* Without thinking, she used the speech of the mind. But Halasaa was sunk deep in the trance of becoming and couldn't respond.

With a surge of joy Calwyn realized she had used mind-speech to call Halasaa, and he had answered her. She could speak to her friend in his own way!

Shada, Oron, and the two boys from the dungeons, Vin and Haid, were huddled together, growling out a throat-song of iron-craft. Mica and the children all looked expectantly to Calwyn. She took a deep breath. If Darrow were here, he could tell them what to do. But he wasn't here; she would have to be the leader. She stared back at them numbly.

Before she could find words, Heben spoke. "Mica, Calwyn, take the children who can walk. You must find a way out now, as quickly as you can. Halasaa and I will follow with the others. If you see any people on your way, warn them!"

"Why should we care about them? They never cared about us!" said Oron.

"No, Heben's right," said Calwyn. "We have to warn everyone we can. I don't want any more deaths on my conscience."

"I'll warn 'em if I see 'em, Cal," said Mica loyally. "Even though they ain't worth it."

Calwyn gave her a quick, grateful smile and turned to Heben. "Perhaps Keela can help warn the court, if I can find her."

Heben looked at her appraisingly. "Very well. If the children sing until moonrise, will that give you enough time?"

Calwyn nodded. "I think so. You all go together, as soon as Halasaa has healed Ched and Oron. The children can use their craft to open the walls for you."

"I'm runnin' down to the kitchens," put in Mica. "We'll need food."

"No!" said Calwyn. "It's too dangerous. I want you to stay with Heben and Halasaa."

"I ain't your servant now!" cried Mica, her golden eyes blazing. "You can't tell me what to do!"

Calwyn could have shaken her. "*You'll* be trapped!"

"I'll go with her," offered Shada. "We'll get out all right."

"What about *you?*" Mica stormed on. "You'll get trapped!"

No one had noticed Ched, his feet mended, creeping closer to listen. Suddenly he piped up, "You don't know the way, and you can't open the walls. You won't be able to get out. The others can hold up the Palace without me for a little while. I'll come." Ched slipped his thin hand into Calwyn's. "I don't care if everyone in this place gets crushed into dust, but you saved me. I won't leave you."

Calwyn squeezed his hand. "Ched, thank you! Are you strong enough to run? What's the quickest way to the Summer Quarters?"

"Be careful, Calwyn," said Heben. There was a light in his clear blue eyes, a keenness to his face that Calwyn hadn't seen before, almost as if he were looking forward to the danger ahead.

"And you," answered Calwyn, and touched her fingers to her lips in the Merithuran salute.

It was long after midnight, and in contrast to the day, people were milling everywhere. Ched led Calwyn to the very heart of the Summer Quarters, the Courtyard of Three Fountains, a large open plaza overlooked by a colonnade. Breathless, Calwyn leaned on the railing with its graceful twists; it gave way under her weight, and she leaped back. The disruptions to the children's chantment had taken their toll; the Palace would not collapse until they stopped singing altogether, but the fabric of its structure had weakened.

Calwyn shouted over the square, "The Palace is falling! All of you, be warned! There's great danger, save yourselves!"

Heads swiveled, and faces turned up toward her. Some were curious, some amused, but most showed a pitying contempt.

"Poor child," she heard one elderly lady murmur. "The shock of the emperor's death has turned her wits. Look at her; she's not even properly dressed!"

"It's true!" Calwyn's voice rang out clearly above the splash of the fountains. "The Palace is about to collapse! Look! The walls are crumbling."

A gentleman said warningly, "Listen, my girl, unless you can tell me where all my servants have hidden themselves, I advise you to save your fabulations for a smoke-party storytelling."

"Yours too, eh?" chuckled the elderly lady. "Still larking about in the Spring Quarters, I expect. It's always the same at festival time."

There was not one servant to be seen in the plaza. All the courtiers in their festival finery were unattended; some even carried their own stools, a dreadful breach of etiquette.

"Can't you see?" cried Calwyn. "The servants know something's wrong! They must be sheltering in the cellars; you must join them while you still can! You're in terrible danger!"

But the courtiers had already turned away indifferently.

Ched plucked at her sleeve. "Let's go," he whispered. "It's their bad luck. It'll be moonrise soon. Let's get out!" Even as he spoke, a chunk of the railing crumbled away; a rain of white dust descended on the crowd of courtiers below. They stared up in annoyance, brushing the dust from their clothes.

But Calwyn had glimpsed a swirl of pink silk on the far side of the colonnade, and she began to run. "Keela! Keela!"

The Third Princess turned her sleek blond head; she looked distracted.

As her gaze focused on Calwyn, a strange expression flickered across her face, and she took an involuntary step back. But in a heartbeat her habitual mask of cool amusement had slid into place. "Calwyn, what a delightful surprise! What in the world are you doing here, and in such . . . unusual dress? Or should I say, undress?"

"I've been looking for you!" gasped Calwyn. Again that unaccountable expression, almost a look of horror, flitted over the princess's face, but Calwyn was too preoccupied to notice. "Listen to me, Keela! I don't have time to explain properly. The Palace is about to collapse. You must help me to warn everyone!"

"My dear, one doesn't say *must* to a princess." Keela's sharp eyes darted about, scanning the crowd. Then her gaze snapped back to Calwyn, as if she'd taken in her words for the first time. "The Palace is collapsing? How absurd!"

Calwyn stared at her, aghast. "I assure you, Princess, the Palace *will* fall, very soon, tonight! Keela, people will listen to you! Please, warn them!"

But Keela was staring at the ragged figure of Ched, and her face had hardened. "Who is this little boy?" she asked, in a voice as smooth as cream. "Is he a relative of yours, another of the Cledsec Clan? Your little nephew, perhaps? The Imperial Court is no place for children. I'll see that he's taken care of."

"No, thank you," said Calwyn, with forced politeness. "I can take care of him."

"Are you sure, my dear?" Keela's eyes were chips of blue ice. "I thought this child had another guardian."

Ched said nothing, but he sidled closer to Calwyn and clutched hard at her arm. Suddenly Calwyn realized that Keela understood exactly what was happening and who Ched was. Trying to keep her voice steady, she said, "His — his guardian is dead."

"Dead!" exclaimed Keela, and her eyes widened as she stared at Calwyn. She made the sign that Heben had made, to ward off evil.

With a sigh, another section of the railing gave way; white dust settled like a snowfall onto the plaza. People moved out of the way. One or two glanced around and murmured anxiously, but most still strolled about, unconcerned.

Suddenly Keela leaned forward and whispered urgently in Calwyn's ear. "It isn't too late for us to be friends, Calwyn, if that is your true name! I know what you've done, and I'm glad of it. But there's no need to work for the sea-towners; they could never give you what my master and I can, when the time comes. We could work together. Why not give me the child? Change is coming, coming soon. If you help me, I will remember —" Every trace of the frivolous, shallow princess had vanished; Calwyn found herself staring into the face of a calculating and ruthless woman. "Give me the child," repeated Keela, and there was steel in her voice.

Calwyn slowly shook her head. Without warning, Keela pounced on Ched like a roancat leaping on a *nadu*. But Ched wriggled out of her grip and Calwyn dragged him away, and at once they were off, dodging through the crowd of courtiers and down a narrow, twisted corridor. Ched scrambled up the wall, finding footholds in the stone. Calwyn followed, just as nimble, hauling herself upward, her hands coated in dust.

Suddenly they were outside, scrabbling across a sloping roof, under the dark sky ablaze with stars and a slender sickle of moon. A moon. . . . "Ched!" cried Calwyn. "The moons are up!"

Ched nodded. Then he slid down a pillar and dived through a tiny window, and they were inside again, facing a wall whose pattern of fern fronds was beginning to blur and melt.

Panting for breath, Ched held out his hand and sang a throat-song of ironcraft, and an opening appeared in the sagging wall. He and Calwyn plunged through it into a suite of private rooms. A noble lord and lady were seated on cushions, huddled in talk; they looked up in surprise, but nothing was beyond belief this day.

"Follow us!" cried Calwyn. "You must escape from the Palace before it's too late!" But the courtiers didn't even rise to their feet as Ched opened a breach in the far wall and led Calwyn through.

"Gotta go down!" cried Ched when they came to a wide, curved staircase. "Gotta get to the ground —"

Calwyn slowly became aware of a very low, quiet groaning, like the roar of a distant forest fire. Every part of her wanted to scream to Ched, *Hurry, hurry!* But they could only go as fast as Ched could open the way, through wall after wall, until Calwyn didn't even notice the rooms they passed through.

And then Ched gasped, "This is the last." His face was pale, and he was stumbling; Calwyn put out a hand to steady him.

They emerged into a hollow space between the outermost wall and the inner ones. It was neither a room nor a passageway but a narrow blank area, unadorned, with walls so high that they couldn't see its roof. Calwyn forced herself to breathe calmly. The immense walls seemed to press together like two hands trying to crush them. Dust was falling all around, white powder drifting down; it coated their hair, their faces, their clothes, so they looked like ghosts. Calwyn called out silently, *Halasaa! Where are you? Are you safe?* But there was no reply.

Ched's thin chest heaved as he fought for breath. The little boy stood before the enormous ivory wall, one hand outstretched, fingers drooping with weariness, as he called up one last low throat-growl of chantment that mingled with the distant groan of the Palace's slow disintegration. A wild fancy flashed into Calwyn's mind: that the Palace itself was singing, singing the low, mournful song of its own destruction.

As Ched sang, a crack opened in the last thick wall. Slowly, painfully, he cleaved the wall in two, and a jagged line grew wider with every note. And finally there was something that Calwyn could do: With a light song of windcraft she brushed away the dust and stones to clear the opening. This last wall was as thick as the length of *Fledgewing*, and as Ched prized it apart with the steady drone of his song, the whole weight of the stone above pressed down on it.

Ched's voice croaked and failed, and he dropped to his knees. Without thinking, Calwyn took up his song, the two notes at once, as Darrow had tried to teach her: one in the back of her throat and the second inside her mouth. The song of ironcraft leaped from her lips like a living creature, and the force of it shuddered through Calwyn's whole body. The crack shifted and held. She sang on, more strongly, and the gap widened. Now she could see all the way through the wall to the other side: the sand, metallic under the moonlight, *arbec* plants soft as beaten silver.

Calwyn knew that she wouldn't be able to hold the crack open long. She swung Ched up in her arms and leaped through, growling the chantment as hard as she could, forcing the breath out of her lungs.

She was just in time. She heard it begin: a tremendous groan of crushing stone that drowned out her chantment, and then a roar like an avalanche as the whole Palace began to collapse.

Calwyn felt the bite of hard rock under her boots, and then she was running down the steep ridge, running faster than she'd ever run, running until she thought her lungs would burst, still clutching the little boy in her arms. A cloud of dust engulfed them, and the roar built and built like a wave about to break, a wave of crushing stone that towered above them. Calwyn ran, without breath; the moment seemed endless. She felt as though she were drowning, her earliest and strongest fear. She was trapped in the dream she'd had often as a novice priestess, the dream that she was crossing the black ice of the sacred pool and the ice opened and swallowed her. The black water dragged her down, and she was fighting, fighting her way to the surface, but it was so far off, she kicked and kicked toward the light . . .

And as she ran, the wave broke.

Before she heard the final deafening roar, she felt the force of it, a hard blow to her back that knocked her to the ground. She lost her grip on Ched; he slipped out of her arms as she rolled down the slope and onto the plain, striking her head painfully on the stony ground. The world turned upside down.

She could see the wave of destruction ripple the length of the Palace of Cobwebs. The vast silvered edifice crumbled, piece by piece, fragile as meringue. Shada's thin spire crumpled, then a smaller spire toppled, and a row of battlements folded on itself. The great dome on the eastern side caved in, and a slow silent cloud of white dust engulfed the ruins. The stately stone of the Palace of Cobwebs was melting, dissolving, evaporating like sea foam. The image of the huge half-eaten marzipan model of the Palace at the Summer Feast flashed into Calwyn's mind. Now the real Palace looked the same. Nothing was left but a rubble of white crumbs.

She lay there while the rumble of the falling stones diminished. She was alive. She took in one rasping breath, then another, and choked. Her mouth and nose were full of sand and dust. Ched lay a few paces away. Behind them spread a mountain of white stone. There were lumps of rock scattered all around, and the desert gleamed with a thick layer of white dust, dazzling bright in the moonlight. Calwyn was reminded of the mountain meadows of Antaris after a snowfall.

She crawled over to Ched. "Are you all right? Can you hear me?"

He was facing away from her; she laid her hand on his shoulder. He rolled over at her touch, and she drew a sharp breath, for his eyes were wide and staring and his body was limp. "No! No!" Frantically she shook his shoulders. "Ched! Ched!"

But she knew. There was no doubt. The side of his head had

been crushed by a falling chunk of stone; he would have died at once. Tears slid down Calwyn's cheeks as she cradled Ched's small, bloodied body. "I can take care of him," she had said to Keela. She bent her head and wept.

Another roar rumbled out across the desert as a final avalanche of white rock poured onto the red sands. Shakily Calwyn stood up; the ruins were so unstable, it wasn't safe to remain here. But she couldn't leave Ched's body exposed on the plain, to be nosed by *wasunti*. Swiftly she gathered stones and piled them over the little boy. It did not take long. She stood with her head bowed for a moment, holding her palms upward to the Goddess's light, and under her breath she recited the prayer for the dead.

When that was done, she took a deep breath. She had to turn all her attention to her own survival. "Halasaa!" she shouted, turning slowly. "Mica! Heben!"

All around, the lumps of white stone lay still and silent. "Mica!" she called, fighting the sobs that threatened to choke her. "Halasaa! Mica! Heben!" But her voice was swallowed by the indifferent desert. She called with mind-speech, *Halasaa! Can you hear me?* There was no reply.

Suddenly she realized how cold it was; her teeth were chattering. She could not stay here.

Ahead, to the left and right, stretched the endless plain, scored with ravines. Calwyn felt a moment of panic. Where was the gully where they'd left the *begesi*? Was it this side of the Palace or the other? She looked up at the moons, and her racing heart calmed.

She was facing north, and the campsite lay to the north of the Palace. She would have to go around to the other side.

Slowly, laboriously, she picked her way across the desert, giving the remains of the Palace a wide berth. The ground was baked hard as rock underfoot; it crunched beneath her boots. Calwyn stumbled onward, looking around for her friends, starting at every flicker of movement, every scratch of tiny *nadu* claws.

Suddenly the earth shuddered beneath her. Calwyn threw herself to the ground; she heard the clink of armor and the stamp of boots. An Army patrol, perhaps ten or twenty men, Calwyn guessed. She pressed herself flat to the red dirt. She was utterly exposed; she could only hope to be overlooked if she kept completely still.

"Halt! Fall out!"

The command rang out some distance away. Cautiously Calwyn shifted her cheek against the hard-packed sand and squinted toward the sound. If only she had the Power of Seeming, so she could hide herself! She could hear the harsh scrape of metal as the soldiers laid down their heavy shields. A murmur of talk drifted toward her, and Calwyn strained to hear.

". . . turn back here."

"No sign of rebels —"

"Rebels? This ain't down to them. Sorcery did this, brother."

"Sorcery? You're dreamin', brother. The generals and the sorcerers work together. This is the work of them sea-town scum . . ."

So the rebels were being blamed for the destruction of the Palace. It was agonizing to lie so still while insects crawled into her eyes and up her nose and sand crept inside her robes, but Calwyn wanted to hear what else the soldiers had to say.

"Know what our next job's goin' to be?"

"I heard we're takin' over the Palace, brother."

"What's left of it!"

Someone laughed. A chill ran down Calwyn's spine as she thought of the polished armor and shining sword blades of the princes. Perhaps they would see some action at last. If the Army was planning a coup, should she try to warn the courtiers? No, she decided. They would have to fend for themselves.

"We'll show 'em who's boss!"

"There ain't no boss, now the emperor's dead. . . ."

"There's always a boss, brother!"

There was hearty laughter.

"My money's on the Fifth Prince."

"Him! He ain't got the wits to tie his own bootlaces!"

"That's why the generals are settin' him up on the throne, you idiot —"

"Watch your mouth, brother."

"All right, men, that'll do! Fall in!"

There were grumbles and groans, a shuffle of feet and the muffled clank of weaponry, and then the steady rhythm of marching boots shook the ground once more. Calwyn made herself count ten full breaths before she scrambled to her feet. She had to keep moving. Soon it would be dawn.

DARROW 4

Darrow leaned on the tiller, and *Fledgewing*'s white sail puffed out before the wind. Tonno, standing by the mast, his curly hair ruffled by the breeze, turned to grin at him. They had come a long way since leaving Teril and they were not far now from the mining town of Phain. But Darrow was not yet ready to land. He and Tonno would sail on for some days more, past Phain and Geel, through the Southern Straits, along the meandering golden shore around the Heel of Merithuros, as far south as any ship from the Westlands or the Isles ever sailed. But *Fledgewing* would go even farther, sailing through those hostile seas, toward the bottom of the world.

Tonno had been shocked when Darrow abandoned his own boat in Teril.

"*Heron* has served me well," said Darrow brusquely. "But *Fledgewing* is faster."

"Don't expect her to be waiting for you when you come back," growled Tonno. "Teril's packed with thieves like a melon full of pips."

Darrow did not reply. As they drew closer to Merithuros, closer to the Black Palace, the ruby ring that Samis had worn began to burn in his pocket like a hot coal.

* * *

Heron.

"Your name is not your own," says Samis. "I will give you an-other. You will be Heron." Darrow didn't know what a heron was until Samis told him: a bird of the marshes, lean, keeping to itself, stalking the water in solitude. "Except, of course, there's no water here," drawls Samis.

Darrow says nothing. The description is wrong in another way too. He is not solitary anymore: He has Samis. The two are always together. Darrow is freed from the dreary round of daily tasks and lessons. He and Samis go where they please, demand answers to their questions from whichever chanter Samis chooses to sum-mon. They practice their chantments extravagantly, for the plea-sure of wielding power, ignoring rules that bind the other sorcerers. They go hawking in the desert and on hunting expedi-tions to the shore. Unlike the other sorcerers, cloistered in their dim rooms with their murmured secrets, the prince and his com-panion leave the Black Palace and return at will; they have a wild freedom that Darrow has never dreamed of.

The sorcerers hate and fear Samis, yet they dare not gainsay him, not just because he is the emperor's son but also because he is stronger than any of them. It is exhilarating to Darrow to live in the shadow of such casual power, as if he walked beside a whirl-wind or a lightning bolt and called it friend.

For they are friends. After several years of mistrust, Darrow has lost the fear that Samis will tire of his company. And he knows that he is no mere servant, no matter what the other sorcerers mutter behind Samis's back. He is adviser, confidant, companion, brother. When the two traveled together to the Palace of Cobwebs, the courtiers treated Darrow with almost as much respect as Samis himself. Samis speaks of future journeys, away from Merithuros, across the seas to the Westlands, or north to Baltimar.

The world, which had closed around Darrow like the walls of the Testing room, has opened itself out like a flower after rain.

Darrow and Tonno guided *Fledgewing* into the harbor of Hult. The little town barely earned the name: a motley collection of dilapidated buildings, patched together out of driftwood, gray and cheerless. Darrow and Samis used to come here on their hunting expeditions and drink wine in what passed for the tavern. Darrow suspected that the gold coin that Samis carelessly tossed to the innkeeper was the only income the place mustered from one year to the next.

"Wait here till I fetch you," he told Tonno. He stepped ashore onto the sands of Hathara for the first time in five years, grim-faced, and strode in the direction of the rickety tavern. Grubby children watched him from behind an upturned fishing boat and snickered into their hands. In a doorway a woman sat mending. She stared at him with narrowed eyes and, without hiding her gesture, made the sign to avert bad luck. Darrow's mouth twisted in a half smile. How different it was from the welcome he'd received on Ravamey. And yet this was supposed to be his home.

The tavern was as he remembered it. The innkeeper sat at

a trestle table, gambling with two slow-chewing men. He looked up sharply at the entry of a customer. The smell of slava was thick in the air, and the men shook their dice slowly, reflectively, and let them fall without interest, hardly bothering to keep the tally.

Darrow ordered a jug of wine. The innkeeper said, "Haven't seen you for a goodly while."

"No."

"Didn't have *that* last time." He gestured to the scar that dragged Darrow's eyebrow toward his cheekbone. "Get that hunting? With your friend?"

"Yes," said Darrow briefly. "Hunting." He did not say that he himself was the prey in that hunt.

The innkeeper looked sly. "Looking to hunt again?"

"Maybe." Darrow poured himself a beaker of wine; it was as sour and thin as ever.

"Come from the court?"

"Not this time." Darrow looked up and held the man's shrewd gaze for a moment. "I am not welcome at the court anymore. I killed a prince of the Royal House." As he spoke, Darrow saw again the body covered in the gray cloak, lying amid the silver towers and domes of Spareth, and his heart beat hard.

The innkeeper straightened up. "I know someone. You might call him a hunter. Think he'd be interested to meet a man who's killed a prince."

"Yes," said Darrow. "I thought you might. I would like to meet your friend."

Again the two men's gazes met, and held for an instant.

"Be here at sundown. I'll make sure he comes."

"Thank you," said Darrow. He drained the beaker and went outside to wait.

The road that ran along the shore was red and dusty, littered with small stones. He walked up and down. It was not so hot here on the southern coast, but it was warm enough, and the sun glared as fiercely as in the middle of the desert. The sea was a sheet of white metal, painful to look at. Some little stones pattered into the dust at his feet, and he heard children giggle and run away. Thirsty, he found a fountain in the deserted marketplace and sat for a while on its dusty edge in the sunlight, conscious of the eyes that watched him from every hut and every shadowed doorway.

The sorcerers gather in the dark corridors, in whispering knots. When they see Samis and Darrow approach, they turn away, silenced.

"The old Lord is dying," says Darrow. "They must choose the next wearer of the Ring."

Samis strides along. His high hunting boots strike like flints on the black marble.

"In all my time here, I have never met this old Lord. It's time we paid him a visit, Heron."

"They won't allow it."

"Heron, you disappoint me! Have you not learned that lesson yet? *They* cannot prevent us from doing anything. Come."

The two friends sweep along the polished corridors. Samis is right: The sorcerers do not stop them. Samis's arrogance is like a torch of fire, scattering those who might oppose them.

Only at the very door to the room where the old Lord lies does someone say no.

"You shall not enter," says the Spider, malignant in his dark robes, his long fingers curled already around the ebony staff that the old Lord carried.

Samis's eyes narrow. "You have hopes, my friend," he says softly. "Do you truly think yourself worthy to be the next Lord of the Black Palace, with all its mysteries, all its sorrows? Are you strong enough?"

"I am no princeling," spits the Spider. "But I have earned the right to rule here. The old Lord has promised that I will be his successor."

Samis smiles his lazy smile and inclines his imperious head. "Ah, well, if the old Lord himself has decreed it, we must offer you our congratulations," he says. "Come, Heron. Let us leave our friend to enjoy his inheritance." The two men turn away. They are some distance from the doorway when Samis begins to sing beneath his breath. Darrow hears a strangled cry. He spins about to see the Spider collapse, in a flurry of black robes, his mouth gaping in horror. The ebony staff protrudes from his chest. Samis has stabbed him, with chantment, through the heart.

Darrow rushes back to the fallen sorcerer, but the man is already dead. Blood trickles from the mouth, twisted in its final leering grimace. Darrow cries to Samis, "What have you done?"

Samis is not there. Darrow turns his head and sees him emerge from the Lord's room. "Come," he says briskly. "The old man is dead too. Time for us to go a-hunting, my Heron. There's nothing more for us here." Samis's eyes gleam as they hurry down the corridors. "Ha!"

"What have you done?" Darrow asks again. He follows his friend, of course; he would follow him to the rim of the world, but his hands tremble.

"Heron, my Heron. There is no calamity. Two evil old men are dead. They stole children and tortured them. The world is a better place without them, is it not?"

Darrow does not reply. His heart is troubled. He and Samis do not stop to pack their bags. Before noon, they are riding *hegesi* to the shore. Before nightfall, they have found passage on a boat bound for Geel.

It is not until they are on board the boat that Samis shows Darrow what he stole from the old Lord's hand. Darrow never asks him whether the old Lord was alive or dead when Samis took the Ring from his finger. He is afraid of the answer.

At sunset Darrow went back to the tavern.

The place was crowded, but he saw at once the man he sought. He was lean and alert, weathered and keen-eyed, a desert dweller in desert robes. He stood as Darrow entered, and deliberately drew back a fold of his robes to show the curved knife that hung at his belt. Darrow went to sit at his table.

"They tell me you are a hunter," said the rebel fighter.

"I used to be. I would like to be so again."

"I think I can help you." There was a pause. "My name is Fenn."

"Darrow."

"So. You have killed a prince. How? An accident?"

"No," said Darrow. "It was no accident."

Fenn nodded slowly, with respect. "You are a brave man, to show your face inside the Empire."

"Perhaps," said Darrow wryly. "But my task is not finished."

"Ah." Fenn poured them each a beaker of sour wine. "These are interesting times, my friend. They say the Palace of Cobwebs is fallen. Perhaps the whole Royal House lies crushed beneath its ruins."

"I had not heard that," said Darrow evenly. "I have been at sea."

The rebel shrugged. "It may not be true. There are all kinds of stories." He leaned forward intently. "However, this much is true: The towns of Geel and Phain, the mines and the harbors, have fallen to us. The revolution has begun. Had you heard that tale, at sea?"

"I had not heard that tale," said Darrow. "But I am not sorry to hear it. The Empire of Merithuros is rotten to the core. The miners and town dwellers toil and starve while the emperor's courtiers grow fat. It's time for change."

"I am glad we agree." Fenn grimaced as he swallowed a mouthful of the thin wine. "Why did you wish to meet? Do you want something, or do you have something to give?"

"Both, I hope." Darrow twisted his beaker but did not lift it. Suddenly he asked, "Do you know of the Black Palace?"

"The Black Palace?" Fenn looked startled. "Yes, I've heard stories of the sorcerers' nest. But the Black Palace is just that: a hearth story."

"The Black Palace is real," said Darrow quietly. "I can take you there."

"Into Hathara? No one who goes into Hathara has ever come out alive."

Darrow smiled. "I have."

"Why?" asked Fenn abruptly. "What do you have to gain?"

"The same as you. I want to see change in Merithuros; I want to see the Empire dismantled. The brotherhood of sorcerers is as much a part of the corruption as the emperor himself."

Fenn shrugged. "I don't know anything about sorcery, and I don't wish to know anything about it. But if you say that marching on the sorcerers' nest will hasten the revolution, I am prepared to risk it. But —" In a warning gesture, Fenn put his hand again to the knife at his belt. "I advise you not to trifle with us. If you lead us into Hathara, into the dead lands, for nothing, we will kill you."

"Agreed," said Darrow calmly. "My friend Tonno will come with us. He is not Merithuran, he is a son of Kalysons, but you can trust him. And by the way . . ." He sang a low note, and the beaker of wine leaped from the tabletop. A dark stain spread across the floor. "Do not trifle with me either."

Fenn started to his feet; his hand flew up in the sign to ward off evil. He looked quickly at Darrow with a mixture of wariness, loathing, and respect. It was a look that Darrow had often seen before, and he returned it without emotion. "Yes, I am a chanter. Does that alter your decision?"

For a long moment the two men stared at each other. At last Fenn put out his hand. "I am a man of my word. We will go with you to the sorcerers' nest."

Darrow shook Fenn's hand, then motioned to the innkeeper to bring them more wine. "Sit down, brother. I have much to tell you."

In Gellan, the red city, it is dusk. The jumbled spires and tenements glow in the light of sunset, the same color as the ruby ring that Samis wears. Samis stands on a bridge above a sluggish river, the color of blood, as if it ran from a slaughterhouse.

Darrow stands beside his old friend and stares down at the swirling water. He is a boy no longer. He cannot believe the words that Samis has just uttered; he feels as though he has stepped into a dream, or a nightmare. Yet he knows that his friend is in deadly earnest, though his voice is light.

"Well, my Heron? What do you say? Are you with me in this quest?"

For a heartbeat or two he cannot speak, and his heart is

gripped with dread. Can it be possible that for a third time his inability to act, to speak, to move, will take him helplessly down a path he has no desire to follow? Will he shake off this paralysis in five years, or ten, or fifty? Will he find himself an old man, Samis's deputy, heart's brother to the tyrant of Tremaris, the Emperor of the World, nodding and smiling beside the throne of a madman?

"I will be the Singer of All Songs, my Heron." Samis looks into Darrow's eyes, as cool and arrogant as the night they first met, up on the roof of the Black Palace, with the moons shining behind his head. "And you will be with me."

Darrow finds that, after all, he is not paralyzed. He cannot speak, but he can move. He takes one step backward, then another. He shakes his head.

Samis frowns. Then he holds out his hand. "Heron. You know you are more truly my brother than any of the emperor's sons. Everything I gain, I will share with you."

Darrow finds his voice. "No," he croaks, still shaking his head. "No."

He turns his back and begins to walk away down the narrow streets that lead from the river, the noisy, crowded streets. He walks faster and faster until he breaks into a run, and he does not stop running until he reaches the docks, and the dark, cold, cleansing sea.

The Madness of the Sands

It was dark down in the cellars. Keela had never known such darkness. The Palace of Cobwebs was always lit, by moonlight or filtered sun, or by thousands of candles. But this was thick, choking darkness, hot and stinking of fear.

Keela patted herself all over. She was unhurt, but in the scramble to safety she had lost her shoes, and her beautiful gloves were in tatters. The gods alone knew what she must look like!

Now that the roar of destruction had stopped, Keela could hear whimpers of panic, moans of pain, and weeping from the other trapped survivors. She had lost Immel, lost her friends; they were separated from her by fallen walls. Keela was not afraid. It would be only a matter of time before her followers came to find her. They couldn't all have been killed! She was alive; others were alive. She had only to wait. Though she had never been good at waiting. . . .

Far above came a rumble of falling stone as part of the ruins settled. Keela winced. If only she had managed to hold on to that chanter child! He would have been able to shift all these rocks and burrow their way out in an instant.

Something shifted in the blackness nearby. "Who's there?" called Keela sharply.

"Lord Haigen, First General, Fourth Division of the Imperial Army, born into the Clan of the Darru!" a gruff voice barked out. "Who goes there, woman?"

"Mind your manners, sir! You're addressing the Third Princess of the Imperial House!"

"I beg your pardon, my lady." There was a pause. "Never fear, my lady. My soldiers will be here presently to dig us out. Stay close to me, my lady. I'll see you're looked after as you deserve."

Keela almost laughed aloud. She could hear it all in his voice, in his crafty, stupid, soldier's voice. He wanted to use her, this general; like all those ambitious men, he thought he could wear her like a jewel to enhance his own power. It never occurred to these men that Keela might have ambitions and plans of her own, that *she* could use *them*.

"Oh, General!" she purred. "I'm so glad you're here, I'm so glad there's a strong man here to take care of me! Where are you, Haigen? Let me hold your hand!"

"I'm afraid I've mislaid my gloves, my lady," confessed the general.

"Never mind about that. We have survived a catastrophe. We mustn't let a little thing like *gloves* stand between us."

For a time they sat in the dark, hand in hand, flesh against flesh. Keela could hear the general's breathing. She moved a little closer, aware that Haigen could smell the perfume of her hair, her clothes, her skin.

"Do you know what caused this?" she murmured. "An earth-quake?"

"I won't lie to you, my lady. It was no earthquake." The general's voice swelled, became important; like all men, in Keela's experience, he loved to explain things to a woman. "The rebels from the sea-towns are behind this. Nothing more certain."

"They must be very strong to destroy the Palace!"

"Not so strong that we can't defeat them."

"But you couldn't have expected this!"

"Our intelligence did not rule out the possibility of an attack," said the general, but there was a glimmer of uncertainty in his tone. "Though an attack on this scale seemed — improbable."

Keela fell silent. She must be very careful now. It was clear to her that the sharp-toothed little *nadu*, Calwyn, must have been working for the sorcerers and not the rebels. Only the sorcerers knew about the children. Had they plotted to assassinate the emperor and remove the children, to bring down the Palace? They might have suspected that Amagis had betrayed their secrets, and ordered the little *nadu* to kill him too . . . In the darkness, she began to stroke the back of the soldier's roughened hand. At last she said, "Perhaps the rebels had help from elsewhere. From the sorcerers?"

The soldier stiffened. "And what does my lady know of sorcery?"

Keela squeezed his fingers. "What will become of us? With the emperor gone, and the Palace destroyed? It grieves me to say it, but my brother, the First Prince, is not fit to take my father's place."

The general's voice was very cautious. "The Army will ensure that the stability of the Empire is maintained."

"Of course . . ." They both jumped as a thunder of falling rubble sounded overhead. There were muffled shouts, and someone screamed. Keela held the general's hand firmly in hers. She said, "Do you know the Hatharan ambassador?"

"I have met the man."

"He and I were very good friends."

"Indeed?"

"He told me certain things, secrets that only the emperor and the sorcerers know. Would you like to hear them?"

"My lady," breathed Lord Haigen.

"I can make you a powerful man, sir, once we get out of here. First among generals. Even able to choose the next emperor. But —" Her fingers tightened warningly around his. "I have my price."

"What price is that?"

"I will share your power." She did not say: Until another comes, a greater man than you, who will brush aside whichever puppet you have chosen, and make me his empress.

The soldier sucked in his breath as he considered. "Very well," he said abruptly. "It shall be as you wish."

"Do you swear it, by the blood of your fathers?"

"I swear."

So she told him, there in the darkness, her mouth close to his ear, as they waited for the soldiers to come. She told him everything that Amagis had told her: the ancient bargain between the emperors and the sorcerers, the chanter children who had held the Palace up with ironcraft. She told him about the Black Palace, deep in the barren lands of Hathara, where the sorcerers nursed their strange powers and where, no doubt, they plotted to overthrow the Empire. She promised him the support of three of the Seven Clans, all she could speak for.

At last, there was a scraping of stone, and shouts, a shower of white dust, and a lantern thrust through a gap in the roof. The troops had come, just as Haigen had promised. The general was revealed as a red-faced stout man, of middle age, who snatched his hand away from the princess's as if it burned him.

"Lord Haigen, sir!" The young lieutenant saluted smartly. "Glad to see you still alive, sir! There's a council of generals, at dawn, on Martec Plain, to discuss the situation, sir. They'll be glad to see you too."

"A council? Excellent." Haigen tugged at his clothes. "I have much to tell them, urgent information, important information."

"Lord Haigen?" Keela called sweetly. "Surely you have not forgotten?"

"Yes, of course." The general turned back. "See that the princess is fed, and — and so forth. The men will take care of you," he said, over his shoulder.

Keela's voice trembled with rage. "What of your oath, sir? Sworn on your fathers' blood?"

"Oh." Haigen smiled. It was an unpleasant smile. "A vow sworn to a woman is not binding, my lady. Or else where would our honor be?"

The young lieutenant stifled a laugh behind his hand, but as Keela wheeled to face him he soon became sober. "You dare to smirk at me, you dog?" she hissed.

"No, my lady," he stammered.

Keela's eyes narrowed. "Give me your cloak. Then, if you want to make yourself useful, you can find my manservant."

The sky had begun to lighten when Calwyn found the gully. She'd almost given up hope, crossing and recrossing her footsteps as she searched for the hidden path. Several times she'd struck a dead end against blank walls of red rock or found herself out on the moonlit plain again. She felt a renewed admiration for Heben and the confidence with which he'd led them across the trackless sands, and she wondered again how they would manage without him.

Now when she looked toward the remains of the Palace, she could see tiny antlike figures swarming around its base: The courtiers who had managed to survive? The Army, preparing to take over? Or the rebels, starting their revolution? Whichever it was, she wanted to keep out of their way.

Eagerly she pushed down into the ravine, toward the stream and the fronds of green that fringed it. There was the campsite, tucked beneath the overhang, and the *hegesi*, rounded up and tethered loosely to a tree.

And there was Heben, filling a waterskin at the creek. And there — Calwyn broke into a run. Halasaa strode toward her with his arms outstretched. Mica was chattering excitedly to Shada, and Oron splashed his face in the stream, while Haid and Vin crouched by a tiny fire, slapping out rounds of flat bread.

Halasaa hugged Calwyn and swung her around. *Calwyn!* She hid her face in his shoulder and held him tight, unable to speak.

Why didn't you answer me after the Palace fell? I thought you were dead!

I answered, my sister. But your mind was too unquiet to hear me.

Heben came up, pushing the stopper into the waterskin with the flat of his hand. "I'm glad to see you safe, my lady," he said, retreating to the safety of politeness in his relief.

Halasaa let Calwyn slide to the ground. "Yes, I'm safe," she said soberly. "But Ched — he was killed, as we were running away."

The children clustered around, solemn but not surprised. "We all would have been dead soon enough if you hadn't come," said Vin.

"At least he died under the sky, not locked up inside a box," said Haid, and Vin nodded gravely.

"Those two had it the hardest of all, down there in the dungeons," Shada whispered to Calwyn. "With all the weight of the Palace on top. That's why there were two there, in the dark." Indeed, Vin and Haid were very pale, and as the sun rose higher, they hid their eyes and blinked in the strong light.

"Have you seen our work?" asked Heben, gesturing in the direction of the Palace.

"Yes," said Calwyn. "There are people all around the Palace now. Or what's left of it."

Heben nodded. "I've been up to look. There are courtiers, coming out. And servants, looting, I think."

"I seen 'em, too," Mica put in. "They all look stunned, like slava-chewers. Like it's a bad dream, and they're waitin' to wake up."

"We must move on," said Heben abruptly. "There are soldiers everywhere. And now there are so many of us —"

Calwyn frowned. "I'm not sure we should go yet. Perhaps there's something we can do to help. There must be people injured. And there might be fighting soon." She told them what she had overheard the soldiers saying.

"We can't stay here," said Heben. Calwyn thought, *He is very tired. We are all very tired.* "We have already agreed. We must move on, we must start out for Hathara without delay. If there's to be fighting, we mustn't be caught here."

"We ain't got much time." Mica looked around the campsite. "We got to pack up everythin' —"

"We haven't decided anything yet." Calwyn's voice was icy, and the others drew back a little at the sudden flash of authority in her eyes. "Halasaa? What do you say?"

Halasaa had hung back, making no contribution to the debate. Now he shrugged. *We need you, Calwyn. We will need your chantments. If you stay, I will stay with you. If you go, I will follow.*

Stubbornly Calwyn said, "Darrow would say that we should stay and help."

"Darrow ain't here," said Mica.

Shada piped up shrilly, "You promised we'd rescue Gada and the others! You *promised!*"

Calwyn made herself stand straight-backed, though she felt sick and helpless. The others stood, watching her, and she realized with a shock that if she insisted, they would obey her.

Halasaa's words sounded quietly in her mind. *You blame yourself for the child's death. But remaining here will not bring him back. What of the other children? You have made a vow. You should not break it.*

Calwyn let out a deep breath. "Yes. We'll go, as soon as we can."

Heben nodded and laid a hand briefly on her shoulder before he turned away to begin packing up their camp. Wearily Calwyn trudged to the little fire and the waiting rounds of flat bread. She longed for a day's rest and a deep and dreamless sleep, but she would have to make do with a few moments snatched in the shade while she chewed on the warm bread.

"Ain't you glad now me and Shada went to the kitchens and got flour?" Mica said challengingly.

"Yes, I'm glad," said Calwyn dully. She didn't have the energy to argue. She watched with a pang as Mica ran off with Shada to untie the *hegesi*, joking and laughing, as if the two girls had been friends for years.

Calwyn. Halasaa was looking down at her.

"We're not leaving already?"

Not yet. He gestured to her to remain where she was. *There is time to rest awhile.* He sat down beside her, somber-faced.

"You look tired too, Halasaa."

It was difficult to heal the children, in body and in spirit. There was so little time. The last boy, Oron, may be still broken within.

"There'll be time to finish the healing later." Calwyn put her hand on his arm.

Perhaps. But I fear this next journey will not be easy.

"None of our journeys are easy, Halasaa," she said, but he didn't smile. Her friend had lived all his life in the impenetrable forests of the Wildlands. He and his people dwelt on platforms that sailed high in the trees, but much of their time was spent in the dim shadows of the forest floor. Calwyn ventured, "The desert must seem very strange to you, after Spiridrell."

Strange!

Calwyn almost jumped backward at the vehement force of his unvoiced word.

This place. It is a place of death. Do you not feel it? Not in this gully, where the water flows and the plants still grow, but all around us, on the plain. Their spirits are here, spirits of the dead.

Calwyn stared at him in dismay. "Who died, Halasaa? Whose spirits are here? Was there a battle?"

Halasaa looked at her, his eyes filled with sadness. *The spirits of the trees. I hear them moaning. I sense the ghosts of the trees, the murdered forest.*

"A forest, in the middle of the desert? But there's no rain to nourish even a single tree, let alone a whole forest."

He shook his head. *There were trees here, Calwyn. Long, long ago, as far back as the first coming of the Voiced Ones to this place. I hear them crying out to me, in their pain and their sorrow.*

Calwyn shivered, and she thought she could hear it too: a heartbroken, tormented moaning. But then the sound faded into the murmuring of the stream and the bleating of the *hegesi*, and she heard it no more.

Calwyn. Halasaa touched her arm, and his eyes were bright again. *I have an idea.*

They spent the rest of that morning gathering rushes that grew by the stream. With chantments of iron, it was simple to weave three large, sturdy mats; the three tents would act as sails, each held up by one child's chantment, while Calwyn and Mica could summon a spellwind to propel them across the sands. And Mica thought of fastening ropes to the corners of the tents so that they could steer.

They worked swiftly, despite their fatigue, aware that their safety depended on escaping the vicinity of the Palace as far and as fast as they could. Calwyn labored steadily, sorting rushes for the children to weave, not speaking to anyone. From time to time she glanced up at the white shape of the ruined Palace on its red ridge. They were too far away to distinguish any people. Her conscience burned for both Ched and the inhabitants of the court. Could she have done more to warn them? Had she been right to rescue the children, even if it cost the lives of the courtiers?

Heben's voice broke in on her thoughts. "Calwyn? We're ready to try them."

They dragged the ungainly rafts to the top of the gully; there was no sign of a patrol. The plain looked as flat as Merithuran bread. Haid droned a chantment to lift up the first tent-sail, and Vin wound the steering ropes in his fists. "Ready!" he called.

Calwyn tipped back her head and sang up a light breeze, but the tent-sail flapped uselessly. As Mica added her voice, the wind strengthened, the sail billowed out, and the raft began to scud along the sand. Shada yelped with delight and leaped onto the next raft with Heben and Mica, while Calwyn, Halasaa, and Oron climbed onto the last. Mica and Calwyn set the wind to take them southwest, around the mountains that lay between the Palace of Cobwebs and Hathara. That way, they could take advantage of the flat plains where the rafts could sail swiftly.

It was not comfortable traveling, though much faster than they could have moved by foot or on *hegesi*. The ride was rough, for though the rush mats were strong, they were not well padded, and the ground was often stony. The passengers soon discovered that it was better to crouch on their haunches than sit on their behinds. There were two *hegesi* on each raft; they did not enjoy the sensation of flying across the sands and bleated with distress. It took all the strength of one person to hold the wriggling beasts.

From necessity, the two windworkers had to sing up one wide wind to blow into the sails of all three rafts at once, and they suffered for it. Even if the three rafts sailed in single file, the edges of the wind threw up enough sand to keep them wiping grit from their eyes, and soon they all tied cloths across their faces. One good thing was that the tent-sails offered some shade from the burning sun. After days sheltered inside the cool cloisters of the Palace of Cobwebs, Calwyn had forgotten how cruel that sun could be.

They stopped just before nightfall. They didn't scout out a campsite; the desert was the same wherever they stopped. Mica and Shada went in search of fuel for a fire but came back with a pitiful bundle. "Not enough to keep us warm," said Heben. "But with the *hegesi* dung we'll have enough to make bread." He crouched over the flames and skilfully smoothed out the mixture of flour and water over a hot stone, one round after another. The children squatted nearby, tearing hungrily into the bread as soon as it was ready.

Calwyn sat apart and quietly sang up some soft snow to replenish the waterskins. The air was very dry, and it was not easy work. Halasaa dropped down beside her and rested his forehead on his knees. His hair had come unbound and hung around his face like a tattered curtain.

"Halasaa? Are you all right?"

He raised his head and tried to smile. *I am weary. And I do not like this place.*

"I know. I wonder how long it will take to reach Hathara."

Too long.

Calwyn gazed anxiously at her friend. "Eat something," she urged him. "And rest. No wonder you feel tired, after the last day or two."

Oron came up to them, holding out his arm. "I cut myself on some dry-grass."

"Let Halasaa rest," said Calwyn sharply. "The cut isn't deep."

"Dry-grass cuts go nasty," complained Oron. "Unless I wash it out with water, and there's not much of that."

"I can sing you as much water as you like," said Calwyn, but Halasaa struggled to his feet.

I will heal the cut. He laid his hands on Oron's arm, but his fingers moved sluggishly; usually they danced too quickly to see.

Calwyn's face felt scorched by the sun, but she didn't ask Halasaa to heal it. *I'll be more careful tomorrow,* she thought.

Soon after nightfall, they crept into the tents to sleep, the children tangled together like puppies for warmth. Calwyn lay awake next to Halasaa, listening to the uneven rhythm of his breath in the dark. Tentatively she called to him with her mind.

Halasaa. Are you asleep?

I cannot sleep, came the prompt reply.

Why not? We're safe here, and Heben is keeping watch.

I fear my dreams.

Even in the midst of her concern, Calwyn felt a thrill that she could speak with her friend in his own way. *Tell me.*

Halasaa's voice came to her reluctantly. *I will show you.*

As Calwyn lay staring into the dark, he put pictures into her mind. She saw through Halasaa's eyes and felt herself walking in his lithe long-limbed body.

She was in the desert, at night, and she was utterly alone. The three moons were behind cloud, and it was difficult to see. The barren plain stretched on all sides, specked with dry-grass and loose stones. The cold air was still, the dry-grass motionless as if it were made of stone.

There was a very quiet whispering, and then she was aware of movement behind her. She whirled around, in Halasaa's body, with all Halasaa's senses, and she knew, as he knew, what made the sound. He had spoken of the murdered forests. And now she could hear the anguished moans of trees, voice upon voice in never-ending torment. And she understood that just as a river was made up of countless drops of water, so the land was made up of the trees, the animals, the web of all living things, and when the life of the land was killed, the land itself died, in slow agony. . . .

"No!" Calwyn sat bolt upright in the dark tent, unaware that she'd cried out. By her feet, Mica murmured and turned over in her sleep.

Halasaa's dark eyes gleamed out of the shadows. *I should not have showed you.*

No — no. You were right. Calwyn lay down again. *But it's only a dream. It can't hurt you.*

Yes, it can. Halasaa got up, wrapping himself in the long desert robes. *I will take watch outside.*

Calwyn lay awake for a long time, but he did not return.

* * *

On the fourth day, not long after noon, Halasaa touched Calwyn on the arm as she guided the raft. She didn't interrupt her chantment but glanced at him swiftly. *What is it?*

There are people nearby.

Calwyn could not stop her song to concentrate on the sense that showed her the presence of life. *Are they soldiers?*

Halasaa smiled faintly. *I cannot tell.*

Calwyn signaled to Mica to let the wind drop. One by one, the rafts slewed to a stop; children and *hegesi* tumbled off the mats.

"What's wrong?" Heben called.

"There are people nearby." Calwyn closed her eyes and sent out the tendrils of her awareness. At first, tense and hurried, she could sense nothing. She opened her eyes and saw Halasaa watching her; he made a gentle gesture with his thin hands. *Slowly.* She understood and closed her eyes again, this time quietly ready to listen, rather than anxiously searching. She sent out her mind lightly, as if she floated over the desert, like a hawk riding the winds.

After a moment, her eyes flew open. "A large party, perhaps fifty people. Men and women, and children, all together. And —" She gave a small smile. "And *hegesi*. Lots of *hegesi*."

"Herders," said Heben. "We're in the lands of the I'beth."

Vin looked up. "I am a son of the I'beth."

Heben looked at him sternly. "Are you still? Did your people cast you out?"

Vin threw back his head proudly. "No. I was stolen from them.

My father and his brother quarreled. It was my uncle who betrayed me to the soldiers and the sorcerers."

Calwyn sighed. Was there no end to the feuds and squabbles that festered in every corner of Tremaris? Nation against nation, like Baltimar and Rengan; Clan against Clan; desert dwellers against townsfolk; sorcerers and rebels and soldiers and courtiers all struggling against one another. Even within one family, brother schemed against brother.

She said, "This band is to the south of us, not far away. Should we hide, or go to them?"

"We need food; the flour is almost gone," said Heben. "The I'beth are superstitious folk, they believe in the powers of magic. You might be able to bargain with them."

"I can see 'em!" cried Mica, shading her eyes. "I can *smell* 'em!"

"That's the *hegesi*," said Haid, who had adopted a protective attitude to the six *hegesi* of the party. Calwyn could smell a pungent aroma that reminded her of the reek of the goat pens in Antaris. Then she heard the tinkle of the herd's bells as they approached.

When the two parties were close enough to see each other clearly, the herders halted. For several moments everyone waited, staring. All the children unwound their head cloths, to show their faces, and the foreigners hastily did the same. Then Vin walked forward, with Heben. They held out their hands to show they had no weapons, and the headman of the nomads came to meet them. They conferred briefly, and presently Heben came back.

"I've told them we have ironcrafters, windworkers, a healer, and a chanter who can sing water from the air. The headman says if we can fill their waterskins and mend their tents, they will give us a sack of bread flour. And —" Heben looked hesitantly at Halasaa. "They have a sick woman among them. Is there anything you can do for her?"

I do not know until I have seen her, came Halasaa's patient reply, but Calwyn thought his shoulders sagged a little as he went across to the herders.

"Ain't there nothin' I can do for 'em?" demanded Mica indignantly. "Don't they need no windworker at all?"

Calwyn smiled. "You can fetch their waterskins for me."

"If we was at sea, they'd want me over everyone," muttered Mica as she stomped off.

When the two groups parted, Vin had news to report. "They didn't know anything about the emperor dying or the Palace coming down. But they've seen many soldiers massed together on Martec Plain, preparing for a march. There's an uprising in the mining towns of the coast. The rebels have taken over Geel and Phain, and they say they're planning to march on the Palace of Cobwebs too."

"They won't find much," said Heben grimly.

"We could show them the way to the Black Place," said Oron. "They can pull that down." Calwyn couldn't repress a shiver as she looked at his small, sullen face, closed in on itself.

Gently she asked Vin, "Did the herders have any news of your family?"

"They offered to take me back to my father. But I said no. I want to help you first. I want to see the Black Place brought down, like the Palace of Cobwebs."

Calwyn did not reply. Soon they were under way again, and there was no chance to say anything more. But all through that day her feeling of unease grew. She had thought their purpose in going to the Black Palace was to rescue the other captive children, but she feared that Vin and the others might be more intent on vengeance for what they'd suffered. Perhaps not even Halasaa's healing could banish that wish entirely.

That night Oron muttered to Vin, "You should have gone with them! At least *your* Clan will take you back! Mine never will —" He fell silent as abruptly as he'd spoken.

Vin said nothing, and he soon moved away from the other boy, as if he had a disease that he might catch. To be rejected by one's Clan was so great a misfortune that even these children could not forgive it. Calwyn went to Oron, where he sat alone, and offered him her waterskin. He took it and drank, but he would not lift his eyes from the ground, and he did not thank her.

On the fifth day, the mountains came into view, a shadowy mass in the southeast. If the chanter children had not told her they were mountains, Calwyn would have taken the shimmer on the horizon for a trick of the desert light.

"How far is it, Shada?" she asked when they'd stopped for a brief rest and a hurried meal. "How many days did it take to travel between Hathara and the Palace of Cobwebs? Do you remember?"

At once a heated argument broke out. "Ten days and nights, on *hegesi*."

"No! Longer than that! A turn of the moons, near enough."

"But we came through the mountains, stupid. This is the long way round."

"But we're going faster, with the rafts, than we did with *him*."

"We have a long way to go yet."

"How do you know, Vin? You slept on the *hegesu*'s back all the way —"

Calwyn grimaced and passed a waterskin to Vin; there were dark circles beneath the older boy's eyes, and he had let the tent-sail drop three times that day. "Drink," she urged him. "Why don't you swap places with Oron and come onto the raft with Halasaa and me? It will be easier for you, with three on a raft." Vin hesitated, then nodded his agreement.

Haid had milked the *hegesi* at dawn, but there was only enough milk for each of them to take one sour, refreshing gulp. "They don't like traveling on the rafts, Calwyn. Their milk will dry up altogether if we keep on like this."

"We must use the rafts while we can. If the ground becomes rougher, we'll have to abandon them."

"Without their milk, we may as well butcher the *hegesi* and just eat them!"

"If we must," said Calwyn, and ignored the shocked looks that

Haid and Heben exchanged. Haid had been provoking her; he hadn't expected her to take him seriously. To a desert dweller, a *hegesu* was worth infinitely more alive than dead. To kill an animal that provided milk and wool and dung and transport, just for one meal of meat, was sheer folly. Calwyn understood this, but they couldn't go on carrying the *hegesi* indefinitely. There was more dry-grass than *arbec* in this part of the desert; it was poor grazing land. The children, for all their bravado, were weaker every day, especially Vin, and she was worried about Halasaa. He had done his best for the sick herdswoman of the I'beth, but he had come back exhausted. He was sitting now, head bowed. His hands, usually so expressive and full of life, hung slack over his knees; he didn't even brush away the flies that clustered round his face, and she wondered if he were listening to the tormented murmuring of the land.

Yet she wondered if the sighing of the spirits of the trees might not be preferable to the silence that hung so heavy over the desert. There was no birdsong, no rustle of grasses or burbling of streams, not even the gentle breathing of the wind, unless she or Mica set it in motion. For almost a year, Calwyn had lived either on a boat or within the sight and sound of the sea. It was only now that the comforting murmur had gone that she realized how deeply she had come to love it.

Her hands shook as she replaced the stopper in the waterskin. She missed the sea, and the island, and Darrow, and Tonno, and Trout. And oddly, she was missing Mica too. She and Shada spent every moment together. Though Shada was several years younger than Mica, the older girl was protective of her, and they whispered and giggled just as the other novices had done in Antaris, leaving Calwyn out. Calwyn knew this shouldn't make her feel so hurt and lonely, but it did.

Like Halasaa, she had bad dreams, the same dream every night: that she was searching for Darrow in the rubble of the Palace of Cobwebs, desperate to find him, but at the same time dreading she might find him dead. And in the dream, over and over again, she found not Darrow, but Ched's small body, or Amagis, grinning lifelessly up at her.

"Calwyn —" It was Heben.

"Oh, what now?"

He ignored her irritated tone. "I've had the looking-tube out. Something's coming across the plain, from the east, out of the mountains."

"Soldiers?"

"I don't think so." He handed her the tube. "It looks like *wasunti*."

At first, all she could see was a cloud of dust, a long way off, heading toward them. Then the shapes in the dust resolved themselves into striped, muscular bodies, moving fast, heads down. Calwyn lowered the tube. "There must be thirty or more."

Heben nodded grimly. "It's a large pack. I hope we can outrun them."

"We'll have to try," said Calwyn, and Heben called them all to clamber back onto the rafts again.

Periodically through the day Calwyn checked on the position of the pack. For a time it seemed that the *wasunti* were unaware of the presence of the rafts and their cargo. But by late in the day, their direction was unmistakable. The pack was headed toward them to cut them off. Heben called a halt.

"Calwyn, what do you say? Should we keep going, try to lose them?"

"You know more about the *wasunti* than I do. What do you think?"

"They have our scent. I don't think we can lose them now." Heben hugged Shada protectively to his side.

"They can smell death," said Oron, looking pointedly at Vin, who by now could scarcely lift his head.

Vin's weak voice came from Calwyn's raft. "Leave me here, then. I'll make a meal for them. It'll give you some more time."

"Don't talk nonsense," said Calwyn sharply. "We're not leaving anyone."

"You've already left one boy behind," said Oron blandly. As was Merithuran custom when speaking of the newly dead, he did not use Ched's name. "Why not Vin?"

Calwyn felt the sting of his words, but she kept her face expressionless.

"Shut up!" shouted Shada. "They rescued us! You think they'd feed us to the *wasunti*?"

"We could leave them the *hegesi*. That might satisfy them," suggested Heben, but Calwyn could see that he was unwilling.

Calwyn turned to Halasaa. "Can you tell what they intend?"

Dully he lifted his head. *They mean us ill.*

"Then we must prepare to defend ourselves," said Heben grimly. The others stared at him, some trustful, some wary, some too exhausted to care.

Only Oron was openly hostile. "Defend ourselves? With what? We haven't any weapons. *Wasunti* hate fire, but we have nothing to burn."

"Halasaa can speak with beasts," said Calwyn. "He'll be able to keep them away —"

But Halasaa spoke silently, to her alone: *My sister, I cannot. I hear their thoughts, but I cannot fend them from us.*

Oron couldn't hear his words, but he saw Halasaa shake his head. "He can't help! What will we do? Blow them away with wind-spells?"

Mica thrust her face close to Oron's. "You want me to practice on *you*?" she spat. "Calwyn can drive 'em away. You'll see! Can't you, Cal?"

The sight of Mica's face turned to her, bright with trust and hope, made Calwyn's breath catch. "It's true," she said shakily. "Heben, I have some knowledge of the Power of Beasts, the magic that tames animals. Perhaps I can keep them at bay."

Heben nodded. "Very well," he said brusquely, then he began to call out commands. "Haid, Shada, gather the *hegesi* together. Mica, Vin, Halasaa, prop the rafts in a circle; we'll stretch the tents between them. Vin? Did you hear me? Oron, you collect some stones. You know how to throw a rock, don't you?"

"*Wasunti* aren't afraid of stones," said Oron sourly, but he obeyed.

While the others made ready, Calwyn watched through the looking-tube as the cloud of red dust drew nearer. Her heart beat as fast as the swift legs of the *wasunti* could run. If she couldn't hold them off, if the magic failed, then they would be helpless prey for those strong jaws and savage teeth. Oron was right; a pile of stones wouldn't keep them away for long. *Taris, give me strength!* she called silently. But the moons were invisible, and Calwyn felt as if the Goddess were far away.

The rush mats were propped in a ring, with the tents pulled tight between them to make a thin barrier. Calwyn could have wept at the pitiful inadequacy of their defense. Haid and Vin knelt at the center of the circle, trying to keep the *hegesi* calm, but the animals sensed the approach of predators and strained at their tethers, bleating hysterically. The children stood facing out, weighing stones in their hands, each with a waiting heap of rocks piled at their feet. Mica caught Calwyn's eye and gave her a grin of encouragement. Calwyn smiled back, close to tears.

"*Wasunti*," she called. "*Wasunti.*"

They came at dusk, in the time of the longest shadows, when cold air fell like a shroud over the plain. They came in silence, not running now, but padding slow and soundless across the red dirt, their muzzles at the ground. Calwyn saw their golden eyes on all sides, unblinking, watchful. Watching her.

Oron bent his arm to throw.

"Not yet!" barked Heben, and a growl rose from a *wasuntu's* throat, warning them. The *hegesi* bleated frantically, rearing and rolling their eyes. The other *wasunti* began to growl softly. Like a chantment of iron, thought Calwyn wildly. Her voice had dried in her throat. They were watching her, the children, Mica, Halasaa, and Heben. Their eyes flickered anxiously between the prowling beasts and herself. They were waiting, all of them, human and animal, waiting for her to act.

Calwyn began to sing.

The ancient song rose in the crisp air, the song she thought of as the song of the bees. Slowly Calwyn turned as she sang, directing the chantment to the beasts that prowled around their fragile circle, trying to push them away with the force of her magic. She held up her hands as she used to in Antaris, to draw the power down from the air, from the moons, from the sky, the realm of the Goddess.

But something was wrong. The chantment was thin and feeble, not grasping firm. The others didn't know it; Heben and Mica watched, wary but confident, and their hands that held the stones were relaxed. But the *wasunti* knew, and perhaps Halasaa, though when she stole a glance at him, his eyes were closed and he swayed to and fro, far away from her.

The *wasunti* crept closer. Imperceptibly the circle tightened.

The menacing growls threaded through her song, but her chantment did not touch them. It floated over them like smoke.

Goddess, help me! Calwyn breathed deep, trying to force the power through the ancient words. The ring of amber eyes surrounded them, mocking her. The *wasunti* bared their teeth; ivory gleamed wet in the light of the setting sun. They were very close, their hot breath steaming in the chill air. Behind her, Calwyn heard one of the children sob. The magic would not hold; the power drifted out between the notes like water flowing through a net, like sand trickling between her fingers —

That was it. She had called on the Goddess, in her realm between the stars. But this chantment belonged to the land, to the life that sprang from the mud, and the power must come from below.

Tremaris, Merithuros, mother of the wasunti, *give me strength!* Calwyn breathed in again, drawing up power from the soles of her feet into her whole body and out into her song, and then, only then, she felt it come true. The *wasunti* heard her. She stared into their amber eyes, strong and commanding, and she felt she could understand the ancient words whose meaning had dissolved generations ago:

> *"Hear me, beasts, and obey!*
> *Go about your work;*
> *I will not interfere with you.*
> *Be at peace in your place*
> *And I will leave you in peace."*

She sang, and the *wasunti* began to whine softly. They stopped prowling; Calwyn could see them in the fading light, seated on their haunches, tongues lolling. She remembered the fierce winged arakin of the Wildlands and how they had returned her song, and now the *wasunti* did the same. They raised their muzzles to the sky and began to howl with mournful dignity, showing the soft white fur of their throats. Their howling filled the night.

Then, one by one, they lowered their heads and trotted away, each in a different direction, and vanished into the gathering dark. As the last one disappeared, Calwyn's song died away. Then she dropped to her knees and let her head fall to the dirt, and she wept as if her heart would break.

"Calwyn! Calwyn!" Shada threw her arms around her neck. "Why are you crying? It's all right, they've gone away, they've all run away!"

Calwyn couldn't answer; she was sobbing too hard.

"Let her alone!" She heard Mica's fierce whisper as she pulled Shada away. "Let her cry."

The tears flowed and flowed. Calwyn didn't try to check them. She lay there helpless while spasms of sobbing shook her. She longed to feel Darrow's arms around her, and a wave of rage surged through her. Where was he? He should be here, by her side, helping. . . .

At that moment she felt the warm weight of a hand on her shoulder, and she jerked round, almost believing that she'd see

Darrow smiling down at her. But it was Halasaa's clouded eyes
that stared into hers.

Come.

Too exhausted to question him, she wiped her eyes and followed.
He led her away from the ring of mats to where a low boulder
stood shadowed in the twilight. Oron sat stiffly in the dirt beside
it, his eyes wide with shock. His tattered robe was soaked black with
blood; gingerly Calwyn lifted the cloth. The boy's leg was gashed
from knee to ankle, ripped open by a *wasuntu's* jagged teeth.

Calwyn shut her eyes to the sight; she felt almost too tired to
care. She forced herself to ask, "What happened?"

She spoke to Halasaa, but Oron answered. "I — ran after."
The boy's voice stuttered, and his hands twitched convulsively on
the red dirt. "Threw — stone. Bit — bit me."

Halasaa knelt beside Calwyn. *I cannot heal him.*

What? Calwyn felt a stab of fear sharper than anything she'd felt
when the *wasunti* were near. Instinctively she spoke in silence, not
wanting to frighten Oron further. *What do you mean?*

I have tried. But I am not strong enough.

*You're tired, that's all. We'll bind his leg. You can try again later, when you've
rested.*

I need more rest than you can give me. Halasaa's eyes were steady, bor-
ing into hers. *You must heal the boy.*

"Me?" The word burst from Calwyn before she could stop herself. *But I can't! I don't have that power, I don't know what to do!*

I will show you. But the magic must come from you.

I can't, Halasaa! How can I? The Power of Becoming is a gift of the Tree People, not the Voiced Ones.

Halasaa picked up her hands and turned them so they lay, palms upward, loosely clasped in his. *You speak as a Tree Person does. You speak with the beasts. Perhaps you can dance like a Tree Person too.* Halasaa took her hands and laid them over the gaping wound in Oron's leg. *Feel the flow of the river through the boy. Do you feel it?*

Calwyn had no strength left to argue. Wearily she allowed her hands to rest on the gash. She felt the slow throb of Oron's blood as it pumped from his body, leaving him weaker at every moment. There wasn't time for this; she would show Halasaa that it was no use, then she would bandage Oron's leg. . . . But while these thoughts ran through one part of her mind, with her other sense, the sense of becoming, she could feel the light within the boy, the light that was part of what Halasaa called the river.

Go slowly. Breathe with him; let your blood flow in rhythm with his.

Calwyn obeyed. It was not easy at first; the light of Oron's being was not steady. Fear and pain and mistrust made it flicker and jump, but she found that the unwavering pressure of her hands helped to calm him. She breathed; she heard Oron breathe; then they were breathing together. His heart beat, and hers beat, and they were beating together.

Let your strength flow into him, Halasaa prompted her. *Let him draw strength from you. Let it flow into his body.*

And she felt it, with a jump of surprise, like a spark flying. At the place where her hands rested on his wounded leg, she and

Oron were one, connected, as her energy, her light, flowed into him. The boy moaned and leaned back against the boulder with his eyes squeezed shut. Calwyn felt a similar sensation as in Halasaa's dream, that she was inhabiting Oron's body. Yet at the same time, she was outside it, holding it —

You know where the hurt is. Go to where the river is disturbed.

Yes, she could sense the injury with her inner awareness, like a rough place in a piece of weaving, like a shadow cast across a patch of lamplight, like a fallen log in the middle of a stream, the water bubbling and eddying around it.

Follow me. Halasaa's hands were on top of hers now, and as he lifted his fingers, she moved hers in response, tapping out the complex rhythm that was the dance of healing. His hands moved much more slowly than when he worked alone, so she could follow the movement. *Knit up the wound, Calwyn. Make it whole.*

She couldn't tell whether the power flowed from Halasaa through her to Oron, or whether it came from herself alone, or if she merely shaped the force that lay within the boy, but she felt it, in the tips of her fingers and behind her eyes. She felt the healing as the flesh knit under her hands. Slowly, slowly, the wound drew itself together, and as it did, Calwyn recognized the nature of the chantment. It was the same as the magic they used to heal and restore the great ice Wall of Antaris, making whole what was damaged, making strong what was weak. Marna's long-ago words darted into her mind: *All the chantments are aspects of the same unknowable mystery, just as each face of a jewel strikes light in a different direction.* Calwyn sat on the red dirt, so far away from the mountains of her homeland, and felt the familiar power flow through her.

At last the chantment was complete. The river's flow was untroubled, the cloth smoothed out, the light undimmed, flawless and whole. Oron's wound was healed.

It is finished. Halasaa's voice was calm, but Calwyn saw a desperate, exhausted relief in his eyes as he lifted his hands from hers. She took her hands from Oron's leg. The moons had risen, and in the silver light she could see clearly that the flesh was intact. There was not a mark to show where the teeth of the *wasuntu* had ripped it open.

Oron lay pale and silent, gasping for breath. Calwyn staggered to her feet. "We must keep him warm — Shada! Take him to the fire. Mica, can you see that he eats?"

She put out a sudden hand to Halasaa as her knees buckled. Now she knew why he had been growing weaker. The Power of Becoming was not an easy magic. Unlike the other chantments she had known, the strength of it came from within the chanter. Calwyn felt as though the marrow had been drained from her bones. She swayed against her friend. *Halasaa — how could you find the strength? All the children, all that healing, bodies and hearts. I didn't know what it was I asked of you.*

It was not you that asked it. Halasaa put his arm around her shoulders and led her to sit by the fire, next to the shivering Oron. *And I am strong. I was strong.*

He lowered himself beside her and stared into the flames. It was a small fire, barely large enough to warm the three who huddled by it. Heben pushed bread into their hands, and Mica brought them cups of water. "Don't you sing up no more water tonight, Calwyn. You done enough. We can last till mornin'."

Calwyn found herself too tired to speak with her mind, almost too tired to use her voice. She whispered to Halasaa, "I'm sorry. I didn't realize — how hard it is —"

The task of the healer is difficult. And I have grown weary these last days. But I am glad, Calwyn. I had thought I was the last of my kind. But I can teach you. The power will not die with me.

Calwyn was silent. She was glad too; she knew how heavy a burden Halasaa carried, being the last to hold the secrets of his people. And tonight had shown that the dances of becoming could be taught. But she hoped that they could find others to learn the magic. She and Halasaa were the same age; passing the gift to her was no real solution. They would have to teach children —

She closed her eyes and a smile flickered over her face as her thoughts drifted. Perhaps she and Halasaa should bear children together, to inherit the gift from both father and mother! She'd never thought of Halasaa in that way. Yet she did love him, and she felt closer to him in many ways than she did to Darrow. Her heart ached. Darrow was a strange and solitary man. She knew that he cared for her, in his own way, and she had no real doubt that he would come back to Ravamey when he was ready. He was a good teacher. Together they could set up the college of chanters she had dreamed of last winter. . . .

Her last confused thoughts were of sitting beneath the tall

trees on the hill behind Halasaa's garden. There were children at her feet, these children, other children, listening, as the novices had listened at Marna's feet in Antaris, the past and future intertwined. The wind sang in the trees at her back, and the sunlight glittered on the bright sea. . . .

She didn't know that Halasaa had wrapped her in a cloak and laid her down beside him to sleep, while far away the *wasunti* howled to one another across the silvered sands.

The next day Calwyn was bone-weary. The chantment of healing had drawn something out of her that sleep alone could not replenish. She sang up some snow to fill the waterskins and helped Mica summon the wind for their rafts, but she had no strength for anything else. When they paused to rest, Shada brought her pieces of flat bread and dried meat, and a mouthful of their precious milk in the bottom of a cup, and coaxed her to eat. "Come on, Calwyn. There's a long way to go, you know."

"I know." Calwyn smiled with cracked lips. It was true, they needed her; she must take care of herself. She forced herself to chew on the dry meat.

"It's wonderful what you did for Oron." Shada settled herself cross-legged on the sand to make sure that Calwyn finished her meal. "Why didn't you do it before?"

"I didn't know I could. I thought only Halasaa could perform that magic. And it's hard, Shada, much harder than singing chantments as we do."

"*That's* not hard. Gada says it's easy as breathing. . . ." A shadow crossed her face.

Calwyn thought back to the collapse of the Palace, when the song of ironcraft had leaped out of her, almost without her willing it. She hadn't tried to sing any chantments of iron since then; in truth, she was afraid. And she didn't want anyone to know that she'd done it, even once. *The Singer of All Songs.* Marna had said that the prophecy of the Singer of All Songs could never be fulfilled, because a man could not sing the chantments of ice and a woman could not sing the chantments of iron. But it was not so. True, Samis had failed to master the songs of ice-call. But Shada had the gift of ironcraft . . . *And I sang it too.* . . .

To her relief, before she could finish her thought, Heben called to her to hurry, and she clambered up to take her place on the raft again.

In the days that followed, they progressed slowly south, skirting the mountains that lay between them and the harsh lands of Hathara. Day by day, the ground became harder and more rocky. At last no chantments of ironcraft could hold the rafts together any longer, and the remnants of the rush mats were abandoned. Now they trudged on, across the dirt.

One day Heben slaughtered two of the *hegesi*, despite Haid's protests. Vin and Oron drank the blood and drew strength from it. The children tried to make Halasaa drink it too, but he would not.

Calwyn forced down a little of the thick, dark liquid, though part of her revolted. They had so little food. All the children had grown weaker. The meat of the *hegesi* heartened them for a day or two, but they were all becoming more and more exhausted and feeble. Even tough little Mica was flagging; she could barely rouse herself to a quarrel. And Heben, whom Calwyn relied on more and more, had begun to falter. He took possession of the looking-tube and raised it to the horizon a hundred times a day, searching for the end of the mountains, which the children said signaled the edge of the vast plain of Hathara.

"I don't understand," he murmured. "We should be almost there."

"We're going in circles," Oron muttered through chapped lips. His face and hands were peeling from sunburn, and his ragged robes were red with dust. "We should turn west, head for the sea, and strike out again from there."

Heben shook his head and scratched a rough map in the dirt with the point of a stick. "No. If we are *here*, it's farther to the sea than it is to Hathara."

"But you don't know where we are. We could be here — or here — or here!" Oron swiped his foot through the map.

"If Tonno was here, he'd steer us by the moons," said Mica. "Then we'd know we was goin' right."

"Or Trout, with his direction-finder," said Calwyn, with a wan smile.

"We are on course," said Heben sternly. "I have lived in the desert all my life, I know how to find my way."

"No one is questioning you," said Calwyn hastily.

"Tonno'd steer us right," muttered Mica. "He's been sailin' and steerin' by the moons longer'n Heben's been — been —" But her sentence petered out, and she lapsed into a miserable silence. Calwyn sighed; it was unlike Mica to let an argument die.

As for Halasaa, he grew quieter every day. Calwyn walked beside him whenever she could. *Do your dreams still trouble you, Halasaa?*

My dreams? He looked at her but didn't seem to see her. *I am always dreaming.*

Even when you're awake? Are you dreaming now?

Always. Always dreaming. He set his lips and walked on into the harsh beating sun.

That night Calwyn couldn't sleep. She wrapped herself in her cloak and crawled out of the tent. It was the time of the Lonely Maiden, with only one moon, and the stars blazed across the sky, horizon to horizon. She had never seen such a huge sky, even at sea. The air was like crystal, freezing cold and clear.

Calwyn clutched the cloak under her chin and knew that her hands were trembling, not from the cold, but from exhaustion and hunger. A dry sob sat in her throat like a stone; she couldn't swallow it. Would they all die here in this barren place? Would their bones lie bleached on the parched plain? She thought of Ched's small face, turned sightless to the sky.

She stared up at the endless stars and the single desolate moon. For the first time in her life, when she tried to pray to the Goddess, she found she could not. Words deserted her. Her dry lips moved but formed no sound. She had no sense of the presence of the Great Mother Taris. Calwyn felt utterly alone.

She stood there for a few moments more, staring up at the comfortless sky. Then she turned and went back into the tent, where the children were sleeping.

The next day the terrain began to change. Now the stony plain was cut across with gullies, and they had the weary work of climbing in and out of them, always heading south. Calwyn paused to wipe the sweat from her forehead. How could she be so thirsty and still make sweat?

"These are old streambeds," said Heben. "Flowing down from the mountains to the sea."

"Streams!" Mica grimaced. "You're jokin', ain't you?"

A long time ago. Halasaa stared straight ahead, his eyes unfocused, seeing things the others could not see. *No longer.*

"Come, Sukie, come, Heggy," Haid coaxed the *hegesi.* "Come now, come home now."

Home! Would they ever see home again? Calwyn dragged her feet, one step after another. She squinted at the horizon. The land dipped about a hundred paces ahead. "Another gully," she called over her shoulder.

Shada moaned. "I can't — I'm so tired —"

"Come on, come on, Sukie," said Mica, trying to make her smile, but Shada was beyond that.

"We'll be with Gada soon," said Heben, but he spoke without conviction.

Calwyn looked up, blinked, and looked again. It had come at last, the moment she'd been dreading. She'd begun to see what Halasaa saw, she was sharing Halasaa's dreams. She could see trees walking over the slope, wavering shapes that moved inexorably toward them. A dry sob broke from her throat.

Heben shouted. One of the children cried out. Calwyn rubbed her eyes and saw that the dark shapes were not trees, but people. Soldiers, she thought. She parted her lips to sing a chantment to keep them away. But her mouth was so dry that no sound came out. Her head swam, and she sank to her knees. They had struggled so far, and now they were lost.

Then she knew for certain that she was dreaming. One figure broke away from the group and came running to catch her as she fainted. Her vision shrank into a black tunnel, and the last thing she saw was Darrow's face bent over hers, and the last thing she felt was his strong arms around her as she fell.

The Black Palace

When Calwyn woke, she thought she was on *Fledgewing*. White canvas stretched above her, and a cool breeze played over her face. Her body ached in every joint, but it was pleasant to lie still, in shade. She closed her eyes and listened dreamily to the soft music of the chantment that made the breeze.

A cool, dry hand touched her burning forehead. The chantment broke off, and Calwyn heard Mica's voice. "How's her fever?"

"Coming down," said a low voice.

Calwyn's eyes flew open. *Darrow!* Feverish, her mouth dry, she used mind-speech without thinking. *Darrow . . . You're here! I have so much to tell you!*

His quizzical gray-green eyes widened as her words sounded in his mind. After a moment he said, "Don't try to talk. Drink this." His strong hand supported her head, and he tilted a cup to her lips.

The water was cool and silvery; Calwyn had never tasted anything so delicious. She struggled to sit up, but Darrow eased her down again. "Rest, Calwyn, you're not strong enough. Just rest. We're taking care of you."

Drowsily she sank back. *Halasaa, is Halasaa all right?*

Darrow looked grave. "He is resting too. Don't worry. Go back to sleep."

For a moment Calwyn resisted. How could she sleep? There was too much to do: the children to care for, Halasaa, Mica, Heben, the *wasunti* to keep away — But Darrow had her hand clasped firmly in his, and she surrendered. Her eyes closed, and she slept again.

She did not see Darrow's face as he stared down at her, the taut line of his mouth, and the tenderness in his eyes.

When she woke, much later, she saw that the white canvas was a tent. Darrow still sat cross-legged by the pile of *hegesu* skins on which she lay. She said weakly, "I dreamed I was on the deck of *Fledgewing*."

Darrow smiled. "We're in the camp of the rebel fighters. Tonno and I joined them in Hult, to take them to the Black Palace. We will all go there together now."

"Tonno is here?" Calwyn sat up eagerly, but her head swam, and she dropped back; she was weaker than she'd thought.

Darrow nodded. "You'll see him soon enough. Mica has been telling us your adventures." He poured her a cup of *hegesu* milk. "Here. This will give you strength."

She sipped it gratefully; she couldn't believe that she'd ever thought *hegesu* milk tasted sour.

"Halasaa and the others? Are they all right?"

He gave her a searching look that she didn't understand. "You asked about Halasaa before. Do you remember?"

She shook her head. Darrow seemed to be waiting for her to say something. After a moment he said, "The children are better off than you. You had the beginnings of sunstroke; we found you just in time."

"*You* found *us*? I think it was we who found you —"

Darrow smiled.

"And Heben?" asked Calwyn. "How is he?"

Darrow's smile disappeared. "I believe he is quite well," he answered coolly. "Tired, and ill-nourished, like all of you." There was a pause. Then Darrow leaned forward and touched his finger to the medallion that Calwyn still wore between her brows. "This belongs to Heben, does it not?"

"Oh — this?" After so many days, Calwyn had forgotten it was there. "I pretended to be part of his Clan to get inside the Palace." She tugged it off and looked up to see a peculiar expression on Darrow's face.

"It wasn't — a love-gift?"

Calwyn smiled. "Of course not! Believe me, Heben would no sooner give me a *love-gift* than — than Halasaa would!"

"Hmm," said Darrow. Then suddenly the grave look returned to his face. "Halasaa is very ill."

"This desert is killing him," said Calwyn.

Darrow was watching her closely. "Mica said that you healed

the leg of one of the children. A great gash from knee to ankle, knitted up without even a scar."

"Halasaa showed me what to do . . ." Calwyn's voice faltered; then she met Darrow's gaze steadily. "Perhaps I could help him."

Wordlessly Darrow held out his hand to help her up. Her knees buckled as she walked out of the tent, and she was grateful for the support of his arm.

The camp was larger than she'd expected. It was a cluster of ten or more long tents and twice as many smaller ones. The bigger tents were ranged about an open space with awnings strung up for shade. Groups of men and women sat cross-legged beneath them. One group, Heben among them, bent over small grindstones, sharpening spearheads. Two men made bread by a fire, and a woman brewed tea in a blackened kettle. Calwyn heard the bleating of a flock of *hegesi* nearby.

As she and Darrow crossed the space between the tents, Mica sprang up with a glad cry. Darrow held up a warning hand, and she fell back, trying to hide her disappointment. Calwyn waved to her feebly. Mica looked bronzed and healthy; with her hair wrapped in a Merithuran scarf, she might have spent her whole life in the desert.

Darrow held back the flap of the small tent where Halasaa lay on a pile of skins. Calwyn gave a cry of joy at the sight of Tonno sitting beside the bed. The burly fisherman pulled her into a hug that crushed her ribs. "It's good to see you safe and well, lass," he said gruffly, but then he looked down at Halasaa and shook his head. "No change." He gave Calwyn's shoulder a rough squeeze as he ducked outside.

Halasaa was not conscious. His face was pale, and his hands rested limply by his sides. Calwyn knelt and picked up one hand, pressing it between her own. She took a deep breath. She wanted so desperately to help her friend, but she feared that her new skill would fail her.

Halasaa! she called to him silently. *Can you hear me? Halasaa!*

But no answering voice echoed in her mind. Darrow watched her, his gray-green eyes unreadable.

Closing her eyes, Calwyn tried to remember what Halasaa had told her. She slowed her breath to his rhythm, seeking the light of his being. It was difficult; she was still weak herself, and she missed his reassuring voice, leading her through each step. This time there was no great wound to draw her attention, no single bodily hurt to be mended. She slowed the beat of her blood to match his. *Halasaa! I am here. Where are you?*

It was no use, she thought; she knew too little of this magic to help him without guidance. Tears prickled behind her eyelids. But she knew that Halasaa was so weak, she might be his only hope of healing. She breathed deep and sent out her awareness again.

After a long time, just as she was ready to give up, she found the flame she sought: weaker than Oron's had been, a dim glow. *Halasaa! Hold on to me!* She tried to channel her own strength into him, as she had done with Oron. But the power seemed to flow right through him, escaping like water through a net, without strengthening or helping him. Where was the injury, the flaw in the fabric, that drained his life away and drained the power she poured into him? She searched, but she couldn't find it, and at last she knew that she would never find it.

Exhausted, Calwyn's head slumped into her arms. "I can't — I don't know enough; I don't know how!" She looked up at Darrow with her eyes full of tears. "I think it must be a sickness of the heart, from his dreams." Carefully she laid Halasaa's hand on his chest. Without looking at Darrow, she whispered, "That's what he said of you, when you went away. He said that there was nothing he could do to heal a sickness like that."

After a pause, Darrow said under his breath, "I'm not sure I am healed even now."

Blindly Calwyn reached out her hand, and he clasped it, and they sat for a long time in silence.

Later that night, after Calwyn had eaten and slept, she and Darrow, Heben, and Fenn sat talking by a small fire.

"There is chaos around the Palace of Cobwebs — or rather, where the Palace of Cobwebs used to be." Fenn looked at Calwyn. "I believe we have you to thank for that, my lady."

"Not only me," said Calwyn uneasily. "Have you heard, were there many killed when the Palace fell?"

"Some were killed," said Fenn evenly. "I don't know how many. And others perished when the Army leaders took over the Palace."

Calwyn lowered her head. Those lives, as well as Ched and even

Amagis, weighed on her conscience. But she could not have left the children to suffer. What was right, and what was wrong? When she was a novice priestess in Antaris, she had always believed that those who had power, like the High Priestess, had the wisdom to match it. But where did wisdom come from? What would Marna have done, in her place? Not for the first time since she'd left her home, she wished she could ask her Lady Mother for advice.

Fenn was still speaking. "The ruins of the Palace belong to the Army, and now that the emperor is dead, there is no clear leadership. But the generals of the Army have proclaimed the Fifth Prince the new emperor."

"That buffoon!" exclaimed Heben. "I met him once last year at court," he told Calwyn in an undertone. "He was a fool."

Darrow glanced at them sharply, and the rebel leader's cool, thoughtful gaze lingered on Heben.

"He is a fool," said Fenn. "None of the Clans will support him. The First Prince and his followers want to rebuild the ruins of the Palace. They do not know that it's impossible without sorcery." His hand twitched involuntarily toward making the sign against evil. He shot the two chanters a challenging glance, not an apology.

"Go on," said Darrow, expressionless.

"Some of the surviving courtiers have dispersed, and set off for the provinces. Certain members of the Royal House have also disappeared into the desert. One party was seen moving south, toward the mountains."

"Heading for Hathara?" asked Heben.

Fenn shrugged. "I doubt it. More likely they seek the shelter of the hills and caves, escaping from the soldiers. The Army is our chief concern. It seems the divisions gathered on Martec Plain just after the Palace fell. Their purpose is uncertain. But if they intend to march on the sorcerers' nest, that is where they would start."

Calwyn frowned. "How would they know where to find it?"

"Amagis," said Heben. He explained to the others, "There was a sorcerer at court, Amagis. He told some secrets to the Third Princess. Maybe he told the generals too. Or perhaps the princess told them what he had told her —"

Darrow gave a low whistle. "Either way, his brother sorcerers will not thank him for that betrayal."

"He's dead," said Heben.

"That's as well for him," said Darrow grimly. "The brotherhood of ironcrafters hold their secrets close. Their secrets are all they have."

Fenn was busy scratching diagrams in the dirt. "Let's assume that the Army does intend to march on Hathara. If they come directly through the mountains, they may soon reach the sorcerers' nest."

"Then we must get there first," said Heben, his thin face resolute.

Fenn said, "My brother rebels are agreed. Whoever rules the Palace rules the Empire." The shadow of a smile crossed his weathered face. "With the Palace of Cobwebs gone, whoever holds the Black Palace will rule Merithuros. We must seize the sorcerers' nest without delay."

"And set the kidnapped children free," said Calwyn.

"That is not our aim," said Fenn.

"It is mine!" said Calwyn hotly.

"And mine," said Heben.

The rebel leader shrugged. "If the children go free, we will not object."

Calwyn leaned forward, staring into his eyes. "You might need those children. They could help you defeat the sorcerers; they could help you win your revolution. Why do you scorn them?"

"I don't scorn them," said Fenn. "They are welcome to join us, if they wish. As are any chanters." He and Darrow exchanged a look. Calwyn watched them, not understanding.

Darrow said, "Taking the Black Palace will not be easy. The iron-chanters have protected themselves for a long time."

Fenn smiled, baring his teeth to the firelight. "I never thought I would accept aid from a chanter of magic."

Again he and Darrow exchanged those enigmatic glances.

"What are you planning?" cried Calwyn.

"We have managed so far without the interference of women," said Fenn abruptly. "This is no business for your ears."

Calwyn flushed and opened her mouth to make a sharp retort, but to her surprise, Heben spoke up first. "Calwyn and Mica and

Shada can endure as much, and are as able — more able — than many men. If you will take the help of chanters, you should take the help of women. It is your loss if you do not."

The corners of Fenn's eyes crinkled very slightly as he looked at Heben. He said mildly, "Do not ask me to change all my ways in one day, brother."

"You talk of accepting our help!" cried Calwyn hotly. "Perhaps you should ask if we are willing to offer it!"

Darrow laid his hand on her arm to silence her. He said calmly to Fenn, "We are with you."

Fenn nodded, then unfolded his legs and strode off to join his companions around the larger fire. Heben followed, asking eager questions about strategy and tactics. Calwyn stared after them. "Are you sure we should be helping them, Darrow? Are the rebels the best people to rule Merithuros?"

"Better the rebels than the Emperor's puppets. Better the rebels than the sorcerers of the Black Palace. And better all of them together than any group alone." Darrow stretched out his legs beside the little campfire. Calwyn was unable to read his quizzical expression. "Never fear, Calwyn. I know what I am doing."

Calwyn stared into the fire. She had wanted so much to be with Darrow again, but he wouldn't confide in her. He had shared secrets with Fenn, but not with her! But she had learned that there was no point pressing Darrow to share his thoughts if he was unwilling.

"Fenn is an arrogant man. How gracious of him, to accept the help of chanters!" She could not keep the hurt from her voice.

Darrow smiled in the firelight. "Do you remember how you showed off your powers to that boy in Kalysons?"

"The one who teased me, so I froze the spittle in his mouth? I remember how furious you were with me."

Darrow was silent for a moment while sparks flew into the night. "I was harsh with you. You were foolish to use magic in such a place. But I made a similar mistake once and paid a heavy price for it. That was how I came to be stolen away to the Black Palace myself."

Calwyn sat bolt upright. "You were one of the kidnapped children?"

"Yes. There is only one path to the Black Palace, and few tread it willingly. There has only been one sorcerer who went there of his own wish, and you can guess his name."

"Samis."

There was silence between them for a time. Calwyn's voice shook as she said, "I can't bear to think of you as a little boy, stolen away —"

Darrow made an impatient gesture, brushing her words aside. "Please, don't pity me," he said brusquely. "But the Black Palace is a dark place. I want to help these people punch holes in its walls and let in some light."

Calwyn stared at his profile in the firelight. Hesitantly she said, "Tell me what happened."

"Another time, perhaps." Darrow's voice was crisp.

Calwyn looked away. After a while Darrow joined the larger group, where Heben's mournful flute sent a thin thread of music to disappear with the sparks into the darkness, and she was left to sit alone.

The next day Calwyn saw what a proper desert caravan looked like. A long row of *hegesi*, laden with neat packs, stretched along the dunes, outlined against the bright glare of the sky. The rebels strode ahead and behind them, swathed in their robes, their heads wrapped in scarves of red and yellow. Halasaa, still unconscious, was carried on a sheltered litter, hung with fluttering scarves. The children, much strengthened and heartened by a day or two's rest and nourishment, formed one tight-knit cluster. The crew of *Fledgewing* formed another, with Heben among them. At the very head of the procession walked Fenn, beating time on the hand-held drum. His deep, clear voice floated back along the line, chanting words that Calwyn strained to hear.

"What is he singing?"

"It's not a song," said Heben. "It's the story of Thanar and Lantrisa, the Father and Mother of Merithuros. Thanar lived on the smallest of the moons, and Lantrisa on the largest, and they loved one another across the gulfs of the sky, and met secretly on the third moon. But her father discovered them and swore to kill his daughter for dishonoring him."

Mica snorted under her breath.

"They ran away to Tremaris, to the forests of Merithuros — there were forests here once, according to the stories — and for a time they hid here in safety."

"Not forever?" asked Calwyn, a little wistfully.

"No. They had many daughters, and when the Seven Warriors came from the sky, they married them, and that was the beginning of the Clans. But Lantrisa's father pursued them, and cut down all the trees of Merithuros searching for them. Lantrisa and Thanar fled deeper and deeper into the forest. Her father cut down every last tree to find them. He slayed them both, and their spirits bled into the dust."

"Cheerful," said Tonno.

Calwyn shivered. She seemed to feel the ancient grief creep up from the land through the soles of her feet and into her whole body. "What a waste. Murder and destruction, and for what?"

"This land was built on blood and sorrow," said Heben severely. "Thanar and Lantrisa died to make way for their children. The forests had to be destroyed so that the Clans could flourish." After a pause he added, in a more uncertain tone, "At least, that's what the stories say."

"Then perhaps it's time for some new stories," said Calwyn. She stole a sideways glance at Darrow. He walked on steadily, as if he wasn't listening, but she thought his face looked sterner than usual, and her heart was heavy. All the old distance of last winter lay between them still; nothing had changed since the day he'd sailed away.

* * *

At the end of the next day, they came to a wall of rock that stretched on and on in both directions, as far as the eye could see. "This is the Lip of Hathara," said Darrow grimly.

The lip was as high as two men, and it curled over their caravan like a petrified wave about to break. Calwyn strained her eyes to left and right, but nowhere could she see a breach or a low place where they might cross or even look over it. Like the Wall of Antaris, it had kept the lands of the Merithuran chanters safe for generations.

Fenn conferred with his fellow rebels. "Get the ropes," he instructed. "With hooks attached, as we use to cross the mountains."

Calwyn swung round to Darrow. He and the children could easily open a way through the rock with ironcraft. But he hung back in inscrutable silence, and the children, looking to him for guidance, whispered to one another but did nothing. Tonno glanced at his old friend and chuckled quietly. "Reckon I might give them a hand, if you don't mind. I know a thing or two about ropes."

Darrow waved his hand, as if to say, *Go.*

Heben glanced at Calwyn. "Why won't Darrow help them?" he murmured.

Calwyn had to smile. Heben's feelings about chantment had changed so much since they'd first met. She said quietly, "Fenn is willing to accept the aid of chanters. But he is still too proud to ask for it."

Heben shook his head and strode forward to offer Fenn his help. The chanters of the company stood by and watched as the rebels, with Heben's and Tonno's assistance, opened the packs and hauled out coils of rope and well-worn slings and pulleys for the *hegesi*. Fenn and Tonno attached a hook to the end of one coil of rope and hurled it over the crest of the lip. But the hook didn't catch, and the rope slithered back, useless, to their feet. Time after time they struggled to secure the rope, without success. At last Darrow went up to Fenn.

"What?" The rebel leader was sweating and irritable.

"The other side of the lip is polished rock. Your hook will never catch." Darrow looked quizzical, or perhaps it was just the scar that tugged his eyebrow down.

Fenn was silent, winding the rope around his arm. Still he could not bring himself to ask for help.

After a moment, Darrow stepped back, and again the chanters stood silently watching while the rebels tried every means they could to cross the high wave of rock. They sent a *hegesu* trotting up the lip, but it scrabbled back before it reached the curl. Then Fenn himself tried to run up it, clutching at the slippery surface with his bare hands. He managed to cling like a barnacle to the rock for a heartbeat, but then he lost his grip and tumbled back in an undignified heap in the dirt.

Calwyn said to Mica, "When I go back to Antaris, I'll tell them to make the ice Wall in this shape."

Mica looked at her in surprise. "Do you think you will go back?"

"Perhaps. One day."

"What for?"

Calwyn was taken aback by the fierceness of Mica's voice. "It's my home."

"No, it ain't. Ravamey's your home, ain't it?"

"Well, yes, but — the place you're born is always your homeland. . . ." Calwyn's voice trailed away. She had not been born in Antaris; she didn't know where she was born. She looked at Mica ruefully. "You're right. Ravamey is the only home I need."

"D'you think we'll ever see it again?" Mica gazed wistfully around at the red desert.

"Of course we will!" Calwyn put her arm around Mica's shoulder, and after a moment Mica leaned against her.

Fenn swallowed his pride at last. Dusting himself off, he strode up to Darrow. "All right," he said. "Show us your tricks."

With a faint smile, Darrow nodded and beckoned the children to stand beside him. The chanters arranged themselves before the towering lip, caught in its perpetual arrested fall. Now it was the turn of the rebels to stand and stare as Darrow raised his hands and let out a low growl of throat-chantment. One by one the children added their voices to his, and the chantment swelled like the roll and rumble of thunder. Darrow swept his hands up and apart, and with a groan, a deep fissure shot through the smooth rock.

Slowly Darrow spread his hands farther apart, and the crack widened, splitting the high wall in two. The chantment grew in intensity, until Calwyn felt that the marrow of her bones was shaken by its vibrations. The chanter children exchanged glances, grinning with triumph. The crack grew wider and wider until it was broad enough for three people to pass through abreast. Darrow, with a nod to the children, brought his hands up once more, then swept them down and together, pressing one palm against the other. The chantment faded like the echoes of a departing thunderstorm and died away.

Only Oron stood back from the rest. He had not joined the chorus of chantment, and his face was closed and brooding. Calwyn laid a hand on his sleeve, but he winced away from her touch. "What is it?"

"I don't want to go back there," he said sullenly. "No one asked if I wanted to go back."

Calwyn felt a pang of guilt. Was it cruel to bring the children back to this place? Yet the others seemed willing enough to return. Since they'd joined the rebels, Vin and Haid had adopted red and yellow scarves and seemed eager to follow wherever Fenn led them. And of course, Shada longed for her brother. . . .

"I'm sorry, Oron," she said. "But we can't leave you here. We have no choice. We must all go on together."

The little boy shrugged off her consoling hand and turned his back on her. Again Calwyn felt that twinge of helpless exasperation. She could not touch this boy, could not speak to him.

On either side of the crack, the rock was folded and wrinkled, as if the chanters had parted the stone with their hands like a curtain. Darrow looked at Fenn, and Fenn gestured to him to be the first to walk through.

Slowly the whole company passed through the opening. On the other side of the lip, Calwyn gasped. They stood on the threshold of a wide, flat, endless crater of red dust, stretching farther than the horizon. It was utterly featureless. The other deserts they'd traveled through were marked by patches of scrub or the folds of dunes; they were scattered with boulders or scored with dry ravines. But this plain was as smooth as a polished platter. Behind them, and to either side, stretched the vanishing embrace of the Dish's lip; ahead, there lay nothing but red dust.

Calwyn looked down. Fine dust lay ankle-deep above a bed of hard rock. Clouds of it puffed up with every step. Already the whole caravan was powdered orange-red.

Mica gave a low whistle. "And I thought the rest of this land were dead and dry! Lucky we got you, Cal, to give us water, or we'd be done for!"

Darrow clenched his hands in his pockets. Without speaking, he nodded in the direction that their shadows fell and began to walk on.

Their camp that night was far from comfortable. Every movement stirred up clouds of the fine red dust, and the whole party kept their faces firmly wrapped in protective scarves. Even Mica was helpless. She tried to sing up a gentle wind to clear the path ahead, but the dust was so fine that it drifted back to envelop the caravan in a choking red mist, and the others begged her to stop.

Only the *hegesi* managed to sleep that night, though even they were restless and bleating, their bellies empty. "*Arbec* grows near the Black Palace, but not here," said Darrow tersely. "They will have to wait."

The human members of the party tried to snatch what rest they could, leaning back-to-back with their heads on their knees. Even when the children swept themselves a clear space, the rock below was bone-achingly hard, and the dust drifted back as soon as it was cleared.

"I thought ironcrafters could command everything of the earth," said Calwyn half-teasingly to Shada. She didn't dare to ask Darrow. His face was hawklike and dangerous.

Shada shifted uncomfortably on her haunches. "We can. But we need to sing to every single particle of dust, and there are so many!"

Presently Shada went with Mica to find some dinner, and Tonno and Calwyn were left alone.

She said, "Darrow looks just as he did last spring, before he left the island. I used to dread that look, Tonno! And here it is again."

Tonno grunted. "He's come a long way to drag the same troubles behind him."

"Coming back here must be hard for him. It must remind him of Samis."

Tonno spat neatly, making a small, clean hole in the layer of dust. "Does he still carry that ring?"

"I don't know. I haven't seen it."

There was a short silence. "How is Halasaa?"

Calwyn grimaced. "No better. No worse."

"You can't help him?"

"I've tried. I can't reach him. It's not like mending Oron's leg; there's no wound to bind."

Tonno gave her a shrewd look. "So you're a healer now too?"

"Not exactly," said Calwyn uncomfortably. "I helped Halasaa heal Oron. I couldn't have done it alone."

"Oh, aye." Tonno sucked on his bottom lip. "Wish I'd brought more pipe-leaf with me. The stuff they sell in Teril's not worth settin' light to . . . So the little lass is an ironcrafter, is she? Darrow was right, it's not just a man's magic."

Suddenly the burden of her secret was too heavy for her to bear alone. In a rush, Calwyn confessed, "I did it too, Tonno. I sang a chantment of iron. When we were running out of the Palace, as it fell."

"Ah." Tonno shifted in the dust. "You told Darrow?"

"No. Not yet." *If he can keep his secrets, so can I.* But she was ashamed to say it aloud.

Tonno uncurled his calloused sailor's fingers one by one. "Powers of Tongue, and Beasts, and Winds, and Ice, you had already. And now the Power of Becoming and the Power of Iron. Six of the nine? Keep it up, lass, and you'll be the Singer of All Songs yet."

"Don't be ridiculous," said Calwyn sharply. "I haven't mastered half those crafts. I used the Power of Becoming once, with Halasaa helping me. And I'm sure I could only sing a chantment of iron that one time because we were in such danger. And besides, I don't know anything about the Power of Seeming. Or the Power of Fire."

"Trout has the Clarion of the Flame safe on Ravamey, he can take care of that," said Tonno comfortably. "As for seeming, you haven't had a chance to learn that yet. When this is over, we'll go to Gellan and find one of them tricksters to teach you, like they taught Samis."

"Stop it, Tonno. It's not funny." Abruptly Calwyn stalked away into the dusk. Her angry feet sent up spurts of dust that whirled behind her like miniature tornadoes. Tonno wrapped his sturdy arms about his knees and stared after her. And Darrow, who had walked up behind them unnoticed and overheard their conversation, stood staring too, his face set like stone, brooding and watchful.

For a long time, Calwyn wandered about on her own. But the sick feeling in the pit of her stomach refused to unclench itself. She didn't want to think about what Tonno had hinted — more than hinted. She wouldn't do it again. She wouldn't even try. She would simply forget. Then no one could accuse her of wanting to be the Singer of All Songs, of being like Samis —

But she found she couldn't banish the idea from her mind. Perhaps if she tried just one more time, to prove to herself that she couldn't do it, then she'd never need to think about it again. She could tell Tonno to shut up, once and for all. . . .

She turned and looked behind her. Everyone was in the camp, moving sluggishly if they had to move at all, staying close to the fires. No one was watching. Calwyn turned to face the flat plain of the Dish and lifted her hand. She let the first low note of chantment, the base note, hum in her throat for a moment. Then, tentatively, she added the overnote, the harmony, and let it buzz on her lips and her tongue, just as Darrow had taught her.

A thin column of dust rose up at the tips of her fingers and danced, swaying gently to and fro as she moved her hand.

Calwyn cried out and flung down her hand. A dry sob tore her throat: She had no moisture to spare for tears. Far above her head, the three full moons, the Lanterns of the Goddess, shone down and bathed her face with silver light.

Keela unwound the delicate veil that shielded her face and hair and shook it free of dust. Once she could have relied on her maidservant to spring forward and perform such a task, but since they'd left the Palace, her servants had grown steadily lazier and more insolent. She would remember that, when she was empress.

Nor would she forget the treachery of Lord Haigen and his fellow generals. They had tossed her aside like a used handkerchief. Those idiot *men* had pronounced the Fifth Prince, her half-witted half brother, the new emperor. Then they had announced their intention to march on Hathara, to subdue the sorcerers who had destroyed the Palace of Cobwebs and seize the sorcerers' nest to take its place.

But Keela had come up with another plan. How surprised the Army would be to arrive at the Black Palace and find Keela already installed there with her followers, the nucleus of a new Imperial Court in place, and the sorcerers doing her bidding! The sorcerers were more powerful than the Army; far better to have *them* under her command than those thick-headed soldiers!

Hastily Keela had convened her faction among the ruins of the Palace of Cobwebs and ordered them to accompany her at once to Hathara. But the lazy wretches were so slow in preparing for the journey, and had grumbled so loudly and so long at the lack of servants to help them, that she'd decided to set off before them, with just a few servants to accompany her.

Keela had only the vaguest idea of what she would do when she reached the sorcerers' nest, but she was supremely confident that she could make those sorcerers obey her. They were only men! Amagis had been an easy conquest. He'd told her that the sorcerers lived without women; they would be utterly defenseless before her charms. And as soon as the new court was established, she would send word to Gellan to tell her master it was time. Then there would be the joint coronation, emperor and empress, side by side —

Complacently the princess patted her smooth blond hair. Despite all the privations and discomforts of this journey, she had surprised herself by *almost* enjoying it. After all, the First Empress must be able to bear hardship as well as enjoy luxury.

The tall, dusty figure of Immel was returning at last, trudging alongside the curved wall.

"Well?" Keela's ice-blue gaze was as frosty as ever, even in the desert heat.

"There is good news, Princess." Immel's bows grew lower every day, as though he were mocking her. "My Clansfolk met a band of chanters some days past, traveling south toward Hathara. There were children among them."

Keela smiled. She had been right. It had been a plot of the sorcerers, working through that little *nadu*. No one else would have even noticed her. It takes one extraordinary woman to recognize another, she thought complacently, forgetting that it was Amagis who had first suspected Calwyn.

"My Clansfolk believe the chanters opened a way through the Dish's lip." Immel pointed to the towering wave of rock, which their straggling party had followed for two days now. "See here, my lady, where the fault lines run? The lines appear whenever the sorcerers come and go from Hathara, though they usually vanish again at once. But these lines have remained. The way still lies open."

"Then why are we standing about here, you dolt?" Impatiently Keela threw herself onto her *hegesu* and urged it into a gallop, following the lines in the rock that pointed southward, to the doorway into Hathara.

It was several days before Calwyn and the others glimpsed the imposing cube of the Black Palace, squat and blind on its raised plateau, a dark speck against the unrelieved expanse of red. The *hegesi* were more excited by the scent of the *arbec* plants that fed the chanters' flocks.

"Will the sorcerers see us?" asked Fenn.

Darrow shook his head. "They don't expect guests. They keep no watch. They won't know we're among them until we are inside the Palace, and perhaps not even then."

Still, Calwyn felt a sense of foreboding when they'd climbed onto the plateau and stood at last at the foot of the towering black monolith. She could see their reflections in the wall as clearly as a mirror. Tentatively she reached out a hand to the surface: It was as smooth as polished marble and hot to touch. She sprang back, singing up a swift chantment to soothe her burnt hand.

"I'm sorry," said Darrow. "I should have warned you."

"It's all right," said Calwyn coolly, though her hand was red and smarting.

The rebels had their weapons at the ready, arrows to bow-strings, daggers drawn, spears poised. Heben stood with them, knife in hand, his whole body tense and strained. The children were nervous. Shada's cheeks were flushed, and Haid waited with the *hegesi*, his eyes fixed apprehensively on the blank black wall. Tonno gripped his short fishing knife. Mica was beside him, eyes shining, with a spear on her shoulder. Calwyn and Vin stood by Halasaa's litter. Slowly Darrow lifted his hands and sang.

A doorway appeared in the shining wall. But this was no rough, jagged crack. It was a high, imposing gateway, framed with grooved

pillars. Overhead, two immense stone ravens stretched their wings
to form the top of the Sorcerers' Door. Their savage beaks were
open, and their blind, pitiless eyes glared down at the intruders.

With a confident gesture, Fenn motioned the rebels inside. The
others followed. Haid gave one of the *hegesi* a farewell pat on the
rump as they left the animals to graze outside. Calwyn and Vin
went in last of all, behind Halasaa's litter.

As she crossed the threshold, Calwyn shuddered. The air inside
the Palace was dank and cold, but that was not the reason for her
unease. She sensed a dark power in this place that wreathed in the
shadows like a poisonous mist. She had the strongest feeling that
if everyone stopped shuffling their feet and murmuring, she would
hear something, something important . . . but the feeling passed.

After the glare of the sunlight, it was impossible to see anything at first. His face closed and grim, Darrow led them through
stark rooms and up wide stone staircases, dimly lit by lamps high on
the walls. Calwyn thought that there could not have been a place
more different from the Palace of Cobwebs, where every wall had
been curved, every nook and alcove cunningly decorated, the over-
all effect light and frothy. This place was all straight lines and
stark angles; it could not have been more simple, or more bleak.

Fenn walked beside Darrow, tense and alert. "Where are you
taking us?"

"Farther in," said Darrow.

But they did not get much farther. They entered a vast, vaulted
chamber with another huge staircase at one end, and an immense

iron grille rattled down and clanged to the floor behind them, cutting off their escape. "Scatter!" shouted Fenn, but a swarm of black-clad figures came streaming from doorways and pouring down the staircase, until a wall of sorcerers circled them, ten deep, each with a glittering handful of sharp blades.

Without a sound, Oron dropped and squirmed through the grille; he was small enough to squeeze through. Then he was gone, vanished into the shadowy bowels of the Palace. Shada and Hajd spun round to wriggle after him, but a swift note of chantment and a flash of steel pinned them both to the stone floor. With a cry, Calwyn sank down beside the children. They were not hurt, but the short, sharp steel blades had plunged through their tunics deep into the polished stone. Already Shada was yanking herself free, ripping her ragged clothes, but there was a harsh growl, and another strong blade flew through the air. Shada screamed as it knocked her to the ground and pinned her down by the hair.

Calwyn couldn't see clearly what happened next, but she had an impression of rushing figures, whirling black robes, shrieks and growls of chantment, and the terrifying rush and lunge of spears and knives. Shada screamed again, tugging at her pinioned hair. Calwyn struggled to free her, to shield Halasaa, and to sing. "Mica!" she yelled. "A wind, a wind!" She sang up a wind, a strong indiscriminate blast that knocked all the wrestling figures off their feet, rebels and sorcerers alike. She heard Mica's high, clear voice join hers. At last the girls staggered to their feet, with their backs against a wall, and Calwyn saw the floor covered with breathless bodies, dozens of black-robed sorcerers writhing like upended cockroaches, and the rebels on their stomachs, flattened by the force of the wind.

"Enough!" cried Darrow in a ringing voice. Calwyn and Mica exchanged a glance and shifted the tone of their song to make the wind flow around him, so he could stand. He stood with his hands upraised and swung around to show them all what he held in his hand.

It looked like a burning ember. It drew the faint light of the vast room toward it, and the gaze of every person there. The dull red glow throbbed slowly, radiating a dense and irresistible power. With a sickening thump of her heart, Calwyn recognized the ruby ring, Samis's ring.

Only the murmur of the girls' song and the eerie whisper of their spellwind disturbed the cold silence of the huge room. The hairs on the back of Calwyn's neck stood up.

Darrow cried, "I have returned to claim what is mine!"

His voice echoed around the polished walls.

From the far end of the chamber, at the foot of the staircase, one of the sorcerers called in a strangled voice, "What do you claim? Your punishment?"

"You have no right nor any power to punish me."

"You left us! You broke the covenant of the Black Palace."

Darrow threw back his head. "I recognize no covenant. What worth has a covenant that is not entered freely? What worth has a covenant imposed on children, stolen from their homes? Every one of you was taken from your family, most of you even lost your names in this place, as I did, and yet you dare to take homes and names and families from other children in their turn! Your covenant is void, and I repudiate it!"

His words rang through the chamber and died away into the hiss of the spellwind. Behind him, Vin cheered, and Shada and Haid whooped and clapped their hands. And high in a gallery above, where they had been watching everything, the chanter children who still lived in the Black Palace cheered and drummed their fists against the stone. Some of the younger sorcerers cheered too. Without turning around, Darrow held up a hand, and they all fell quiet.

A sorcerer shouted, "Where is your friend Samis?"

The words hung in the quiet for the space of a breath.

"Samis is dead," said Darrow in a low voice. "And I have returned to claim what is mine by right of this ring, the Ring of Hathara, the ring that once was Lyonssar's."

At once the sorcerers erupted into agitated murmurs. Calwyn looked at Mica and gestured with her hand. Mica nodded, and they altered their song to lighten the wind. They sent a soft breeze through the chamber, as a reminder of what they could do if they chose, but the sorcerers and the rebels found they could sit up without having the breath snatched from their lungs.

Darrow held up the ring. Then, for the first time, he pushed it onto his finger and raised his clenched fist in the air. Calwyn's breath caught in a disbelieving sob.

Darrow cried, "I claim dominion of this place and all who dwell herein! In the name of Lyonssar, and by the token of Lyonssar!"

His voice rang back from the vaulted roof. Three sorcerers, marked out from the rest by the black cowls they wore, climbed to their feet. The other sorcerers were watching to see what they would do. Calwyn's heart beat hard. Slowly the three cowled heads bent low. Then, soft as the hiss of wavelets running up a beach, soft as sand settling after a windstorm, the sorcerers responded. "In the name of Lyonssar, you are Lord of the Black Palace and all who dwell herein." And one by one, they staggered to their knees and bowed their heads before Darrow.

For a moment he stood motionless, his fist raised high, blood-light glinting off the red stone. His back was to Calwyn. Then he turned to look at her and Mica and said in his dry voice, "You may stop singing."

The first order of the Lord of the Black Palace was to have Halasaa carried to a quiet room; the next, that food and drink be provided for the rebels and the crew of *Fledgewing* and that they be given suitable accommodation.

"And the children, my lord?" asked one of the stiff-backed sorcerers appointed to carry out the wishes of the wearer of the Ring of Lyonssar.

Darrow looked at him coolly. "Treat them as honored guests."

Calwyn said, "Oron must be hiding somewhere. He should be told that he won't be harmed."

"See to it," said Darrow, and the sorcerer bowed stiffly.

Fenn stood nearby, fingering the hilt of his knife, waiting to speak with Darrow. One side of his mouth curled in a half smile. He knew, thought Calwyn with a stab of resentment. He knew what she had not known.

Cautiously Heben cleared his throat. "Er — Lord Darrow —"

"Address him as *my lord*," said the haughty sorcerer disdainfully. Calwyn almost laughed. Were they back in the Palace of Cobwebs, with its ridiculous layers of protocol and etiquette? Could it really be Darrow, her Darrow, at the center of this bowing and scraping?

"My lord," repeated Heben obediently. "Shada's brother, my brother-in-land, Gada —"

"Of course." Darrow turned to his minion. "Have the boy, Gada, brought to this man's quarters."

"What about all the other children?" Calwyn burst out, unable to contain herself any longer. Darrow turned his cool, appraising look on her.

"I will deal with the children in good time," he said. "There is much to be done. Please, Calwyn, enjoy the hospitality of the Black Palace."

It was an order, not an invitation. Her face burning hot, Calwyn opened her mouth, but Tonno laid a restraining hand on her sleeve.

"Steady, lass," he murmured. "He's up to something. Give him some room to cast his line out."

Stiffly Calwyn inclined her head and allowed Tonno to lead her away. But as soon as they reached the sparsely furnished rooms that had been assigned to them, her feelings exploded.

"Is *this* what he came here for?" she demanded. "I can't believe it! No wonder he wouldn't tell me what he was planning! Lord of the Black Palace! Does he think he's Samis, come back to life?" She flung herself into a chair, but the next moment she sprang up again and began to pace furiously.

Mica helped herself to the platters of food that had been brought to them. "He's had that ring all the time, you know," she said. "That were Samis's ring, weren't it? Does that mean Samis were the Lord of the Black Palace too? He never said nothin' about that."

"Samis was set on becoming emperor of all Tremaris," said Calwyn. "Perhaps he didn't think a petty lordship like this was worth mentioning!"

"No petty lordship, I think," said Heben slowly. "With no emperor on the throne —"

"Whoever rules the Palace, rules the Empire, yes, yes, like Fenn said. So Darrow is the Emperor of Merithuros, is he?" Calwyn let out the incredulous laugh that had lurked in her throat since Darrow first pulled the ring from his pocket.

"Back in Spareth, didn't Darrow say that Samis stole that ring?" growled Tonno from the corner.

Shada said, "The sorcerers told us about that ring, the ring that was lost, the Ring of Lyonssar. Without the ring, there was no Lord here, just the Council of Three. We all knew that."

"All that time!" cried Calwyn to Tonno. "All that time, ever since Spareth, he's been thinking. Thinking about whether to come back here and become Lord of the Black Palace —"

"And if he sets them children free, and stops the sorcerers stealing them, and puts chantment to good work, why not?" said Tonno unexpectedly.

"Well —" Calwyn stopped. She couldn't explain why she felt that Darrow had betrayed her. What if she'd gone back to Antaris and been proclaimed High Priestess, as Marna had said would be her own destiny one day? Would she expect Darrow to feel as affronted and wounded as she did now? Abruptly she turned her back on the others and walked to the end of the room. If there had been a window, she would have stared out of it, but there was none.

It was because he had never told her about the significance of the ring. He hadn't trusted her enough to tell her. Instead he'd brooded over it alone, in his whitewashed hut on the cliff, sailing around in his little boat. She was so angry and hurt that if Darrow had appeared before her at that moment, Lord of the Black Palace or not, she would have *kicked* him —

Just then the door did open, and she swung around, heart beating hard. But instead of Darrow, a young brown-skinned boy stood in the doorway, grinning shyly. Shada gave a choking cry and flung herself around his neck, and Heben leaped across the room to embrace them both. Calwyn watched the tight, joyful knot of the three reunited. Then, with a lump in her throat, she turned away.

Between the sand-clock and the central staircase was a hollow, dusty space. Darrow had known it as a boy and had hidden a tiny carving of an albatross there. And Oron knew it too. He had found the albatross without knowing what it was.

He was creeping back from the kitchens to his hiding place with a stolen round of soft *hegesu* cheese when he was seized from behind. He saw a glimmer of pink silk, then a slender but strong hand clapped over his mouth.

"Be quiet!" a voice hissed in his ear. "Or I'll snap your neck like a pigeon!"

He believed her. He went limp in her grasp, and the woman twisted him around to stare into his face. "You're one of those children who escaped, aren't you? The chanter children, from the Palace of Cobwebs?"

Dumbly Oron nodded.

"And here you are, running about loose. Why is that?" She narrowed her eyes. "These sorcerers brag of their mighty gifts, but they can't manage to keep hold of one little boy. They don't even put a guard on their front door! I could have brought a whole Army inside. I didn't need to leave my servants waiting on the plain."

Speechless, Oron stared at her, his mouth agape. The woman tightened her grip on his arm and began to fire questions at him.

"Why are you hiding? Who are you hiding from? Who rules the sorcerers? Where is the girl who brought you here, Calwyn? Do the sorcerers know that the Army will arrive at any time?"

"I — I don't know!" Oron stammered.

The woman's pale blue gaze bored into him. "You're afraid, aren't you? I know the smell of fear. This whole place reeks of it." She gave his skinny arm a final wrench, and let it drop. "Well, little boy," she said softly, "fear no more. I will take care of you for the rest of your days, if you'll be my eyes and ears. What do you say?"

Oron swallowed the acid that had come bubbling into his throat, and nodded his head again.

Calwyn sat beside Halasaa's bed and watched the shallow rise and fall of his chest. Always lean, he was thinner than ever, his cheeks sunken, the flesh stretched like a drum-skin. Helplessly Calwyn raised his dry hand to her lips. She had tried again and again in the last few days to tune her sense of becoming to the flickering light within her friend, but the flame was even dimmer than before. *Halasaa!* she called silently. *Come back to us!*

She sat there most of the night; she thought that perhaps it was dawn now. Shadows clotted in the corners of the black polished room, and the guttering lamps gave off a smell that made her head swim. Wearily she sank her head onto her hand.

"Is he any better?"

Darrow had let himself quietly into the room, but she didn't raise her head. She said dully, "He's dying. You know that, don't you?"

There was a pause.

At last Darrow said, "I've not seen you since the day we came here."

"I thought the Lord of the Black Palace would send for those he wished to see."

He let out a soft breath. "Calwyn, Calwyn. You must know you need no invitation from me."

"I don't know anything about you anymore." She turned to stare at him. "Why didn't you tell me about the ring?"

"I intended to tell you. I came back to Ravamey to tell you, but you were gone."

She gestured impatiently. "You could have told me before that. You had the whole of winter to tell me!"

"And you could have told me that you had learned some more powers of chantment! Healing, and mind-speech, and ironcraft. You told me nothing! Instead I had to find out from Tonno and Mica. I suppose you've been too busy sharing confidences with Heben to find time to mention it to me."

"*Heben?* What has any of this to do with Heben?" cried Calwyn. "I didn't think the Lord of the Black Palace would take an interest in such things!"

Darrow's gray-green eyes were narrow with anger. He said, "I didn't plan to become Lord of the Black Palace, and I may not wear the ring for long. But while I wear it, I can do some good here. Isn't that what we talked about on Ravamey, doing good?

Perhaps I can bring peace in this troubled time, and not only to the Black Palace."

"Isn't that what Samis said?" flashed Calwyn. "That he would bring peace and prosperity to all Tremaris?"

Darrow spread his hands in a gesture Calwyn hadn't seen him use before, a Merithuran gesture, and she had a sudden strong sense of the distance that lay between them. "What would you have me do, Calwyn? Without power, we can do nothing, neither good nor evil. Yet you would have me give up power lest I misuse it."

"I don't think you're going to misuse it," faltered Calwyn. Wasn't that exactly what she feared? Who was being mistrustful now? She pressed Halasaa's thin, cool hand to her forehead. *Halasaa, come back, help me!*

For a few moments Darrow was silent, watching them. Then he said, "Calwyn. Let me explain." His voice was hesitant, searching for words. "For the first time in my life, I do not feel like an impostor. As a pupil here, as Samis's friend, even after Spareth, I have never felt that I have earned what has been given to me. Even with you —" He broke off and looked away. "But here, as the wearer of the ring, I am sure of myself. I know what must be done, and I know how to do it. You may think that I have no more right to wear the Ring of Lyonssar than Samis did. Perhaps that's true. But this is a gift that will never come again. I must seize it, I must make the best use of it that I can."

Darrow held out his hand to her, the hand that bore the square red ring. "Come up to the roof," he said, and there was a new note in his voice, an imperious tone that expected to be obeyed. Calwyn heard it with a pang of misgiving, but she followed him out of the room.

Neither of them noticed as a small figure detached itself from the shadows outside Halasaa's door and scurried silently after them.

They climbed endless shadowed stairs and ramps, moving ever upward, toward the heat. In some places, the lamps had gone out, and they moved in darkness. Then Darrow would reach back and seize Calwyn's hand, making her heart lurch. His hand was firm and warm as he led her confidently onward, never missing a step, and she wondered how many times he had come this way before.

At last they emerged onto the rooftop, blinking in the piercing glare of morning. Darrow led Calwyn through a wilderness of pipes, vents, and rickety shacks, birds' nests, and discarded rubbish to the edge of the roof. "This is where I used to come, when I was a pupil here, to look at the stars."

Calwyn stood close to the black marble wall; it was already too hot to touch. She remembered how she used to climb the western tower of the Dwellings of Antaris to gaze out over the forests. How long ago that seemed. . . . Even in the blazing heat, she was aware of the warmth of Darrow's arm close to hers. The distance between them seemed less out here, in the clean air and the iron-bright light. From somewhere among the forest of vents and air ducts came a high-pitched, eerie sound, as the wind whistled across one of the pipes.

Far off across the flat red sand of the Dish of Hathara, Darrow pointed to a dense black line, like a column of ants, that steadily advanced toward the Palace.

"I wish we had the looking-tube!" cried Calwyn.

"We don't need a looking-tube," said Darrow. "The Army is coming." He stared out across the plain, his eyes narrowed against the sun. "I left the way open. They will all come: the soldiers, the courtiers, the rebels, the Clans. They will follow our tracks. The peoples of Merithuros are accustomed to a center, to one ruler, to being ruled from one place. They will try to reconstruct the Palace of Cobwebs here, even those who fought to tear it down. That is a thing that can't be done. The Black Palace was not built as a place for people to dwell. The sorcerers live in it as termites live in a fallen tree, or mice in a barn. Those who call this place the sorcerers' nest speak more truth than they know."

"What is it for, if not for people to live in?"

Darrow looked at her. "Samis discovered the secret of this place. We are the only ones who ever learned it." He paused, staring hard at Calwyn. In a low voice he said, "It is a war engine."

Calwyn stared at him uncertainly. "A war engine like Trout used to build? For throwing bolts, or hurling balls of fire?"

"Not quite." Darrow hesitated. "It is more like an armored cart, or a shielded boat. Do you remember, I once told you of the war boats of Gellan?"

"With great speed and hulls of bronze that no weapon can penetrate. Yes, I remember — But this is a building! It can't move."

"Yes, it can." Darrow glanced around, though there was no one in sight but a fierce-eyed eagle, who gave one harsh cry and launched itself over the edge of the roof, to soar across the desert.

"I don't understand," said Calwyn helplessly.

Darrow swung around, pointing to the black polished pipes of various heights and widths that thrust above the jumble of shacks and piles of debris. "Do you see these pipes? They are the key to it, to the machine. They are blocked now, all but the Pipe of Lyonssar, but if they were to be unblocked, the winds would blow across them. It would make a chantment of iron."

"Like Heben's flute?" Calwyn stared up in awe at the towering pipes.

Darrow grimaced a little at the mention of Heben's name. "Yes, like a flute. Exactly like a flute. Each pipe holds a different note, but if they all sing together, it would be a complete song of chantment. And that chantment would be powerful enough to move this entire Palace across the sands."

"And Samis discovered this?"

A shadow crossed Darrow's face. "Yes. The Black Palace is infused with strong magic, dark magic. It is not a happy place. It is a fortress, a war machine, designed to crush and to kill. No wonder those who live here are so dark of spirit."

Calwyn shivered. "Who made it, Darrow? The Ancient Ones, who built Spareth?"

"I believe so. But perhaps they were wiser than we think, Calwyn. Perhaps they abandoned it here, in the middle of the wilderness of Hathara, so it could never be used again for any destructive purpose."

"They would have done better to destroy it completely," said Calwyn with a shudder. She tried to imagine the vast bulk of the Black Palace advancing across the plain of Kalysons, flattening crops and mills, destroying everything and everyone in its path.

Darrow gave the half smile she knew so well. "It would not be an easy object to destroy. And in a strange way, it has its own beauty."

"Perhaps," said Calwyn skeptically. Even in the sun's heat, she shivered. "How did the sorcerers come to live here?"

"Lyonssar himself brought other chanters here, at the time of the great persecutions. That was long ago, longer than anyone can say. The sorcerers struck a bargain with the emperors. They would keep the Palace of Cobwebs intact, if they were left alone, and safe, here in Hathara."

"All alone," said Calwyn slowly.

"As are your priestesses in Antaris." Darrow shot her a sideways look. "The brothers of the Black Palace have kept their chantments safe here for generations, just as the sisters of Antaris have done behind their Wall of ice."

"We must break down all these walls!" cried Calwyn impatiently. "The chanters of Tremaris must come out of hiding!"

Darrow nodded absently, but he didn't seem to be listening; he frowned toward the north. The black line was still there, moving imperceptibly closer.

Calwyn took a breath. "When will they arrive, Darrow?"

"By sunset perhaps. Not long."

Behind them, a small, ragged figure slipped unseen from behind a pillar and darted away, down into the shadowy interior of the Palace.

Calwyn and Darrow stood side by side and watched as the creeping tide of the Imperial Army crawled nearer and nearer. Unglimpsed and unsuspected, some remnants of the Imperial Court, Keela's faction, followed in their wake.

Darrow turned to Calwyn. "I must ask you," he said, in a strange, strangled voice. "What are your feelings for that boy?"

Calwyn's mind was a blank. "What boy?"

"Heben."

"Oh, by the Goddess!" cried Calwyn, stamping her foot in despair, and impulsively, without thinking, she turned her face up to his.

At first she thought he was still angry with her, he kissed her so hard. But then his arms folded around her, and she knew that he wasn't angry anymore. Nor was she; she felt as if she could never be angry again.

After a while, she became aware of a slight tugging on her long plait; the great ruby ring had become caught in her hair. But it was a long time before either of them bothered to untangle it.

The Ruby Ring

The noon bells clanged out, and the great funnel of the sand-clock turned ponderously. The sorcerers, the rebels, and the children gathered at Darrow's summons. Since his arrival, the normal rules of daily life were suspended; there were no lessons, and the children wandered freely through the Palace, scuffling and skidding along the polished floors, talking about what had happened in hushed, eager tones, and comparing stories. Some spoke of going home. Once or twice Calwyn heard the sound of muffled laughter.

But no one was laughing now. The black-robed sorcerers and the children in their dark tunics all wore the same sober expression as they flocked to the hall in the heart of the Palace where Darrow had proclaimed his lordship.

Gada and Shada were there, close to Heben, whose serious face had glowed with quiet joy ever since they'd been reunited. Vin was there, wary but defiant, and Haid, looking lost without his *hegesi*. The other children — except Oron, who had not yet been found — sat cross-legged on the floor, whispering. Fenn and the rebels leaned against the walls, hands resting with careful nonchalance on their sword hilts. They were dressed in their desert gear, and they watched the sorcerers with eyes full of suspicion. The sorcerers stared with equal loathing and mistrust at the rebels and stood clustered together like a flock of crows, rustling and muttering in their black robes.

Calwyn and Tonno stood apart from the rest, toward the back of the room. Tonno laid his big hand on Calwyn's shoulder. "How is Halasaa?"

"Worse, I think. He seems to be dreaming, bad dreams. We can't wake him. Mica's with him now."

Tonno nodded his curly head soberly. "The sooner we can take him home, the better. Reckon you and me and Mica can manage the voyage back. If we leave in the next day or two, we'll be home again before the moons turn."

"Oh — Tonno —" Calwyn's eyes shone and then clouded. She said, "You think Darrow will stay here, then?"

"Reckon he might, lass. This is his place, this is where he belongs. Ever seen him stand so straight?"

Darrow made his way to the foot of the stairs; the crowd parted for him. There was indeed something different about the way he carried himself, an air of quiet authority that no one dared to argue with. Perhaps Tonno was right and this was where he belonged. *But I don't belong here — anywhere but here!* Her longing for green trees and blue water was like a physical ache, and the parched and mutilated land seemed to cry out with the same yearning. Calwyn knew that if she remained in Hathara, she would dry up and wither inside just like Halasaa. And yet what had happened on the roof made everything more complicated. Her whole body was singing; she felt as if she'd dived into the sea after a long day's work. She knew that to tear herself away from Darrow now would be the most difficult thing she had ever done. But Halasaa needed her; he needed her more than Darrow did. . . .

The whirl of thoughts exhausted her. She was very tired in any case, and the nights spent sitting by Halasaa's side had taken their toll. She leaned back against the comforting bulk of Tonno's body as Darrow mounted partway up the broad stairs. A hush fell over the crowd as his voice rang out, clear and confident.

"Hear me! For three days, I have worn the Ring of Lyonssar. Many of you have wondered what use I will make of my lordship. I tell you this: I will remake the Black Palace. For many generations, it has been a source of fear and hatred, and that fear and hatred has spread out from Hathara like a cancer, eating at the whole of Merithuros.

"Some of you believe that the Empire fell when the Palace of Cobwebs fell. It is not so. For the heart of the Empire was never there. It lies here, within these walls. Without the Black Palace, without the secrets and the lies and the abuse of chantment, there could have been no Palace of Cobwebs, no Imperial Court, no emperor, no Empire. If we are to remake Merithuros, then we must begin here, here and now!"

Darrow was a slight figure, and he looked lean and spare in the simple black clothes he had worn since he came here. But in the dim light of the oil lamps, his fair hair shone like silver gilt, and his gray-green eyes flashed as he threw his head back. The great square ring on his hand glowed with its uncanny blood-light.

"Will we transform the Empire of Merithuros into the Republic of Merithuros?" His voice echoed through the vaulted chamber. "Are you with me?"

Calwyn felt a chill of memory, thinking of Samis as he'd stood in the tower in Spareth and called on them to help him, to unite Tremaris —

One of the rebels spoke from where he lounged by the wall. "We've been patient with you so far, Lord Sorcerer. But why should we share power with you, with the chanters? We want to take power for ourselves. That's what we've worked for. Why should you cheat us out of that?"

"You ignorant upstart!" hissed one of the cowled Council of Three. "Our brotherhood is the true keepers of the Empire! Iron-craft built Merithuros, and we are the guardians of the Power of Iron. Our knowledge is sacred and infinitely precious. The question is, why should we share power with you savages?"

Shada called out shrilly from the crowd of children. "We don't want anything to do with you — we'll join the rebels! You should never have sent us to that place!"

"Selfish, ungrateful child! Your sacrifice was necessary so that we might all survive in peace! You forget, we *saved* you children. You think you would have survived as chanters *out there*?"

At once shouting broke out from all corners of the room. Darrow said nothing but stood in grave silence, a slim upright figure, and gradually the silence spread out from him to the rest of the chamber. Into the quiet he said, "These debates are necessary, but later; there is no time for them now. The Army is on its way here."

The shouting began again. "Impossible!"

"He's lying!"

"I suppose all the Seven Clans are coming as well!" sneered one of the sorcerers.

Again Darrow waited for silence to fall, then he growled out a throat-song of chantment. Slowly he swung around to face the outer wall and swept his arm in a series of wide arcs. At once a buzz of excitement rose as everyone, rebels and chanters alike, surged forward.

Darrow was opening windows onto the desert. As his song droned out, gaps began to form in the outer wall, small perforations in the black polished stone that grew into a long row of graceful arched apertures, until the whole side of the huge room was transformed into a colonnaded terrace high above the ground.

The sorcerers staggered back, shielding their eyes from the flood of bright light. Some of the children yelled out and ran forward to hang over the edge of the windows, shouting and pointing. But Fenn and his fighters were less startled by the appearance of the windows — for anything was to be expected from these uncanny magic-workers — than by what they could see through them.

Long rows of soldiers were clearly visible and moving closer to the plateau. Calwyn could make out their scarlet banners and the plumes on their bronze helmets. The lines of troops stretched back and back across the plain, a moving mass of metal, flesh, and armor. And behind them Calwyn glimpsed another straggling procession, less disciplined than the soldiers and far gaudier: bright curtained litters and rainbow silks that could only belong to members of the court.

The chamber was in uproar. Hundreds of voices shouted at once, the black robes of the sorcerers rustled in agitation, and the rebels' boots drummed as they stampeded to the arched windows and jostled for a view.

Darrow stood immobile on the stairs, arms crossed, watching the commotion he'd caused; a faint smile played around his lips. Calwyn swallowed hard. She whispered to Tonno, "He looks — he looks like Samis, that day he blew the Clarion of the Flame. Do you remember, Tonno? How Darrow tried to make him speak, but he stood there, with his arms folded, just like that, and wouldn't answer — And the ring shone on his finger —"

"Aye. I remember," said Tonno grimly, and he tightened his grip on Calwyn's shoulder until it hurt.

But now Fenn had drawn his knife and leaped up the stairs beside Darrow. He shouted, "We must prepare for battle! We'll fight beside you, you magic-men, if you have the stomach for it! Or are you soft-bellied as worms, locked up in this dark box all your lives?"

"Oh, no," hissed one of the Three Councillors, and though his voice was soft, everyone in the room heard it. "We will fight beside you, filthy and stupid as you are. If the emperor's spawn think they can take over our Palace, our sacred home, we will show them —"

But then came a voice that Calwyn had not expected to hear: Diffident, reserved Heben called out from the thick of the crowd. As he spoke, a space cleared around him. His face was flushed, and his words tumbled out, brimming with passion.

"Must we fight?" he cried. "Must we have war? For what?" He waved his hand toward the windows. "Before we knew *they* were coming, we were ready to tear each other to pieces! Now we see a common enemy, we're happy to work together. Can't we work together *without* the enemy?"

"But the enemy is out there, boy!" exclaimed Fenn. "Do you want us to turn our backs and hope they'll go away?"

"No — no! That's not what I mean." Heben was calmer now, but there was something in his voice that made everyone fall silent. "The emperor is dead. The Palace of Cobwebs is fallen. Nothing will ever be the same! The Army shouldn't be our enemy — we should work with them —"

"Heben is right." Darrow spoke quietly, but every head turned to listen. "We have the chance, here, now, in this place, to make a new Merithuros. We can build a land without emperors and princes. A land where chantment is no longer secret and despised. A land where the Seven Clans will live and work together, rather than quarreling. A land where the Army is put to better use than marching around the Empire demanding food and dancing women —"

"They'll find no dancing women here," said somebody sourly, and everyone laughed.

"We must begin again!" cried Heben, and his eyes blazed in his thin, ardent face.

Darrow nodded. "As soon as we begin to fight, we begin to make the same mistakes all over again. The Army and the court, the rebels and the chanters, the miners and the Clans. . . . You may despise them, they might hate you, but they have much to teach you, just as you have much to teach them. If we are to build a true republic, we must welcome them. And then we must begin to talk to one another."

The chamber erupted; everyone shouted at once. Darrow stood in the eye of the storm with a calm half smile. Fenn tried to control the uproar, hauling some speakers up to stand beside him on the stairs, holding up his hands for quiet. From time to time there was a lull in the noise, and individual voices could be heard: pleading, persuading, bullying, cajoling, fierce, and passionate voices. Heben's voice was prominent among them, and before long he stood beside Fenn and Darrow on the steps, arguing fervently. The din roared around Calwyn, and she swayed against Tonno's sturdy side.

"Let's go outside, lass," he said in her ear. "This is no argument of ours."

Calwyn nodded and allowed him to shepherd her from the room, with his strong arm around her shoulders. They slipped out into the quiet of the polished corridor and at once saw Mica hurrying toward them, her sandaled feet pattering on the black stone. "What's all that racket?" she cried. "I could hear it all the way from Halasaa's room!"

"Is Halasaa all right?" asked Calwyn anxiously.

"Just the same — he ain't no worse. Maybe better. He's sleepin' now, a proper sleep, none of them dreams."

Calwyn bowed her head; she felt that she couldn't face that oppressive little room where Halasaa lay lost in his wilderness of pain and shadows.

"The Army's right outside," Tonno told Mica. "Darrow opened up windows."

Mica's face lit up. "Let's go out and see 'em! Oh, let's get *out*!"

Calwyn said, "Perhaps the doorway Darrow sang is still open —"

Impulsively they set off through the hushed rooms, leaving the echoes of the debate behind them, until the only sound they could hear was their own footfalls. Calwyn hurried ahead, down ramps and staircases. Now that Mica had suggested it, the confused longings and clamoring in her head had firmed into one desire, to get out of the Palace. Partly she was impatient to escape from the stale air and the stifling shadows, but it was more than that. Something tugged at her, like a chantment of iron that pulled at her mind. Faster and faster she hurried on, until she was almost running and Tonno and Mica had to trot to keep up with her. The temperature rose steadily as they approached the outside of the building, and before long they stood in front of the imposing doorway that Darrow had opened.

For two days it had stood ajar, but a disapproving sorcerer had sealed it again only the night before.

"Oh, no!" cried Mica, her face pinched with disappointment.

"I can open it!" exclaimed Calwyn wildly. "I can, I can open it!"

Behind her back, Tonno and Mica exchanged a look; Tonno shrugged. Calwyn closed her eyes, stretched out her hands, and let her mind fall into a state of relaxed attention. Her longing to be outside was so strong that it overwhelmed her misgivings about practicing ironcraft. The chantment murmured in her throat. She felt for the crack where she could insert the delicate wedge of her song and found it. Slowly the crack began to split apart. The notes of her chantment were a lever that gently, almost imperceptibly, forced the stone asunder.

Her eyes were still shut as she felt her way. But she heard Mica give a gasp of excitement behind her, and Tonno's indrawn breath. And then came another noise, a long low groan, like the breath of the Black Palace itself, as the huge stone door swung open.

Calwyn opened her eyes. A bright square of red sand and azure sky gaped before them, and at once Calwyn ran out into it. Mica followed, whooping and throwing her arms into the air. Tonno shook his burly head as if to clear the clinging shadows of the Palace. A flock of *hegesi* grazed on the plateau not far from the doorway; they lifted their heads for a moment and gazed blankly at the intruders.

Calwyn stepped back, shielding her eyes, and stared up at the smooth black wall of the Palace. There, about a third of the way up, was a series of small holes: the arched windows that Darrow had punched into the wall of the meeting chamber. A few little faces peered out: some of the chanter children, enjoying the view they'd never seen before. Mica waved, and the children waved back.

"Look." Tonno stared to the north. "They're not far off."

The nodding plumes and banners were at the very foot of the plateau, splashes of color that bobbed and fluttered against the red dust, and the late afternoon sun glinted off the helmets and spearheads of the soldiers.

Shouts of command began to drift toward them. "Halt!" "Siege stations!" "Load catapults!"

The soldiers broke ranks and swarmed forward to assemble their weapons. Calwyn recognized the Mithates war engines that Trout had described: catapults for hurling fire, and huge sledges, piled with boulders that the soldiers must have collected on the other side of the Lip of Hathara. The cohorts teemed around the foot of the plateau like ants around their nest. Behind the catapults were other troops, equipped with ropes and hooks, ready to scale the escarpment when the Palace had been breached. There were archers with their bows already raised and soldiers tending huge iron cauldrons, filled with flaming tar.

Calwyn stood watching, with her hand above her eyes. She felt paralyzed and dizzy, as if she were floating away from her body. The whole scene was drenched in thick orange light from the declining sun.

Tonno touched her arm. "Better go in, Calwyn. We don't want to be caught in the middle of the fighting."

"We are in the middle," said Calwyn, dry-mouthed. "If not for us, none of this would be happening. Fenn was right. I can't make it go away by shutting my eyes."

"We can see everythin' — and we can run if we have to!" cried Mica, her eyes shining.

"Come inside!" urged Tonno once more, but Calwyn shook off his hand.

"No! No!" Something like panic rose in her. She *had* to stay outside. She allowed Tonno and Mica to lead her behind the shelter of a low wall of stones that marked the boundary of a garden, but she would not crouch down. She had to see, she had to stay here, with her feet on the ground. She didn't know why it was so desperately important, only that it was.

The soldiers moved rapidly, with terrifying efficiency. Already a boulder had been loaded into the cup of one catapult, and Calwyn heard the cry go up: "Release!" The restraining ropes flew free, the cup rose majestically upward, and the boulder, the size of *Fledgewing*'s dinghy, soared into the air. There was a sickening crash as it slammed into the black marble wall of the Palace, punching an ugly splintered hole.

"Can't you stop 'em, Cal?" cried Mica. She believed that Calwyn could do anything.

A shower of sparks flew between the Army and the Palace: a hail of arrows, their gleaming heads caught by the sun. Most glanced off the stone and fell back, useless, into the dust, but some whistled with deadly aim straight into the hole. Calwyn gasped and flung out her hands to the soldiers, as if pleading could bring a stop to this.

The soldiers with ropes were writhing up the edge of the plateau, hauling one of the catapults after them. "Get *down!*" roared Tonno, shoving Mica behind him. But Calwyn stepped forward, inexorably drawn closer to the battle.

She was dimly aware of a strange sound behind her: a growling, buzzing, unearthly music, howling out across the desert. But it was Mica's cry that made her spin around, even before she heard the noise that followed. It was a noise that engulfed all other sound, a grinding, screeching noise so loud she thought her head would split in two.

Calwyn spun around in horror, clutching her ears. It took her a moment to comprehend what she saw, so extraordinary was the sight. The Palace was moving, gliding silent and ponderous as an armored ship across a dry sea of sand. And it was moving toward them —

Tonno grabbed Mica by the arm and pulled her away, his eyes wide with disbelief and horror. Calwyn swayed, frozen to the spot, as her mind whirled. The engine, the demonic engine — only Darrow knew the secret — Darrow must have set it off —

"Calwyn!" Faintly Mica's desperate scream reached her, and at last she found she could move her feet, and she ran.

Breathless, she stumbled after Tonno and Mica, feet pounding across the dirt. Clouds of red dust swirled around them until they coughed so hard they could no longer run. "It's all right," gasped Tonno at last, tears streaming. "It's not coming after us —"

Calwyn spun round: He was right. The three had run to the west, toward the setting sun, and their shadows stretched back to where the Palace loomed close to the edge of the plateau, scattering the troops who had scaled the rise. As they watched, the vast war engine halted, then changed direction, gliding back across the plateau, crushing the sorcerers' gardens to pulp.

The procession of courtiers had almost caught up to the soldiers on the plain, but the sight of the moving Palace had thrown them into bewildered chaos. Curtained litters were dropped, and courtly ladies and gentlemen peered out, covered in dust and exclaiming in distress. Servants fled in every direction, and laden *hegesi* bolted, bleating. Through it all, Calwyn could hear the shouted orders of the Army commanders, the clash and clatter of arms, and the hiss of swords being torn from their sheaths.

"There must be war now!" she cried in despair. "What's Darrow thinking?"

"Darrow? Darrow never done this!" said Mica vehemently.

"But he must have!" Calwyn was almost in tears. "No one else knows how!" With her heart in her throat, she stared up at the roof of the Palace. Was that movement there, a small dark shape darting? She squinted in the thick light of sunset. The Black Palace, engine of war and destruction, sailed inexorably onward. "Release!" yelled the soldiers, and another huge boulder smashed into the Palace. Black splinters showered Calwyn, Mica, and Tonno, and they flung up their hands to protect their eyes.

Calwyn gasped. With that impact, she'd seen movement again, at the very edge of the roof, and this time a dash of color too: pink. She stared, and blinked, and stared again. "Mica, look! The roof! I think — I can see Keela!"

Mica peered upward. After a moment she said, "That's her all right. You think *she* set it goin'?"

"It's impossible," said Calwyn. "Only a sorcerer —" She stopped. There was that splash of pink, and beside it, another, smaller figure, difficult to see in the fading light. The one in pink was Keela, she was sure of that. How did *she* get here? And who was that with her, that small figure — small enough to be a child —

Mica jumped and gave a little scream. "Calwyn! It's *Oron*! Ain't it? Can you see?"

"Yes," breathed Calwyn. Oron and Keela, in league together, somehow . . . It was Oron who had set the Palace going, not Darrow. She felt as if a great weight had lifted from her.

The soldiers loaded the catapult on the plateau, but before they could release the cup, the Palace swung around again and they were forced to scatter. The sharp polished corner of the cube crunched down onto the catapult, splintering it into a thousand pieces and grinding the boulder into dust.

What must it be like inside the Palace? Calwyn had been on a boat tossed by a fierce storm. She remembered her terror as she'd slid helplessly along the deck, not knowing which way the ship would pitch next. She pictured how the Palace's inhabitants would slip on the polished floors, how their heads and limbs would slam into those unforgiving marble walls. Halasaa, Darrow, Heben, the twins — *Goddess, let them be safe!* She put her hands to her head. Was that a voice in her mind, pleading for help? *Halasaa? Is that you?*

"Calwyn, can't you do nothin'?" begged Mica.

Calwyn swayed and clutched at Tonno's hand. She whispered, "I don't know — perhaps —"

"What are you planning, lass?" asked Tonno quietly.

She couldn't reply. The silent cry for help was all around her, vibrating up through her body, pulsing in her blood. It was not Halasaa; it was a greater force, a shapeless power that called to her. *Halasaa! Help me, help me!* But there was no one who could help her. Whatever she did, she must do it alone.

Abruptly she let go of Tonno's hand and sank to her knees in the red dust. She pressed her palms flat down through the thick red dirt to the rock beneath. Just as when she'd sung to the *wasunti*, she felt the power of the land flow into her. The land, the sand, the rock, the desert. Merithuros. The wounded land, the suffering land.

"Calwyn? What are you doin'?"

Mica's voice came to her faint and dreamlike. The clamor in her mind, the call for help, was more insistent: She must answer.

She closed her eyes. *I will try. I will try.* The power flowed through her hands, into the land, and from the land back into her, a seamless circle, a looping river.

> *From the river, the sea;*
> *From the sea, the rains;*
> *From the rains, the river.*

Her lips moved, but she did not know what she sang. Halasaa's voice came back to her. *Breathe.* And she breathed. The rhythm of the land's breath was infinitely slow, as slow as a generation passing. Calwyn could not match that rhythm, but she could begin to sense the immeasurable respiration, a gentle wind that blew past her, around her, through her, an infinite slow *aaah.* In response, her own breath slowed, her heartbeat slowed. Now she was infinitely heavy, connected to the sorrow of the land, and she was infinitely light as she rested there, a dandelion seed, a speck of dust.

Down she reached, deeper and deeper still, through the layers of rock, through seams of gold and emerald, through underground lakes and seas, through rock that crumbled like cheese and rock that was hard as flint, and, at last, the roiling, unquiet liquid rock that flowed beneath all the lands and united them, as the sea flowed and united the surface of Tremaris. That was where Merithuros ended, the land floating like a raft on that red-hot sea. Calwyn held the land beneath her dancing hands as she had held Oron's wounded leg, aware of the whole, aware of the injury to the whole.

But holding on to that awareness was like trying to ride a furious tempest. Oron had been one small being; the life that pulsed through the lands of Merithuros was vast and seething. Trying to grasp its immensity, Calwyn was as helpless as a straw in a gale, as fragile as a scrap of snow in a blizzard. Terrified, she struggled for control.

But at the next moment, the tumult ceased. Suddenly, miraculously, it was as if she herself had become the storm; the wild, surging power was part of her, as she was part of it. Seamlessly, joyfully, she flew, soaring on the currents of becoming, and she saw it all, understood it all, as the power surged through her. In that single instant, she comprehended the whole.

Effortlessly her attention rose, up through all the layers of the land, up again to the surface, and traveled out across the spreading sands. This was where the wound lay, on the land's skin. She saw, she grasped it all. Near the Palace, the troops, the scattered courtiers: fear and confusion. Beyond, in the mountains, the herders and *hegesi*, tracing their wandering tracks across and across the barren plains. And beyond, far beyond, the Clans, and the townsfolk, and the miners, the depleted lands, *arbec* and dry-grass, scuttling *nadi*, and eagles that swooped, across and across the empty sky.

Halasaa's voice echoed from deep in her memory. *Let your strength flow — make it whole!* Exhilarated, she felt the power stream through her. She would, she could knit up this wound!

But even as she allowed herself to form the thought, the thought itself unbalanced her. Her attention slipped. She lost her vision and all her confident sense of power. With a sickening wrench, she was helpless once more, hurled into the teeth of the storm, choking in a boiling cloud of dark poison gas: hatred and fear, the poison that steamed like sulphur from the wounded land. Thrashing panic rose, a part of her, inside and out; she breathed it with every choking breath.

Helpless in the grip of the deep magic she had called up, she knew she could not control it. The hurt that drained the land was too vast. Such a wound could never be healed; the Power of Becoming could never knit up such an injury. She was not strong enough, her gift was too small, and she was alone. Just like Samis, who had tried to summon up chantment greater than he could master, she was overwhelmed.

"Calwyn! Are you all right?" Tonno's voice was warm and urgent in her ear. "Calwyn! The Palace! We have to run!"

Briefly Calwyn returned to herself. The Black Palace loomed above her, the shriek of the pipes piercing her skull. Everywhere people were shouting and screaming. She tried to stand, but she couldn't move.

Black panic engulfed her again, and as she lost herself in her own terror, all the pain of Merithuros entered into her. Unknowing, Calwyn gave a shuddering scream that pierced through the tumult that surrounded her. All her strength, all the light of her being, all the power of her magic, was pouring out of her, through her open hands and out, down into the ground. In that moment, there was no Calwyn; she was part of the land, part of its pain.

The magic flowed from her and through her in an ever-changing, endless circle. *From the river, the sea; from the sea, the rains; from the rains, the river.* She was the river, and the sea, and she was the rains, the black deluge of suffering, the roar of blind rage, the endless weeping of oblivion.

"Calwyn!" Mica screamed. The Palace had changed direction. That uncanny music moaned across the plain as the engine bore down on them. The two tiny figures, one in pink, one in black, were at the very edge of the roof now. Both gestured frantically, flinging out their arms in helpless despair.

"They can't stop it!" gasped Mica. "Reckon they can't steer it neither!"

As if to confirm what she said, the Palace swayed off balance as it careered toward them. Calwyn still knelt on the ground, blind, deaf, paralyzed. In desperation, Tonno seized Calwyn's arm and tugged at it.

"Don't!" screamed Mica, sobbing. "Don't you see, she *can't!* It's chantment — it's *swallowin'* her!"

Calwyn's hands had sunk deep into the rock, and she gazed straight ahead, with unseeing eyes, like a statue. Her face was dead white.

"She's not breathing!" shouted Tonno, white with panic himself, and he shook Calwyn's rigid body by the shoulders.

The sun had all but disappeared. There was a line of vivid red along the western horizon, but that was all. Directly above them, the sky was deep blue-black. It shaded down to the edge of the plain, paler and paler, bleached bone-white where it met the desert sand. The Palace, sleek and inexorable, loomed only three hundred paces away.

Suddenly Calwyn gasped a deep, shuddering breath, as if she had swum up from the depths of the ocean and sucked in the life-giving air as it burst over her head. Dazed, she stared at them, terror and bewilderment in her eyes. Her hands were trapped up to the wrists in the solid rock.

"Calwyn, your hands, free your hands!" shouted Tonno. The Palace was within two hundred paces.

Uncomprehending, Calwyn stared down at her arms, at the rock that had closed over her hands. She moved her lips without a sound, swallowed, and moved them again. A faint croak issued from her throat, and she shook her head.

"I can't," she murmured faintly. "I can't sing. . . ." Limp as a rag doll, she swooned forward into Tonno's arms.

"Calwyn, Calwyn!" cried Mica.

"Like Halasaa," muttered Tonno, his face creased with concern.

As they bent anxiously over Calwyn's slumped body, a lean figure sprinted toward them across the red dust from the Palace. Before they knew it, Darrow was at their side. He threw himself onto his knees beside Calwyn.

"What happened?" he demanded, laying his hand on her pale forehead. Her eyes were closed, her breathing shallow.

"She done some chantment, it were some chantment like Halasaa's, but now she's all sung out, and all for nothin', and the ground's eaten her!" Mica wailed, barely coherent. "And that *thing's* still comin'!"

Darrow stood up. The vast engine leaned toward them, slowly sliding across the red dirt, obliterating garden beds and low stone walls, closer and closer. The soldiers had ceased their attack; they circled the Palace warily but held their fire. And the sorcerers inside the Palace were silent, their chantment hushed. Courtiers hovered, unsure whether to stay or run. The Palace reared above them, only a hundred paces away.

"Mica!" Darrow's voice was quiet but firm as steel. "Stop the winds above the Palace. Hold the air still."

Then slowly, calmly, Darrow raised his hands and sang. Puzzled but obedient, Mica sang too, and as she held back the desert winds that drove the engine, one by one, invisibly, the blocks that had sealed the pipes on the roof of the Palace slid back into place. There were pipes as wide as the trunks of spander trees, and pipes as slim as Darrow's wrist, and every size in between. He knew them all, and one by one, unhurriedly, he sang them shut.

Still the immense cube of the Palace came on, its razor-sharp edge only fifty paces away.

"It's still movin'!" screamed Mica, abandoning her chantment. She flung herself down beside Calwyn and scrabbled with her bare hands at the rock that trapped her friend.

Darrow held up a clenched fist, the hand that bore the ruby ring. He growled out a chantment, and as Tonno and Mica stared, the red stone of the ring wrenched itself free of the gold claws that gripped it, and hung suspended in the air, glowing in the last fiery light of sunset.

For a heartbeat the ring hovered there, between the flat plain and the dome of the sky. Then Darrow flung up his arms toward the looming black silhouette of the Palace, stamped against the emerging stars. The radiant bloodred stone shot up, up, to the roof of the Palace.

Darrow threw back his head and watched it go. "The last pipe," he whispered. "The Pipe of Lyonssar, which is always open. The ring is the only way to seal it, the only way to stop the engine."

As they watched, the Palace slowed, the black edge grinding through the red dirt, forty, thirty, twenty paces away, sliding slower and slower. And then, at last, it was still. A profound silence filled the Dish of Hathara.

In the midst of the silence, a low growl of chantment from Darrow crept across the desert. For a long moment nothing seemed to happen. Then Mica saw the dark-shining speck of the ruby come spinning out of the night to Darrow's clenched fist. The tiny golden claws of the ring reached up to grasp the stone, and it settled back in its place, dark and secret as blood.

Darrow said, "It is finished."

The soldiers stood about, uncertain and whispering. The courtiers began to creep back in fascination to the Palace in its new resting place, close to the edge of the plateau, slightly tilted down the slope. Mica saw that more and more openings had appeared in the walls of the monolith, so that the sheer cliff-face of

the cube was pocked and laced with holes, windows and doors
and peepholes. A face was staring down from every aperture; one
of them was Heben, watching intently, and beside him stood
Fenn, one hand on Heben's shoulder.

For a long frozen moment it was like a picture in a tapestry; the
chanters and the rebels gazed down, and the soldiers and the
courtiers gazed up, trying to read one another's faces.

Night had fallen suddenly as it always did in Merithuros. The
three moons shone brightly, flooding the scene with silver light.
The huge black cube of the Palace loomed at the edge of the escarpment; all around it lay the destroyed walls and gardens of the
plateau, the smashed remains of military equipment, abandoned
helmets and scraps of banners. A great crowd of soldiers and
courtiers was massed at the base of the plateau. Catapults and
courtly baggage littered the red dirt, and bewildered *hegesi* galloped
across the plain. Soldiers stood about in aimless groups, helmets
pushed back, hands on their hips. Here and there, someone stood
stoically having his head bandaged or wincing as a cut was
sponged clean. Disheveled courtiers clutched their embroidered
robes close against the evening chill and picked their way gingerly
across the battlefield to stand with their acquaintances. No one
knew quite what to do.

Darrow stooped to where Calwyn lay; he sang a swift chantment to free her hands from their manacle of rock and lifted her
in his arms.

"We must take her inside," he said.

"Inside there again?" Mica's sharp little face grimaced in reluctance.

Darrow said, "The Black Palace is not what it was. It never will be again. Inside and outside are not so different now."

Tonno lifted his boots, squelching, in . . . could it be . . . *mud*?

Mica gave a sudden yelp and clutched his sleeve. "Tonno! Look!" She pointed down with a shaking hand.

"By the gods," muttered Tonno, dazed and blinking. Surely his eyes were playing tricks on him. It must be one of those chantments of seeming that made you see what wasn't there, because this was impossible.

A spring of water was bubbling up from the place where Calwyn's hands had been. Silent and unstoppable, a clear stream crept out toward the edge of the plateau, then trickled over the escarpment. As Tonno and Mica watched in amazement, the rocks around the mouth of the spring crumbled; Mica leaped back as a sudden roaring rush of water poured out in a silver torrent. She held out her dusty hands to the spray and eagerly splashed her face. She was a child of the ocean, and she had been missing the sea.

Darrow walked steadily around the side of the Palace to the still-open door, carrying Calwyn in his arms. Mica trotted to catch up to him. "Darrow, where'd it come from? Look, it's still spoutin' up!"

Darrow turned his head, and a brief smile flickered across his stern face. "Perhaps the uprooting of the Palace has freed the spring that fed the wells, like pulling a cork from a bottle. Or it might be Calwyn's doing."

"What is it she's done, Darrow?"

A shadow crossed his eyes. "I don't know what she has done, Mica."

A sheet of water spread across the plain, wider and wider, until the plateau where the Palace stood seemed to float on a pewter plate that mirrored back the sheen of the moons' light. Tonno paused to duck his head into the river and shook his wet curls with a sigh of satisfaction. Mica danced with delight.

"It ain't never goin' to stop! It'll be the biggest lake in Tremaris! It'll fill up the whole of Hathara!"

"Perhaps it will." But Darrow was less interested in the lake than he was in taking Calwyn to safety.

The soldiers and courtiers clustered about the sloping walls of the escarpment and shouted up to the chanters. They were not like Mica and Tonno, relishing the embrace of the water. There was real panic in their voices as they yelled, "Let us in, for pity's sake! We'll drown out here!"

One of the chanters leaned far out of one of the new windows and called down to Darrow. "My lord! What would you have us do?"

Without breaking his stride, Darrow called, "Have them throw their weapons into the water, and the rebels' too. Then let them come up."

Children hung out of the windows and laughed at the sight of the bedraggled courtiers as they stumbled through the deepening water, wet hair tumbling over their shoulders, their fine clothes sodden and heavy with mud. But the courtiers responded to the children's giggles with good-natured shrugs rather than insults. The soldiers of the Emperor's Army were surprisingly nonchalant as they tossed their weapons into the widening lake and hurried to the shelter of the tilted Palace. The chanters opened gateways in every wall and waved the invaders inside almost as if they had been looking forward to their arrival. And the rebel fighters chuckled as they threw their sheathed knives from the windows far out into the water, turning it into a game.

Mica saw all this and wondered at it. "What's happened?" she whispered to Darrow. "Why ain't no one fightin'?"

He glanced down at her with a strange expression. "I think we will have to ask Calwyn that."

Soberly Mica looked at Calwyn's pale face as it rested on Darrow's shoulder. "Will she be all right?"

"I don't know," he said grimly.

They had reached the doorway; recognizing his authority, the soldiers and courtiers cleared a path for him to pass. Inside the hall, the chanters welcomed him. And there was someone else too. At the sight of the tall, gaunt figure at the back of the crowd, Darrow's face lit up with joy and relief. "Halasaa! Halasaa, my friend! Welcome back to us."

Calwyn brought me back.

"But — she said she could not heal you."

She has healed far more than what ailed me. She has been part of a powerful chantment. It may be the most powerful magic ever attempted in Tremaris. Halasaa stepped forward with his arms outstretched. *I will take her now. Do what you must. Make her work complete.*

Darrow hesitated, confused. "You mean, she has performed a chantment of healing? A great healing?"

Halasaa nodded, his face both grave and joyful. *She has begun the healing of a land.*

Darrow held Calwyn's limp body close for a moment before he surrendered her to Halasaa's arms. "Thank you, my friend. Take good care of her."

Halasaa bowed his head and bore Calwyn away, vanishing into the shadows. After spending all his life in the treetops, he was more sure-footed than most, for the floors of the Palace were all slightly sloping now. The sorcerers had hastily sung up some chantments to make it easier to walk around, singing some inclines into steps and roughening the slippery floors to give more grip. The children scrambled about, shouting with wild laughter as they skidded and slid, but the sorcerers found themselves suddenly ridiculous, clutching at the long robes that tripped them up and sometimes tumbling down altogether.

Tonno chuckled and said in a low voice, "Won't do them any harm to look foolish for once in their lives."

Darrow gave him a brief, distracted smile, then said abruptly, "I must go. There is much to be done."

Tonno gave him a bow that was only half in mockery. "Be off with you then, my lord."

As he watched his old friend hurry away, instantly surrounded by a murmuring crowd of chanters seeking instructions, he said thoughtfully to Mica, "I reckon this life might suit him. Lord of the Black Palace. If he throws his dice right, he might find himself ruler of Merithuros yet."

"What'll he be if there ain't no more emperors?" Mica frowned. It was a serious matter to be a friend of an almost emperor.

Tonno clapped her on the shoulder. "We'd best go after Halasaa, see if there's anything we can do for Calwyn."

But they were only partway down the corridor when they were halted by a cry of "Wait!" and saw Heben loping after them. "If you please, Darrow wants us to go to the roof," he panted. "We're to find the two who opened the pipes and bring them down."

It took the searchers a long time to find them. The moons had wheeled through half their nightly journey and the bells for midnight had chimed, before Mica heard a faint noise from within one of the star-seers' huts.

"Over here!" she yelled, and Tonno and Heben came running.

Keela was crouched inside, her pink silk dress stained with dust, her hair a ruined tangle. She lifted her wide ice-blue eyes arrogantly to the silent group at the door of the hut.

"It wasn't me," she declared at once. "I didn't have *anything* to do with it. It was *him*." She pointed to where Oron huddled, nearly invisible, in a corner. He lifted a sullen face to them.

Heben gripped Keela's arm. "Dog!" she exclaimed. "How dare you touch a princess of the Royal House!"

Wordlessly Heben hauled her to her feet, and when she spat in his eye, he wiped it away without flinching.

"How'd you know what to do?" demanded Mica. "How'd you know how to start it?"

Keela indicated Oron with the merest twitch of her hand. "He heard your master talking."

"Our master?" Mica's forehead crinkled. "Oh, you mean Darrow!"

"*She* told me to spy on them!" blurted Oron. "*She* made me un-block the pipes! I didn't know what was going to happen!"

"Enough!" said Tonno sternly. "Save your stories for Darrow."

All the soldiers, all the courtiers, had come inside. There had never been so much noise and bustle in the silent corridors of the Black Palace.

Through the night Darrow was the calm center in a storm of activity. With Fenn by his side, and the Council of Three, and the commander of the Army, he directed the distribution of bedding and food and other necessities. But when they brought Keela and Oron before him, he waved everyone else aside.

"We found 'em on the roof," said Mica eagerly.

"She made me do it," repeated Oron sullenly, staring at his feet. "She said she'd kill me if I didn't do what she wanted."

"Surely you won't take the word of a dirty, lying little boy over that of the Third Princess of the Empire!" exclaimed Keela with a toss of her head.

At that Darrow raised an eyebrow. "It may have escaped your notice, my lady, but there is no Empire anymore. Perhaps that means there are no princesses, either."

Keela's eyes narrowed. "You speak treason," she said haughtily. "There will always be an Empire. And I will *always* be a princess." As she spoke, her gaze swept about the room, searching for familiar faces. Suddenly, imperiously, she called out, "Immel!"

A tall man on the other side of the room turned to look at her, but his face registered nothing. There were other courtiers in the room, but though they had been her followers at court, they also avoided her gaze, as if they were embarrassed. One or two even shuffled from the room. Keela stared after them, momentarily nonplussed. Then she drew herself upright and curled her lip with as much arrogance as before.

Mica put in, "Her name's Keela. She was friends with Calwyn when we was at the Palace of Cobwebs."

Keela patted the ruin of her hair. "I only befriended her because Amagis begged me. Such a dull little thing!" She glanced at Darrow flirtatiously from beneath her long lashes, but he stared back at her, unmoved.

"Tell me why you set off the engine."

"Well, I was so frightened when I saw all those soldiers! I do *hate* fighting!" Keela smoothed her skirts with a coy smile, a gesture that belonged to another time. She realized it and stopped. "I thought if they saw the machine move, then everyone would stop *attacking* one another — I wanted to stop people being *hurt!*"

"She's lying!" Oron burst out. "She wanted to find a way to rule the sorcerers, and to show the Army how powerful she was! She made me follow Calwyn and spy on you! She made me tell her about the engine and how to set it going!"

"So we made it go." Keela shrugged. "But he couldn't make it stop." She gave Oron a scornful look. "I was only trying to *help*," she wheedled, her head on one side.

Darrow said dryly, "I think not."

"There's more!" cried Oron. "She wants to be the empress! She wants her half brother, the prince, to be emperor! *That's* her plan. Make her tell!"

Keela was staring at Darrow. "I know you," she said slowly. "I have met you before." She began to smile. "My brother introduced us!"

Darrow's face was expressionless. "It is many years since I visited the Palace of Cobwebs. I'm afraid I don't remember you."

"You don't remember *me?*" Keela echoed incredulously. "Are you sure?"

But Mica had turned pale beneath her golden tan; she clutched at Tonno's arm.

"Her *brother*! A prince!" Suddenly she flung herself at Keela and pummeled her with her fists. "Who is it, what's his name? Is it him, is it Samis?"

Keela tried to push the furious girl away. "Stop it, stop it! How dare you touch me? Yes, yes, his name is Samis, our true prince, my half brother, the emperor who *will be*. You'll all be sorry when he comes to claim what's his!"

"Mica, let her alone!" barked Tonno.

Freed from Mica's breathless attack, Keela smoothed her hair. "It makes no difference, you silly little girl. None of you can stop him. When he returns, he will knock down all *this* like a pile of children's blocks." She waved a derisive hand around the bustling room, then turned to Darrow. "As for *you* —" she hissed. Flirting had not worked; she let her hatred blaze forth. "*You* will be especially sorry. You called yourself his friend! Traitor!"

Darrow said, "I have bad news, Keela. Your prince is dead this half year."

Keela tossed back her head. "You're mistaken," she said silkily. "Amagis saw him, and spoke to him, not three turns of the moons ago."

"Liar!" cried Mica. "I seen his dead body myself!"

Keela smiled, a secretive, infuriating smile. She twirled a lock of hair around her finger and said nothing.

"Liar!" said Mica again, but with less conviction. She darted a look of alarm at Tonno and Darrow. Darrow's face was closed and unreadable.

"Where is he then?" demanded Tonno. "Here, in Merithuros?"

Heben, who had not spoken, said softly, "Mica, didn't you say, at the Palace of Cobwebs, that Amagis had just come back from Gellan?"

Keela's impudent expression did not change, but her smile froze, and she turned her face away.

Darrow drew Tonno and Mica aside. He said, with a trace of bitter humor, "It would not surprise me. He always did feel at home among the tricksters of Gellan."

"But he can't be alive!" whispered Mica passionately. "We saw him killed, we all did, when Trout brought down the tower in Spareth!"

Soberly Tonno shook his head. "We saw him lying there, lass. But don't forget, he's a master of seeming. Mebbe he made it so we'd believe he was dead."

"But Trout ain't never tricked by spells of seemin', and he thought he were dead."

"Trout never went close to his body. None of us did except —"

They both turned to look at Darrow. His gray-green gaze was level and enigmatic. "The Power of Seeming works best when you want to believe what you are seeing," he said. "On that night, I cannot deny it, I wanted to see Samis dead."

"He ain't alive." Mica's mouth became a stubborn line. "He *ain't.*"

Darrow made an impatient, dismissive gesture. "There will be time enough later to find out."

"What'll you do with 'em?" Mica nodded back to Keela and Oron. The boy shuffled from foot to foot on the sloping floor, but Keela had found a bench to perch on and preened herself under Heben's watchful gaze.

Darrow ran a hand through his hair. "Guard them, until it is time to bring them to judgment. Tonno, I entrust you with that duty. Heben, I have other work for you, once the prisoners are secured."

Heben bowed his head solemnly. Darrow turned to Oron, and his stern voice was tempered with gentleness. "You are young, and you have suffered. That does not excuse you, but it will be remembered when it is time to decide your punishment. Keela —" His voice grew more steely. "There can be no excuse for what you have done this day. Take her away."

"On your feet, my lady," said Heben, with only a shade less than his usual courtesy.

As they left the room, they passed close to one of the new windows, and they paused to look outside. The silver pool had edged out and out, wider and wider, deeper and deeper, until it lapped at the very horizon, a vast rippling lake where the dry dust had been. The three moons sailed high in the sky, and three moons glimmered on the water.

Keela shivered and turned her head away. "I don't like it," she whispered, and for once she spoke from the heart. "It frightens me. It's not natural, so much water in one place."

"This is nothing," said Heben, with a touch of world-weary pride. "Wait until you see the ocean."

Even before the disgraced pair and their guards had left the room, Darrow was besieged once more. That night, he listened until his ears rang and talked until he was hoarse. "I'm sorry, my lady, there are no scented soaps or private bathrooms here. But one of the children will show you the washing rooms downstairs. . . . Brothers of the Army, I appeal to you, for the sake of Merithuros, to remain true to your ideals of courage, and service, and mutual help. . . . Children, I need you to open more windows, more colonnades. Let in the air and the moonlight. . . . Those of you who want to stay are welcome. Yes, I will arrange for the rest of you to return home. . . . Yes, Lord Sorcerer, I understand that the ancient grievances still rankle. But if you can lay them aside, we will build a future where chanters do not need to hide away. . . . Fenn, your brother and sister rebels will have a most important role in building the new republic. Tell them to think carefully about the shape it will take. I will speak to them soon. . . . Heben! I have a task for you. I need to send messengers to all the Clans. Tell them what has happened, and invite them to join in the building of the new Merithuros. Word the messages with care. We will need the Clans, but they must realize that they will have to work with the others. The days when the Clans lorded it over the rest of the Empire are gone."

"I understand," said Heben solemnly, and there was a glow of excitement about him as he set off to see to his task. Darrow watched him go with a thoughtful expression in his eyes.

Finally, just before dawn, Darrow asked each group to choose representatives to meet in a grand council the following day. "And then our real work will begin."

Somehow Calwyn had created a precious space of goodwill and calm; he could not know how long it would last, and they had to act quickly. The new Merithuros could not be built in the space of a single night, but they could lay a foundation, while the precarious healing held, to secure a peaceful future for the years to come.

When at last Darrow was left alone, he sat for a time with his hands pressed to his eyes. He was weary beyond imagining; he feared that if he relaxed even for a moment, the whole delicate structure would collapse again into chaos. And yet he was alive with a strange energy: the energy of a power that was not magic, a worldly power, an authority he had never suspected in himself.

Presently he took his hands from his eyes. He covered one hand with the other, the Ring of Lyonssar between them. He had taken the ring from Samis's cold, bloodless finger. Was it possible that Samis still lived, that even now he was in Gellan? Darrow could well believe that Amagis had lied to Keela for reasons of his own. But he would have to find out for certain. He could feel the steady, reassuring pulse of the jewel, like a second heart.

Slowly he rose and crossed the room. Between the doorjamb and the wall was a crack, only as wide as a hair. With a careful chantment he prized it apart, inserted his fingers into the hollow, and drew out a tiny carving. It was a wooden hawk, as high as his thumb, wings folded, head turned, like the birds that perched on the roof of the Palace and scanned the desert for prey.

Samis had called him Heron. But Calwyn always said, *You look like a hawk.* He would never be Heron again.

He closed his hand around the little carving and went to Calwyn.

She lay in the bed that Halasaa had occupied, and Halasaa had taken her post beside it. He looked up as Darrow entered.

"How is she?"

She is sleeping. The swoon has passed.

Darrow drew up a stool and clasped the hand that lay limply on the covers. He looked at her pale face, the dark plait over one shoulder.

"I'm glad you are here to watch over her, Halasaa. I'm glad you are recovered. We were afraid for you."

The sickness in this land has begun to heal, and I am healing with it. Thanks to Calwyn.

"Have you ever heard of anyone healing a land before?"

No. It is a remarkable thing. But every chantment of healing has its price. And this has cost her dearly.

Darrow looked up; Halasaa's bright eyes watched him across the bed. Gently Halasaa touched Calwyn's face with the tips of his brown fingers: her eyes, her mouth, her forehead.

She has lost the gift of chantment.

Darrow looked down at her hand, and his own hand holding it. The ruby ring seemed dull now, an ordinary stone, dark and colorless, like muddied water. He said blankly, "But that can't be. The gift, once given, cannot be taken away. And besides —" He stopped.

Go on. Halasaa's voice was gentle.

Darrow looked at him keenly. "You know it, don't you? She is the one. She should be — what Samis wanted, the Singer of All Songs. She will be, one day."

Halasaa shook his head. *Not now. She has lost it all. Like Samis, she reached beyond her strength. She was not ready for such a powerful magic. It almost consumed her.*

"No!" said Darrow fiercely, and he leaped to his feet, letting Calwyn's hand fall. He strode around the small, dark room. "No. No."

The Power of Tongue remains, perhaps. Perhaps not even that. The flame has almost gone out.

Darrow stopped pacing and gave a bitter laugh. "All this time, I would not see it, I did not want to see it. I would not speak to her of it, I never *helped* her. She bore that burden alone. I was too proud. And now — now it is too late —" He sank down again on the stool and buried his head in his hands.

Halasaa moved silently to his side, and laid his hand on his friend's shoulder. *It is not too late for you to help her. She has never needed your help more.*

Darrow felt the pressure of Halasaa's hand lift from him and heard only the faintest sound as he walked from the room and left him alone with Calwyn.

He put the little carving of the hawk into her hand and folded it in both of his. And whether it was the warm clasp of his hands or the words he whispered to her, by the time the bells struck for sunrise Calwyn had opened her eyes.

From the River, the Sea

Some days later, Calwyn sat with Mica on a newly opened terrace on the southern side of the Palace, where the sun was warm but not too strong. The Palace stood straight now; for the first time, all the iron-chanters had sung together to haul it level. The children had decorated the walls with friezes like those that had adorned the Palace of Cobwebs, and the long wall behind the two girls bloomed with stone flowers and fruiting vines and *nadi* frozen in mid-scamper.

"Do you want another cushion, Cal? A glass of that cordial?"

"No, I don't need anything. Don't fuss, Mica." Calwyn turned her head restlessly. For all her protests, she still felt shamefully weak. And the raw pain of the loss of her powers was as keen as the first moment she'd realized they had gone. The loss of a limb or the loss of her sight could not have been more devastating. It was like a terrible dream, a dream from which she struggled to wake but could not.

That first morning, she had sent Darrow and Halasaa away, not wanting them to witness what she knew, deep in her heart, would happen. She sat up in the narrow bed, in that dim room, with a tin cup of water in her hand, and she had sung the simplest of all the chantments of ice, the first song that the novices learned in Antaris. The words seemed to stick in her throat; at first she thought that was the trouble. But soon the words returned to her. She sang the simple chantment again and again, staring stupidly at the water that would not harden into ice. Not the third time, nor the tenth, nor the twenty-seventh. Nothing she tried could unlock magic that refused to flow.

Even as she sang, she knew it was all wrong. The song fell dead from her lips. Nothing stirred within her; the familiar thrilling tingle of her skin as the power rose never came.

At last she'd fallen silent, still staring into the cup. Someone had knocked at her door, and she'd screamed, "Go away! Go away!" With her eyes screwed shut, the cup hurled away and the water spilled, the noise of her screaming filled the inside of her head with red light, until Darrow came and held her tightly and muffled her desperate cries against his shoulder. He held her until her screams became dry, racking sobs, and then she thrust him away.

Since that morning she had not let him touch her. She could see that it hurt him, but she couldn't help it; it was more than she could endure.

Mica could only guess at what her friend felt, but Calwyn preferred her clumsy sympathy to the bluff incomprehension of Tonno, who had never known chantment and could not understand what she had lost. She'd heard him mutter to Darrow, "I can't sing. Never hurt me. Life's simpler without it, I reckon. Nothing to break your heart over, anyway."

"It isn't *your* heart, Tonno," Darrow had retorted sharply, and Calwyn had felt a fierce stab of gratitude.

But it was painful for her to watch Darrow. He moved about the Palace so briskly and wore his power so lightly. At every moment he was surrounded by petitioners and beset by large and petty demands. He kept Heben always by his side, and soon Heben was swamped with supplicants too. The first Council of the new Republic was held. Representatives of the Seven Clans and the miners of Phain and Geel were expected within days for an even greater council.

Heben had surprised everyone by insisting that women be included in the councils.

"They've all agreed — for now," Darrow told Calwyn wryly. "We must establish Council practice before they remember that they despise women even more than they despise sea dwellers. Ah, well. Perhaps the generation that comes after this one will be more tolerant."

"The next generation!" Mica widened her eyes, and Darrow had laughed.

"I must plan a long way ahead. An Empire might be destroyed in a day, but it will take twenty years to build the Republic to replace it." He looked at Calwyn, and his face became serious.

"Without you, Calwyn, none of this would be possible. You have given Merithuros the most valuable of gifts: a space of generosity and willingness to listen."

He put out his hand to her, but she did not take it. She said nothing. Empire or Republic, it made no difference to her. What did she care for Merithuros and its councils and its votes and speeches? Darrow cared passionately; Darrow belonged here. She had never seen him so full of purpose, so energetic, so cheerful. He was happy. She had never, in all the time she'd known him, seen him happy before.

Her hand went to her throat, where the little hawk hung from a silver chain. She thought of another gift Darrow had carved for her, over a year ago, the wooden globe that she kept beside her bed in the cottage on Ravamey. *At home,* she told herself. The word tasted strange on her tongue. But many words seemed strange to her now; even the gift of speech had been tainted.

Mica's voice dragged her back from her thoughts. She was leaning over the edge of the balcony, peering through the looking-tube across the shimmering lake.

"Look at Tonno down there! He's teachin' 'em how to make boats! They don't like it one bit!" She gave a gurgle of laughter. "Halasaa's there too. Can't see what he's doin' —" She craned her head. "He says he'll plant trees, and more *arbec,* and —" She stopped. "What was that other thing? Pearl-grass?"

Calwyn looked up listlessly. "He wants to sow pearl-grass in the lake," she said. "It's a marsh plant, a grain. It grows in shallow water."

"He says he'll make a garden, good as the one at home." Mica stole a glance at Calwyn. "Sounds like he's plannin' to stay here a good long time. Who'd have thought it?"

Calwyn shifted restlessly on her cushion. Halasaa was happy too. What kind of person was she, that the happiness of others only seemed to deepen her own misery?

"The twins is stayin' too, with Heben. Shada reckons Darrow wants to make Heben his — what do you call it? Like first mate to the captain."

Calwyn shook her head mutely.

"His deputy, that's it. Heben and Fenn together, if the Council agrees." Mica slid onto a neighboring cushion and gave a sudden giggle. "Remember when Heben first come to us askin' for help, and he said he never wanted to be emperor? Looks like he might end up bein' the next best thing!"

"Marna used to say one of the best signs of being fitted for power is a reluctance to hold it," said Calwyn. She had been thinking of Marna more and more in the last days.

"Cal," said Mica suddenly. "What if we take some of them chanter kids home with us to Ravamey? Start that college you was talkin' about last winter?"

Calwyn stared at her. "How can we possibly do that?" she asked sharply. "When I can't even sing anymore?"

"Well, I thought . . . maybe you could still *teach* 'em." Mica shrugged and looked away, embarrassed. Then, with relief, she caught sight of someone approaching and smiled. "Here comes

Darrow!" She sighed. "I can't never remember to call him 'my lord,'" she said plaintively. She scrambled to her feet and waved cheerfully to Darrow, who for once was alone.

Calwyn looked up in alarm. "Don't go, Mica!"

"I'm not sittin' here like a third oar in a rowboat when you two want to talk to each other."

"But I don't —" cried Calwyn desperately. But Mica had already skipped away.

At first it seemed that there had been no reason for Mica to go. Darrow settled himself beside Calwyn and stared out at the silver lake. The ruby ring gleamed on his finger. For a moment Calwyn was seized by a vivid desire to see him hurl the stolen Ring of Lyonssar into the shining water, to throw away the Lordship of the Black Palace with all its duties and its glories and be her Darrow once more. As she watched, Darrow twisted the ring around his finger, and she almost believed he would do it. But then he let his hands rest on his knees, foursquare, like a king, with the ring still in its place.

"How are you feeling today, Calwyn?"

"Quite well, thank you," said Calwyn irritably. She was tired of people asking her how she felt, as if she had a fever, when what ailed her was a different kind of sickness entirely.

"This is a pleasant spot." Darrow spoke with exaggerated cheerfulness, ignoring her tone. "I wish I had more time to enjoy these splendid views."

"I don't want to keep you from your duties," said Calwyn, tight-lipped.

Darrow looked at her. "I wish there was something I could do."

"Well, there isn't. You can't help me. Halasaa can't help me. No one can."

There was a pause. From far below floated the sound of a splash, and hearty laughter. Darrow smiled. "Tonno's boating lessons are progressing well."

Calwyn pleated the hem of her tunic between her fingers and said nothing.

Darrow stretched his legs out in front of him. "Have you heard the news? Your friend, the princess, has escaped."

At that Calwyn looked up. "Keela's escaped? How?"

"The soldier assigned to guard her could not resist her charms. The current spirit of forgiveness was very useful to her! None of Tonno's boats is missing, so she must have waded through the lake." Darrow grimaced. "She has some courage, I will grant her that. I sent searchers after her at once, but I fear we've lost her."

"Where do you think she's gone?"

Darrow looked at her. "To Gellan, I imagine," he said dryly. "To join her brother."

"You believe her, then? You think Samis is alive?"

"Keela believes that he is. Nothing else could make her cross that water. Before this, I was not inclined to believe her. But now — I am not sure."

"You know, when we were in Spareth, after — when we thought he was dead —" Calwyn spoke slowly, feeling for the elusive words. "Do you remember Halasaa's dance? I had such a sense of the life in everything, after that. And I did think, I did think I could still sense the flame in Samis. But I thought it must just be that the sense was so new to me, it was all jumbled up —"

She stopped abruptly. That day, the sense of becoming had been so new to her, so exhilarating. For the first time, she had been able to perceive that flicker of life in all beings, the glow, the energy that animated everything. She had been so filled with joy; she remembered how she'd laughed with delight as she caught Halasaa's eye, sharing their gift. But now — now everything was dead to her. The light, the flame had gone. It was all dull, all disconnected. Savagely she wiped at her eyes. How she hated Darrow to see her weep!

"I will go to Gellan," said Darrow. "I must."

Calwyn looked at him in horror. So helpless herself, the thought of Darrow going into danger clutched at her heart. "But . . . your work is here!" she stammered.

"All our work will be undone if Samis lives. I must be sure."

"Then send someone else!" cried Calwyn. "Send — send Heben!"

Darrow laughed. "I could not send anyone to face Samis who was not armed with chantment. This is a task I must undertake myself. Heben can stay here. Since his father has disowned him, he does not owe allegiance to any of the Clans, but he understands

them inside and out. He and Fenn will fill my place until I return."
He looked at Calwyn swiftly. He said, "I would ask you to come
with me, Calwyn. But —"

Calwyn laughed bitterly. "There's no need to say it. I'd only be
a burden to you, like *this*."

"It isn't that," said Darrow, but he couldn't meet her eyes.

"I wish I could go!" she cried with sudden passion. "I wish I
could fight him! I wish I could do *something*, anything! I wish my
hands had been cut off, rather than this!"

Darrow opened his mouth to speak, hesitated, and closed it
again. He shifted on his cushion, folding one leg beneath him. At
last he said, "I know this is small comfort, but there are many
things you can do in the world without magic. Not one in a thousand people in Tremaris has the gift of chantment. The rest must
find some way to live."

Calwyn gestured impatiently. "I know. Tonno has told me how
lucky I am to have my youth, to have — friends — who care for
me. . . ." She did not look at Darrow. "But I'm not *whole*. I will never
be whole again." She dropped her head, and this time she didn't
bother to dash away her tears. "Perhaps it's a punishment from
the Goddess," she whispered. "For Ched, and Amagis, and the
ones who were killed when the Palace fell. Halasaa says that every
healing has its price. Surely every death must have its price too."

Darrow frowned. "The Goddess would never punish you for
what you have done here. Calwyn, in helping to heal this land, you
have saved many more lives than you've had a part in ending!" He

reached for her hand, but she flinched from his touch. "I came to ask if you would stay here, until I return from Gellan."

"No," she said at once, surprising herself. She hadn't realized that she had made up her mind already, and so firmly. "No. I can't."

In a low voice, he said, "I would like you to stay. I would like to think of you here — safe —"

"Oh — Darrow." She looked up at last. "I can't stay here."

There was a pause. "If you are sure," he said carefully. "I will not try to persuade you. Tonno will sail with me to Gellan. We could take you and Mica home to Ravamey, and Halasaa perhaps, though he might remain here a little longer, I think. Trout will be missing you. . . ." He saw her face. "What is it?"

She shook her head. "I had — such dreams, on Ravamey. I can't bear to go back there, not while I'm like *this*." She gazed bleakly across the bright sheet of the lake. "But where else is there for me to go?"

From somewhere behind them came the sound of children's laughter and the patter of bare feet as they chased each other across the polished floor.

Darrow said, "You might go to the mountains. Back to Antaris."

Calwyn looked up at him quickly, and he saw a light in her eyes that he had not seen for many days. "The mountains! Oh, I have been so homesick for the mountains!"

Slowly Darrow nodded. "If there's anywhere you might be healed, that will be the place."

The light in her eyes died, like a candle blown out, and she looked away. "I can't hope for that."

"I understand." His voice was quiet. "Calwyn. If you can wait until I return, I will come with you."

Her breath caught in her throat. *He will come* — There was nothing she would like more in the world. To make the same journey in reverse that they had made together the previous summer, across the plains and up into the mountains, to walk day after day with Darrow at her side. And perhaps, at the end of it, to be healed — She had to speak quickly; if she waited, even for a heartbeat, she couldn't trust herself to give the answer she must give.

"No," she said firmly. "No. I couldn't just sit here, not knowing what was happening to you. I couldn't bear it. And you couldn't come back and then leave again so soon. Your place is here. You must finish the work you have begun."

"The work *you* have begun," he said, and there was such tenderness in his voice that the silver water danced and blurred before Calwyn's eyes.

"I want you to make me two promises," said Darrow, with the note of steely command he had recently acquired. "Firstly, that you will be careful. Do not travel alone. Take someone with you, Halasaa, or Mica. Even Trout, if you can drag him from his workshop."

Calwyn nodded mutely.

"And secondly, if you don't find what you are seeking —" His voice dropped. "Or if you do find it — whatever happens — promise me that you will come back."

Calwyn found that she couldn't answer. Darrow touched her cheek. His gray-green eyes were half-smiling, half-stern. "If you don't make that promise, then I will have to exercise my authority as the Lord of the Black Palace, and keep you imprisoned here."

She tried to smile. Words choked in her throat just as they did when she tried to sing chantment. She whispered, "I would like to promise, but —"

"You can't?" Darrow's voice was suddenly harsh.

Calwyn stared at her hands.

"Well," said Darrow, after a pause, in the same dry, brittle voice. "If you will not promise to wait for me, then I must wait for you." He stood up. Softly he said, "You were the one, Calwyn, who taught me never to give up hope."

Blindly Calwyn reached out a hand to him, but already he had turned and begun to walk back along the terrace.

"Darrow!" she whispered, but he didn't hear her, and as she watched, his lean black-clad figure merged into the shadows of the Black Palace, and only the golden light of the dying sun remained.

Look for Book Three in The Chanters of Tremaris Trilogy

The Tenth Power

The forest was a sheet of white, streaked with charcoal and daubed with blue shadow. Snowdrifts were heaped beneath the trees, and each twig was outlined with a silvery coat of frost. Day after day the freeze had continued, and the sky was a clear, crisp blue. Here and there, the tracks of birds and burrowers marked the coverlet of snow, but bears and other animals dozed, waiting for the sun's warmth to wake them. They could not know that this winter had lasted too long, and the time for spring's return had already passed.

The only sign of movement in the vast silence of the forest came from three small figures, stark shadows against the snow, their breath puffing in the air.

Calwyn tucked the end of her dark plait securely into the hood of her fur-lined cloak and kicked snow over the remains of the fire. Smoke and steam rose with a hiss. It was midday, but the sunlight was weak and watery where it filtered through the trees.

Calwyn's face ached with the cold, and her eyes were sore from squinting into the glare. Under her cloak, she wore a padded jacket, thick trousers, and several layers of woollen undershirts and tunics. A sharp hunting knife hung from a sheath at her belt, and she wore a small wooden hawk on a silver chain around her throat. Rabbit-skin mittens protected her hands, and a woollen scarf partly hid her face. Her dark eyes stared out beneath straight eyebrows, level and watchful. Calwyn did not often smile these days.

Balanced on iron blades strapped to her boots, Calwyn crunched across the snow to where her companions squatted by the bank of the frozen river. She was taller, stronger, and, at eighteen, a little older than her two young friends. This was her journey. She was taking them to the place she thought of as home: Antaris, locked away behind its great Wall of Ice. They had been traveling for more than twenty days, almost a turn of the moons. They'd been lucky with the weather; in all that time the freeze had held, and there had been no snowstorms. But even so, the journey from the coastal city of Kalysons had not been easy: They had skated along the shore of the Bay of Sardi — frozen across for the first time in living memory — then upriver through the mountains.

Calwyn watched as Trout and Mica, heads close together, struggled with Mica's skate blade. Trout looked tired, and when Mica glanced up, Calwyn saw the bruise of shadows under her eyes.

"You see the moons last night, Cal?" she asked eagerly. "It were the Whale's Mouth."

It was the formation that the priestesses of Antaris called the Goat and Two Kids. "Yes," said Calwyn. "The middle of spring."

"So why's it still winter?" Mica shivered. "It ain't right. I don't like it. Remember when you sung up ice for me that first time, Cal, and I got so excited? Reckon I've seen enough ice and snow now to last me all my life."

"I remember," said Calwyn shortly. Mica's face fell.

"Don't wriggle, Mica." Trout frowned with concentration as he tugged at the leather thong that fastened Mica's skate to her boot. He was seventeen now, a serious young man, no longer the nervous boy that Calwyn had met almost two years before. But his blue eyes were still round and questioning, and his thatch of brown hair still flopped untidily over his forehead. As usual, his bootlaces were strung through the wrong holes, and one of his coat buttons dangled by a thread. He sat back on his heels. "There, that should hold it."

"Trout, it's too tight! My foot'll fall off!" Mica winced as she wriggled a finger through the lacings. She too had grown up in the past year; she had become a striking young woman, with her golden eyes and thick, honey-colored hair. But she looked miserable now; her nose was red and swollen, her lips were chapped, and her eyes streamed with the cold.

"Better too tight than too loose," said Trout mildly. "You'll twist your ankle again if you're not careful."

"Look." Calwyn opened her mittened hand and showed them a prickly sprig. "It's bitterthorn. Ursca uses it to dull pain and help bring sleep. It grows near the Wall."

"So there ain't far to go?" Mica's face brightened.

"We'll reach Antaris by nightfall."

"At last!" muttered Trout fervently. "Hot baths, clean clothes, a proper bed!"

"The beds in the Dwellings are hard, Trout," said Calwyn. "The sisters of Antaris live simply. Don't expect luxury."

"But they have mattresses?" Trout squinted through the glass lenses that perched on his freckled nose. "We won't have to sleep on the ground?"

"Of course not," said Calwyn irritably.

"Antaris must be like Emeran, where me and Grandma lived," said Mica wistfully. "Like when all the men went out to sea, fishin', and all the women was left behind together. Even better, cos there ain't no pirates. We had good times, peaceful, all singin' and that, with no men racketin' around."

"What's wrong with having men around?" asked Trout, slightly hurt.

"I don't mind *you*. Boys is all right."

Trout screwed up his face and hauled Mica to her feet. Born in the Isles of Firthana, where snow and ice were unknown, Mica was far from steady on her skates, though her skills had improved greatly since the start of their journey.

She slid out onto the frozen river, whirling her arms wildly. Layers of wool and fur made her as round as a little barrel, and only a few strands of tousled hair poked out from her knitted cap. In the middle of the river, she wiped her nose on her sleeve and began to sing a high, lilting chantment of the winds. The snow-drifts, fallen branches, and the slush of dead leaves on the ice blew aside, clearing a path for them.

"Mica! Don't forget the Clarion!" called Trout. He held out the precious, golden Clarion of the Flame, the last relic of the Power of Fire. At first, Mica had been wary of using such a powerful artifact, almost too nervous to bring it to her lips, but now the slim little trumpet was an old friend. Without the magic of the Clarion to keep them warm, to start their campfires, to clear the snow from their snug tent, and to light their way when the dark drew in every afternoon, the three travelers could not have survived this journey. Even when it was not being played to summon the chantments of fire, the Clarion glowed with a steady, comforting warmth. Mostly, Calwyn and Trout let Mica hold it; she had to be warm to sing her chantments, and she suffered from the cold more than they did.

Mica skated back, grabbed the Clarion, and tucked it inside her jacket. "Brr, that's better! This'll stop my throat-ache." With a brave grin, she wobbled away again.

Trout was a better skater than Mica. As a student in Mithates, he had skated every winter. He'd told Calwyn and Mica about skating parties on the River Amith, with races and picnics and dancing on the ice. That was strange to Calwyn. In Antaris, where each novice must cross the black ice of the sacred pool to become an initiated priestess, skating was a skill to be exercised with respect, not a matter for fun and games.

But Trout was not reckless. He was a sturdy, dependable skater who never showed off. Now he and Calwyn tugged on the pack harnesses and set off in stride together.

"Wait for us, Mica!" Calwyn called. "How many times do I have to tell you, it's not safe!"

With a tremendous effort, Mica halted her headlong glide. "You say that every day, but the ice ain't broke once yet!" she yelled, her breath a white cloud.

"You don't know the signs of thin ice, Mica. Keep to the edges."

"Don't be cross with me, Cal," said Mica plaintively, but in truth she was tired, and relieved to drop behind the others.

For a time, the only sound was Mica's high, eerie song of chantment, and the steady swish of blades on ice.

"Calwyn," said Trout in a low voice. "Don't be too harsh with Mica. This journey hasn't been easy for her, you know."

"It isn't easy for any of us," snapped Calwyn. "You think it's easy for me?"

"No, no — I mean — I know why you're in such a bad mood all the time. . . ."

"If you know so much, then why talk about it?"

Scowling, Calwyn tucked her chin into her scarf and scanned the river ahead. Once, if she had seen a crack in the ice, she could have sung a swift chantment to seal it. Once, she would have made this journey singing softly all the way. And as Mica sang to clear their path, Calwyn could have sung to strengthen the ice beneath them.

Not so long ago, Calwyn had been a chanter, a gifted chanter. Most chanters of Tremaris could sing the chantments of only one of the Nine Powers. Calwyn had been taught the Power of Ice by the sisters of Antaris, and then she had learned the chantments of the winds from Mica. She had also sung the songs of the Power of Beasts, which tamed animals. And in Merithuros, half a year ago, she'd begun to learn the chantments of ironcraft, the power that moved everything of the earth except air, fire, and water.

It was all gone. All her gifts of magic were lost. *Merithuros stole them from me*, she thought bitterly, though at the time she had given herself freely to try to heal that dry and troubled land. But the task had overwhelmed her — and now this never-ending winter seemed a cruel joke at her expense, reminding her every day of what she'd lost. Her fists clenched hard, and the crushed fragments of the bitterthorn twig crumbled and blew away across the ice.

Trout ventured a change of subject. "Steel blades would be better than iron. Stronger. Lighter too. Do you ever use steel skate blades in Antaris, Calwyn?"

"We have steel knives," said Calwyn, dragging her thoughts from her own misery. "But metal's very precious in Antaris: The traders have to carry it to us all the way through the mountains. We use bone blades for skating."

It felt strange to Calwyn to say *we* of the priestesses of Antaris. Almost two years had passed since she had run away with Darrow, the Outlander who had breached the ice Wall. So much had happened in that time. She had traveled across oceans and through deserts. She had seen the fabled Palace of Cobwebs and walked the desolate streets of Spareth, the city abandoned by the Ancient Ones. She and her friends had fought Samis, the most dangerous sorcerer Tremaris had ever seen, and they had defeated him — or so they'd thought.

There were reports that Samis was alive and hiding in Gellan. Certainly his half sister, Keela, believed so; she had fled from Merithuros to join him there. Now Darrow, with Tonno and Halasaa, had traveled north to the Red City.

The thought of Darrow was, as always, bittersweet. Darrow had carved the little wooden hawk that Calwyn wore at her throat. He had become her friend, then more than a friend. But now she was not sure what they were to each other. What had happened to Calwyn in the deserts of Merithuros had changed everything. Darrow was Lord of the Black Palace, the ruler of all Merithuros. And she, Calwyn, was nothing.

After the loss of her chantments, she had pushed Darrow away. She knew that had hurt him deeply, but her despair and her misery were so great she couldn't bear anyone near her. Sometimes she thought she almost hated Darrow; at times, she hated herself. She wouldn't have blamed Darrow if he'd begun to hate her too. It might even be a kind of relief if he did. But mostly she was numb, beyond feeling.

Now Calwyn was returning home, as an injured animal crawls back to the safety of its den. She was sure of only one thing: Marna, the High Priestess, would be glad to see her. Remembering Marna's smile, the twinkle in her faded blue eyes and the gentle touch of her hand, Calwyn spurred herself to go faster. Her skates bit smoothly across the ice, one long stroke after another.

In one way, it was lucky for the travelers that this fierce freeze had lasted so long. They had skated upriver across the plains and through the mountains, making their journey much quicker than if they'd walked all the way. Calwyn had never known the rivers to freeze so hard, nor so late in the season.

"Cal! Cal!" Suddenly Mica swooped past them. "Come on! Can't you feel it?"

"Mica, *wait*! For the sake of the Goddess!" shouted Calwyn, but as she and Trout rounded the bend, she saw why Mica was so excited.

Ahead, spanning the width of the river, shone a steady, impervious gleam, a shimmer like a vast mass of diamond. The great Wall of Antaris reared over them.

Calwyn's breath caught in her throat. How many times had she stood beside this towering barrier? How many days had she walked along it, singing it into being with chantments of ice-call? She knew it better than she knew the shape of her own face. She knew the Wall in the hot sunshine of high summer and the mellow dusk of autumn, in the clean fresh light of spring, and as it appeared now, in the blue shadows of winter.

But something was different. It wasn't just that she viewed the Wall from the outside now. What was missing was her awareness of the magic that had built and sustained the mighty rampart of ice, the living power that hummed through it and crackled all around it. Mica was a chanter: Mica had sensed strong chantment even before the Wall came into view. Once Calwyn too would have known that they were close to the Wall. It would have called to her, just as it had called to Mica.

But Calwyn felt nothing. The Wall appeared to her as it did to Trout, who stood gazing up beside her, openmouthed. It was a marvel, yes, a wondrous sight. But it was dead, lifeless, no more than a slab of frozen water. It was Mica who shivered, Mica who heard the call of the Goddess, Mica who shied instinctively from the shimmering surface. "Anyone'd feel safe, with *that* protectin' 'em," she murmured in awe.

Trout reached out to the Wall, but Calwyn struck his hand away. "Don't! It'll kill you! It's death to touch the Wall, the chantments that flow through it are so strong."

Trout shook himself. In Mithates, chantment had been outlawed generations ago. And though Trout had been the unwitting finder of the Clarion, the only relic of the Power of Fire, which the people of Mithates had renounced, he still had to be reminded of the possibility of magic. He had a practical mind, interested in how things worked, and making them work better; he had built the direction-finder that they'd used to steer their course. (Mica called it his "which-way," and the name had stuck.)

Calwyn stood staring at the Wall. Then she curled her thumb and forefinger into a circle, as the villagers of Antaris did when they approached the immense shining barrier, and she made the sign that they made, touching the circle to her forehead, her throat, her heart. This was the way the common folk made reverence to the Goddess Taris, Mother of the priestesses. Calwyn could no longer count herself as a Daughter of Taris. She had lost the most precious gift the Goddess had given her.

"Cal?" asked Mica timidly. "We goin' in?"

"Yes," said Calwyn, without moving, and the two girls remained motionless, side by side, gazing upward. Trout waited for a breath or two, then, still balanced on his skates, he tottered up onto the riverbank to explore the Wall as it curved farther into the forest.

A moment later the girls heard a shout. They hurried to where Trout stood by the Wall with his eyes averted, pointing mutely.

Mica and Calwyn didn't scream; they had seen enough horrors to prevent that. But Mica turned away with a shudder, and bile rose in Calwyn's throat.

There was a body inside the Wall. It was a woman; long reddish hair swam around her like a gossamer scarf. Her back was to them, her face hidden, but she wore the yellow tunic and shawl of a priestess. Shafts of blue light trapped the body like the bars of a cage; brilliant diamond cracks in the ice seemed to target the bloodless flesh like arrows.

"You never told us you put dead people into the Wall," said Trout accusingly.

"We don't!"

"Then how did she get there?"

"It must have been an accident —" Calwyn faltered. "Quickly, Mica, the Clarion! We have to set her free!"

"She's dead, Calwyn," said Trout bluntly. "It's too late to help her."

"We don't know that!" cried Calwyn. "A little village boy lost his way in a snowstorm, and we found him, blue and cold, not breathing. But the sisters brought him back to life. Mica, quick!"

Mica pulled out the Clarion and breathed through it as gently as she could. She was the only chanter among them; only she could call forth the power that the Clarion held. As she played, a clear note rang out, and the golden Clarion glowed brighter.

Slowly the ice of the Wall began to melt. Chantment met chantment, fire breathed to ice, as the music of the little horn unfurled. The thick, curdled ice became transparent; puddles of water formed around their feet. "Careful!" cried Calwyn. "Don't burn her!"

They were not skilled at using the last artifact of the Power of Fire; the Clarion's power was far greater than their ability to control it. Mica had grumbled that it was "like tryin' to ride a sea serpent." They had learned through trial and error which notes made heat and which made light, when to breathe through the Clarion gently and when to play a fiercer blast. Calwyn tried to guide Mica, and Trout observed and remembered. Sometimes the Clarion did as they intended; often it did not. After one or two nearly catastrophic accidents, they had learned to be cautious.

"Play it like when you're starting a campfire," suggested Trout.

Mica blew a succession of rapid, staccato notes. Calwyn watched in an agony of impatience as the ice dripped and melted, until the thinnest possible crust of ice remained around the body. "Stop!" she shouted, and simultaneously Trout yelled, "Watch out!"

The head lolled, and the woman's body smashed to the ground, stiff as a wooden doll. A faint blue tracing of veins was visible beneath her pale skin, and her calloused hands were large and strong. Calwyn rushed forward, dragging off her mittens with her teeth. "Give me the Clarion!" The trumpet still pulsed warm with the afterglow of chantment, and Calwyn held it to the woman's breast, her hands, her belly, as she would have held a hot poultice. The priestess's hazel-green eyes stared up unseeing; her mouth was wide, stained with something dark, and one strand of hair was caught between the cold lips. "It's Athala," said Calwyn as she worked frantically over the body. "She's our shoemaker."

Trout looked at Mica and shook his head. Mica, who still had great faith in Calwyn, set her mouth stubbornly. She picked up Athala's cold, stiff fingers and rubbed them between her gloved hands. When Calwyn placed her cheek close to the cold face, she felt no stir of breath or pulse; when she breathed into the blackened lips, there was no quickening response. When she lifted her mouth away, her own lips felt numb, and she tasted the unmistakable aniseed flavor of bitterthorn. So Athala had been drugged, or drugged herself — perhaps the bitterthorn was disguising the presence of the spark of life.

Along with her chantment, Calwyn had lost the special awareness she'd gained with the help of her friend Halasaa. He was one of the Tree People, the first inhabitants of Tremaris, and he was gifted with the Power of Becoming. He could heal injuries and illness, and speak with animals.

Half a year ago, Calwyn would have known, without this blind, desperate groping, whether this woman was alive. She folded Athala's hands around the Clarion and held it to her throat, willing the blood to pump again through the ice-cold body.

She couldn't have said how long they crouched there while the early winter dusk gathered around them. At last Trout touched her shoulder. "It's no use, Calwyn. She's dead."

"It ain't your fault, Cal." Mica slipped an arm around her friend's waist. "You tried your best."

Calwyn shook her off. "I could have done better than that, once," she said bitterly.

"Not even Halasaa could have helped her," said Trout. "She was dead, Calwyn, dead a long time, I'd say. She was past healing."

Calwyn closed the hazel-green eyes and drew the yellow shawl over Athala's face. "Her body should be burned, and the ashes scattered under the blazetree in the sacred valley. We can bring her inside the Wall ourselves, but we'll have to send people to carry her back to the Dwellings." Calwyn pulled on the mittens she'd discarded while she tried to revive Athala; her hands were stiff with cold. "It'll be dark soon. We should go in."

Trout examined the breach dubiously. "Is that gap big enough?"

"Yes," said Calwyn shortly. Part of her was horrified at the blasphemy of melting a hole in the sacred Wall. The voices of her childhood echoed in her mind: *The first duty of every priestess is the care of the Wall.* And now she had mutilated it.

Trout and Calwyn dragged Athala's body inside the Wall and laid it down gently. Mica threw the packs one by one through the gap. Once they were all safely inside, they trudged back to the river and skated on. For some distance, the river and the Wall diverged, but after a time the river veered toward the rampart again. It was so dark now that Mica held the Clarion to her lips. A stream of golden light, warmer than any lantern, flowed from the mouth of the little trumpet and cast a pool of brightness around the travellers.

Suddenly Trout gasped and put out his hand to halt the others. The three huddled together, staring.

Body after body was ranged inside the Wall, a line of the dead as far as the light of the Clarion could reach. Perhaps three dozen of the sisters were held upright in the ice, all robed in yellow, their unbound hair swirling about their frozen bodies.

"Oh, no — *no!*" whispered Mica.

Calwyn covered her face with her hands.

Trout said, "What's happened, Calwyn? Why?"

"How should I know?" said Calwyn sharply. "There must be a reason. Perhaps — perhaps the way to the sacred valley is cut off, and Marna decided to keep the dead bodies here until they could hold the proper rituals." Even to her, that sounded absurd.

"But why so many?" Trout persisted. "Didn't you say about two hundred sisters lived in the Dwellings? There must be thirty or forty here."

Calwyn shivered. "Perhaps it was Samis. Darrow and I escaped, but maybe the sisters . . ." She swallowed. Never in her darkest thoughts had she dreamed that Samis might have destroyed Antaris; never had she imagined returning home to a wasteland.

"Samis done this?" whispered Mica.

"I don't know. Perhaps. It might have — amused him —"

Calwyn turned away, too afraid to examine the faces of the dead. "Take off your skates. We can walk to the Dwellings from here."

None of them wanted to skate past that silent, dreadful file. They thrust their skate blades into the packs, then turned their backs to the Wall and crunched across the hard-packed snow toward the Dwellings.